Daylight came and Isaac concealed himself in the rocks. He watched as four of the men rode off. He recognized Victorio's palamino horse as one of those leaving. They were no more out of sight when one of the remaining Indians went into a leanto type tent and drug out the Mexican girl. He proceded to rape her. She was in no shape to fight off the attack. Once he had finished, the other one took his turn. Both satisfied, they stretched out on the ground laughing.

Isaac watched them for close to half an hour. The girl never moved. One of the bucks finally got up and went over to her and kicked her in the ribs. She moaned and rolled over on her side. He reached down and got her by the waist and pulled her into position, where he mounted her again.

"Animals," Isaac thought. "They even screw like dogs." The anger he felt rose up in his throat. He began to crawl toward the camp.

The Indians had a bottle that looked like whiskey and they began taking turns drinking from it. When they seemed to be half drunk, Isaac had worked to within ten yards of where they sat. His knife was in his hand, when he leaped to his feet taking both men by complete surprise. The knife struck out at one and almost decapitated him. The other felt the toe of a cavalry boot smash in his groin. Isaac then rammed the knife deep into his chest, withdrew it and drove it into him again. The girl had risen to a sitting position and was crying.

"Are there others?" he asked her in Spanish.
"Just the ones that left, but they'll be back!"

BOUND BY BLOOD

CHARLES R. GOODMAN

HOLLOWAY HOUSE PUBLISHING COMPANY
LOS ANGELES, CALIFORNIA

Published by
HOLLOWAY HOUSE PUBLISHING COMPANY
8060 Melrose Avenue, Los Angeles, California 90046

All rights reserved. No part of this book may be reproduced or transmitted in any form or by any means, electronic or mechanical, including photocopying, recording or by any information storage and retrieval system, without permission in writing from the Publisher. Copyright ©1985, 1993 by Charles R. Goodman. Any similarity to persons living or dead is purely coincidental.
International Standard Book Number 0-87067-396-3
Printed in the United States of America
Cover illustration by Roxanne Skene
Cover design by Bill Skurski

*For the light of my life . . .
Louise*

BOUND BY BLOOD

Chapter 1

Four A-4's zoomed overhead and each broke off formation leaving a trail of white smoke behind it. It looked like a growing flower, the way the trails spread. As the roar drifted away, the crash of cymbals filled the air followed by the Marine Corp band playing the Star Spangled Banner.

Lt. Col. John Eric Williams, already at attention, snapped a steady hand salute. He looked like a bronze statue standing there on the parade field. Thoughts of the past twenty-five years flashed through his mind. He had been little more than a child when he enlisted in the Marine Corps fresh out of high school with dreams of grandeur. Through the education programs, he had managed to get a college degree in engineering and even completed his master's, although it had taken years of dedication and determination. It had, in fact, taken the better part of twelve years to complete his master's, but never, not once, had there been any doubt in his mind that he would do anything except succeed.

Flight school had been tough, but the pleasure of the challenge far exceeded the work. Jew, as his friends called him (because of his initials, J.E.W.), would be one of the first black fighter pilots in the Corps to fly the F-9, which was the finest most sophisticated, fighter plane in the world as any Marine would have told you with no reservations.

As the cymbals clashed again, Jew blinked and his mind was once again focused on his surroundings. The order came bellowing from the field as the CO turned to the parade field and called the command, "Port arms."

"Right shoulder arms."

"Pass in review."

As a chain is stretched and the front link is pulled, so will the last link move. That is how it was; 600 to 700 men stepped off on their left foot.

Jew snapped another salute as the colors marched by. Each company of men passed and with the command "eyes right," Jew and the others on the review stand acknowledged their actions with a return salute. The troops, having passed in review, moved around to the opposite side of the parade field where they were positioned to face the review stand.

The senior officer in command, Maj. Gen. David Stahl, moved to a microphone on the field and gave the command, "Lieutenant Colonel John Eric Williams, front and center."

There was silence as Jew made a quick left face, marched to the steps of the stand, moved down them looking neither right nor left. Each turn he made while approaching the General was strictly military—sharp and crisp. As he approached the General, Jew came to a halt. In his most distinctive way, he snapped a salute that caused his hand to quiver like a dagger thrust into a tree.

"Lieutenant Colonel Williams reporting as ordered, Sir."

"Lieutenant Colonel Williams, this day the 16th of April,

in the year of our Lord 1982, I have been given the pleasure of awarding two presentations to you. For outstanding duty and performance of those duties, your diligence and untiring performance in the face of the enemy, I award to you the Distinguished Flying Cross.

"Be it known to all men that Lieutenant Colonel Williams was on his 78th mission over enemy territory when his airplane was hit by a missile. Lieutenant Colonel Williams was forced to bail out behind enemy lines. Once on the ground, he managed to find a fellow pilot who had also been forced to eject. Lieutenant Colonel Williams did administer first aid and carry his fellow pilot to safety. This ordeal took thirteen days and encompassed many dangers to both Lieutenant Colonel Williams and to his friend.

"Lieutenant Colonel Williams, there is no way I could ever thank you enough for your actions. The pilot Lieutenant Colonel Williams saved was Captain David S. Stahl, Jr., my son. His mother and I will never be able to repay you. Not only for your devotion to duty, but for the courage you exhibited in the face of the enemy, where it would have been understandable for one to think of only saving himself. This gentleman's first thought was to save his downed fellow officer and countryman. We applaud you, sir."

Everyone in the stands joined the General in clapping. Jew smiled.

The General took a deep breath. "I said there were two awards. Somehow I really hate to give you this one." He paused and handed Jew a leather folder. "These are your retirement records. Today we have lost a hell of a Marine and a damn good pilot, but we find satisfaction in knowing we will always have a good friend."

The General came to attention and saluted. Jew returned the salute. The band started to play "The Marines' Hymn," an arrangement which sent the sound of a well-trained band, not only into the gathered crowd, but for blocks around.

As the band ended their rendition, it could not have been timed better. Three F-9's came over the horizon. They could not have been over 500 feet off the ground. One had a stream of red smoke trailing behind it. The second had white and the third stream was blue. The three colors drifted together and it gave the entire sky the appearance of a huge flag. Even with the noise from the engines, one could hear the gasp from the people in the stands. The demonstration and flight of the three pilots was a beautiful thing to see.

"Well, Jew, I hope you enjoy your farm and you damn well better have a hell of a lot of quail on it, because I am coming down next season." The General's head was straight forward. His lips barely moved as he spoke.

"You got it, Dave. I only hope you shoot better than you fly."

Both men smiled. Jew turned his head a bit to gain a better glimpse of the General. He noticed what looked like a tear roll down the General's cheek.

"You take good care of yourself, John. You were a good officer. Your command will miss you," he said as they shook hands.

Chapter 2

Jew slowed down and turned the station wagon on to the lane running up to the old stone farm house.

"Is this it, Daddy?" Rhonda asked.

"This is it, sweetheart, and just over that hill out back is a stream. The two of you will have years to enjoy this place. Who knows? You may even catch a fish or two."

"Oh, John," Clara said as they approached the house. "It's more run down than I remember."

"Well, Honey, it's been five years since we bought it and renters can play hell with a place, especially when it needs work before they move in." Jew paused as he slowed to a stop in front of the house. "Would you look at this place. God, it's going to take a lot of work, but it's going to be a grand place when we finish it. We'll have it ready—oh, say," he paused, "ten or twenty years." He smiled at Clara, "It won't take long, Honey. It'll be a labor of love. I think I'll put a greenhouse over there, the pool will go right there." Jew was pointing and walking around the house as he talked.

"Don't you suppose we should go inside and make sure the electricity has been turned on and if the plumbing works first before we get into pools and such?"

"Clara, my darling, you are much too practical. And, as usual, you are right. So let's go in and see what we have."

The house was in bad shape. It was obvious it had been without the necessary repairs for years. But the building was sound. Half of the shutters were broken or gone. The roof needed to be replaced. The outside stone was dirty and a green moss had grown up on the north side from the ground about two feet high.

Once inside, the kids ran about looking in each room. Jew and Clara stood in the living room and surveyed what was to be their dream house. Jew could see disappointment creeping into Clara's expression.

"Hey, not too bad," Jew exclaimed. "Mr. Robertson said he'd have a cleaning crew in before we arrived and that he did."

"Oh, John, this is going to be a lot of work. I expect we can make it into a fine house, but it's going to take time. Lord, is it going to take time!"

"Hon, we ain't got nothing but time."

"Daddy, come quick!"

Jew walked to the rear of the house. There stood Ronnie looking out the window.

"Yeah, son, what is it?"

"An old man just went into the barn."

"Where?"

"Out there. He just came out of the woods over there and walked into our barn."

"Come on, son, it must be a neighbor come to see who's moving in. Let's go meet him."

Jew and Ronnie went out on the back porch.

"Hello," Jew called. There was no reply. He went down the steps, noticing the hand rail would need to be replaced. As Jew and Ronnie crossed the yard toward the barn, Jew had a rush. "Deja vu," he said out loud.

"What, Dad?"

"Oh, deja vu. That's a French term, son. It means, seems like I've been here before or this has happened before. Sort of funny feeling. It comes on one real fast and in a flash, it's gone. That's called 'deja vu'."

"Is that what you call it? That's happened to me before. Sort of scared me."

"Don't worry about it, son. Just enjoy it. It won't happen too often and never as far as I know has it hurt anyone."

They had reached the barn door. "Hello in there," Jew called. There was no reply. The barn door was half open. Jew pulled it open and stepped in. He looked around. No one was in the barn. Jew looked up in the hay loft. A ladder was built next to the wall going up to the loft. Jew climbed up and looked in the loft. It, too, was empty.

"You sure you saw someone come in here, son?"

"Yes, sir. A man with a blue coat on and, oh yeah, a beat up hat. All floppy. One of those like the actors wear at Vicksburg. You know, Dad, those hats that look like a cowboy hat, but not really."

"Yeah. Well, there's no one here now. Must have gone out the other door. Or maybe he walked past the barn and it just looked like he came in. No matter. He's not here now. Let's get back up to the house. I'm sure it was one of the neighbors. Probably cuts through here all the time going home or something."

Jew and Ronnie were halfway to the house when the barn door slammed shut. Jew whirled around.

"What the hell? There's not a leaf moving. How in the

world did that door manage that?"

"Well, Dad, it's an old barn. Maybe the door just fell shut."

"Yeah, maybe. Come on, let's check out the girls and see what's going on in our mansion. We'll check out that old barn later."

As Jew went up the steps, he felt one creak under his foot.

"Well, when I fix this handrail, I had better just go ahead and replace these steps. Can't have your mother falling through one. That could result in my having to cook your supper."

"Yuck," came the reply.

Ronnie jumped past his dad as Jew playfully swatted him on the bottom.

"What do you mean 'yuck,' boy?"

"If you did the cooking, we would wind up eating cold cereal and sandwiches the rest of our lives."

The screen door slammed shut behind them.

"What's this about cereal and sandwiches?" Clara asked.

"Nothing, hon, your son is just giving me a hard time."

"Who was in the barn?"

"No one. Funny, too. The door slammed shut when we left. Really kind of funny." Jew's voice trailed off as he turned and looked out the window. He stood there staring.

"What do you see, John?"

"That barn door. It's open now."

"Well, what do you expect? It's probably been years since anyone fixed the hinges. This old gumbo soil does shift, you know, and I suppose the foundation has settled out there some. Don't you think that would cause a door to swing open and shut?"

"Sure. What else? Has to be something like that."

"Daddy, Daddy," Rhonda called from the front porch. "The movers are coming down the road. Yippee! Here come our things!"

"Right on schedule. The driver said he'd be here about 3:00 and here he comes."

Clara stepped through the front door on to the front porch that ran across the entire front of the house. There was a railing. It, too, needed repair. Several of the rungs were missing.

"Well, I'll be glad to spend the night in my own bed. These last few nights in a motel have just about been all I can stand."

The movers went right to work. Clara showed them which was to be the master bedroom and each of the children's rooms. The fourth bedroom would be her sewing room and Jew's office. It was dark before the last box was taken in.

"Well, you guys earned your money today. Can we buy you dinner? There is a truck stop back toward town."

"No, thanks, Colonel. We need to get on down the road. There's another load waiting for us to Savannah. I want to get home before next weekend. My daughter's in a swim meet. Can't miss that or I'll be in hot water."

"I know what you mean. Be careful and good luck to your daughter," Jew called as the two movers climbed into their truck. The dust settled as the truck pulled out on to the highway.

"Well, family, let's go to town and get us some ham hocks and sweet taters. I'm hungry."

"Daddy, you sound like a hillbilly."

"What yo' mean, chile? I am a hillbilly and tomorrow I'm gonna buy me some bib overhalls and chewin' tobacco."

"Oh, Daddy."

"We'll go for the overhalls, but you can forget the chewing tobacco," Clara said.

"Let's eat. I'm starved," Ronnie added.

After dinner, the family returned home. As the headlights swept the yard, Jew asked, "Did you see that?"

"What, hon?" Clara answered.

"Out there by the barn. Did you see someone?"

17

"No. I wasn't looking."

"I did, Daddy," Rhonda said. "Looked like a deer. Do we have deer here?"

"Sure do. Lots and lots of deer," Jew said. He knew, of course, the deer had been hunted out of this area years ago. Back in the thirties, the local people were forced to hunt the deer and wild hogs for food. When World War II broke out, there was not a deer within 100 miles of the area. He did not want to alarm the family, but felt it might be a good idea to lock the car and he reached over to the glove compartment and removed his 1911 .45 caliber automatic handgun.

"What are you doing?" Clara asked.

"I don't want to leave this in the car." He got a sheepish look and in a spooky voice, he added, "You never know when a big bad bear is going to come out of those woods over there."

"Oh, John, you are a nut. And to think they let you fly an airplane that cost millions of dollars."

"Fooled 'em all, hon," was his reply. "But I got you." He grabbed her and kissed her.

"I love you, you big nut."

"See you young 'uns in the morning. We have a lot of work to do. OK?"

"OK, Daddy," came the reply as the children went into their bedrooms.

"Daddy," Ronnie said.

"Yeah, son?"

"Deja vu."

"Just enjoy it, son. Good night."

"Night, Dad. Night, Mom."

"Good night, son," Clara answered as she turned to Jew. "What's this about deja vu?"

"Oh, I had one of those experiences today when Ronnie and I were out by the barn and I explained what the term meant. I suppose he just had a turn at it. Kind of odd, I'd say. Both he and I having it and on the same day."

"Strange?" Clara said. "It's more than that."

"What's so strange? You've had it before."

"I know, but I had it earlier today myself."

"That is strange. Maybe it's a sign we belong here. You bet. That's what fate is saying. 'You folks belong here on the land where your forefathers lived, worked and died. They cleared the land, plowed the fields and planted the crops. Yep, you folks belong right here. Not in some old stuffy city, somewhere up east.' "

"Oh, hush, and go to sleep. You have plenty to do tomorrow, my man. I need a washer and dryer hooked up, and what's more important, I need the TV antenna up. Do you know I've not seen one of my soaps for three days. Lord knows who's married to whom or who shot who. Three days—my goodness—anything could have happened."

"Oh, poor baby. I'll fix your TV tomorrow. Can't have you missing your soaps, can we?"

Clara pulled the sheet up over her as Jew sat on the edge of the bed. He crushed out a half-smoked cigarette and with a flowing motion slid under the sheet and turned to face Clara. Jew pulled Clara close to him and kissed her on the neck. His hand found its way to her soft, round buttocks. He squeezed and pulled her closer.

"We have to get this tour off to the right start."

"Uh-huh," she said as she leaned over and turned out the light.

Chapter 3

The sun was up and the warm rays were coming through the window in the bedroom when Jew awoke. He lay still, not moving anything except his eyes. It took him a couple of seconds to recall where he was. A flash of fright raced through him caused by the confusion. As he slowly glanced around the room, his mind cleared and he smiled.

"I'm in my own bedroom on my own farm," his mind told him. The smile broadened as the aroma of coffee reached his nose. He turned his head. Clara was gone. He listened. He could hear kitchen noises.

With effort, Jew sat up. He rubbed his eyes to clear the sleep; then with vigor he rubbed his hair and stretched. As he crossed the room to the bath, he scratched his right hip, then his stomach.

"Boy, I slept like a rock last night. Didn't know I was so tired," he mumbled to himself.

The cold water he splashed in his face felt most refreshing. He dried his face and looking into the mirror, smiled and said, "God, boy, but you are a good looking devil."

After slipping into a clean pair of jeans, Jew pulled a tee shirt on with his old outfit's name on it, then strolled into the kitchen.

"Good morning, you pretty thing. Wow! You look good this morning. Care to give me an instant replay of last night?"

"You had your replay. Behave yourself. The kids will hear you," she replied with a smile. "You look like you are ready for some coffee," she added as she set a cup down and poured.

"I am, my love, I truly am for sure."

"John, we've been here on the farm for about seventeen hours and you are already talking like a farm hick."

"I know, honey, and don't it sound good?"

"No, it sounds like a hick."

"It do, don't it?"

"Good morning, Dad—Mom," Ronnie said as he came into the kitchen and sat down at the table.

"Morning, son," Jew answered.

"You hungry, honey?" Clara asked.

"Yes, Mom, I'm starved. Do we have any cornflakes?"

"No, but I'm going to fix some hot cakes. How about that?"

"You bet. Give me about this many." His hand rose about a foot above the table.

"Sure. I'll give you that many," she laughed. "Call your sister and I'll start cooking."

After breakfast, Jew went to the stove and poured another cup of coffee and walked to the rear window. He was standing there just looking for a couple of minutes. In a voice half to himself and half to those in the room, he began to speak.

"Maybe I'll put a garden in over there. The kids have never had a dog. Think we should have a dog. A cat, too. Why not?"

"Sounds good to me, Dad," Ronnie said.

"What? What, son?"

"I said it sounds good to me. I always wanted a dog."

"And I want a kitty, Daddy. A yellow one. OK?" Rhonda added.

"Oh yeah. We'll just do that, Ronnie. We'll get a dog. A bird dog. And you, my little sweet, you shall have your yellow kitten. And you, my little bit larger sweet, you shall have your garden, a flower garden for you. Vegetables for me."

Jew turned back toward the window. He looked away, then snapped his head back.

"There's that guy again. Where the hell did he come from? I was looking right out there. One second he wasn't there and then there he was, walking across the barnyard."

"Where?" Clara said as she walked over beside him.

"He went into the barn. I saw him this time." Jew reached over, picked up his ball cap and pulled it on his head as he went out the back door. As he walked toward the barn, he thought he heard something inside the barn.

Jew stepped through the door expecting to find someone there. It was just as it was the day before. No one was there. He called out, "Anyone in here?" No answer came back.

"I'm John Williams. I own this place. Now I know you are here, so come on out. I am not going to hurt you. I suppose you were wondering who we are?"

There was no reply.

"Hey! Look, man, you can come on out. I can use some help around here if you are looking for work."

Again no reply.

"You hungry? My wife has some hot cakes up at the house. Come on out and we'll go up to the house and have breakfast and some good hot coffee."

Jew waited. There was no reply. He moved through the barn slowly. As he moved, he checked each corner. Slowly he went up the loft ladder. Once at the top, he looked into the loft.

It was empty.

Half under his breath, he said, "Where the hell did he go? I saw him come in here. Had to slip out the back, I guess. Must be some kind of a nut."

Jew walked back up to the house. He went in and walked over to his coffee cup. He picked it up and sipped slowly thinking about the stranger who was not there.

Clara spoke. "Who was it, John?"

"I don't know. No one was there. He must have walked right through the barn and went out back. Crazy. Why would a guy just walk through the barn? He had to see the things on the porch and know someone had moved in here."

"I don't know, John, but you promised to fix the TV antenna. Remember? I suppose you had better go to town and get what you need. I really would like to see my soaps today, honey," she said as she snuggled up and ran an arm around his waist.

As Jew was backing the car around to leave, he thought he saw someone go in the barn again.

"Enough is enough," he said as he pulled the car's shifting lever to drive and pushed down on the gas pedal, causing the rear wheels to spin. Jew drove across the side yard and straight to the barn door. He jumped out and ran into the barn. As before, no one was there.

"Man, I wish I understood what your problem is," he said as he turned and walked back to the car.

Clara came out on the back porch. She stood there with one hand on her hip, the other rested next to the side of her neck.

"John," she called, "what's the matter?"

"Oh nothing. Thought I saw our friend again. Must have been a bird or something. See you in about an hour. Bye."

He slid under the steering wheel, closed the door and backed up. Looking at the barn, he shook his head. "I know damn well he's in there somewhere. Has to be. But where?" he said to himself.

There was not much traffic in town, so Jew just drove around for a little while, up one street and down the next. It had been a little over five years since he and Clara had come down and purchased the farm with the money his grandmother had left him when she died. The town had not changed much and he was glad. The town had a special charm to it. An old south flavor, he thought. Both he and Clara had fallen in love with it the moment they first drove into town looking for a place to retire. They had looked at several areas, a couple of farms in South Carolina, one in Illinois and four or five in Florida. None of them had really moved them like this town and the farm had. It was love at first sight.

Jew saw the hardware store down the street, as he turned the corner onto Main Street.

The store was what one would have expected to find. High ceilings with ornamental trim around the walls where the ceiling and walls met. Three old ceiling fans turned ever so slow. The lighting had been updated to flourescent strips, but the floor was wood and creaked underfoot. Jew wondered how long this old wooden floor had been down. The thing that impressed Jew most was the neatness of the shelves and the items shown for sale on the floor. Everything was in a very military order.

"May I help you find something?"

Jew turned to see a man in his mid to late fifties standing about three feet away. His smile was genuine and Jew felt a warm inner welcome.

"Yes, sir, you sure can," he replied. "I've got to get a TV antenna up today so the wife can watch her soaps or else I'm in big trouble. I hope you have one in stock."

"Sure do. We've got three or four over here." The man turned and Jew followed him to the rear of the store.

"Now, you'll need a mast, too, I suppose."

"Yep. And lead-in wire, too. About fifty or sixty feet, I guess."

"OK. How about guide wire?"

"Yeah, and I had better get one of those clamps that hold it to the side of the roof."

"Let's see. Oh yeah, you mean a U-bolt and clamp. Got it, too. Looks like you are in for a bit of work. One of those 'honey do' days, I'd say."

"What's a 'honey do' day?" Jew asked.

"Oh, you know, honey do this, honey do that, kind of day." The man laughed.

"Yes, sir, that's what I've got all right and it looks like I'm in for a 'honey do' year or two," Jew said with a chuckle.

"You live around here?" the man asked.

"Yes, sir, we bought a place about three miles out the old Moore road."

"There by Willow Creek?"

"Yes, sir, Willow Creek runs through our place."

The man finished adding up the bill and looked up. "I'm Jeff Sanders. This is my store." He extended his hand.

Jew took it and the two men shook hands.

"Pleased to meet you, Mr. Sanders."

"Hey," he interrupted, "call me Jeff."

"OK, Jeff. I'm John Williams. My friends call me Jew."

"Jew, huh?"

"Yep."

"Your middle initial has to be 'E' and you were in the service."

"You got it. I just retired from the Corps."

"A jar head, huh?"

"Yep. For 25 years."

"Well, Jew, we're glad you're here." Before he finished, an old man who had been standing a few feet away looking at the screw bin interrupted.

"Say you moved in on the old Willard place, did you?"

"Well, I don't know, sir," Jew replied. "I bought it from a lady named Carter, Mrs. Elizabeth Carter."

"Yep. That's the old Willard place or at least it's part of the old place. Used to be six or seven hundred acres in that there place. It's been so split up now, I'll bet there's not a tract out there over sixty acres.'

"Well, sir, I don't have near that much. Forty-three acres is what my tract is. Wish it was six hundred, but I'm wondering if I can take care of forty-three. Looks like a lot of work ahead of me already."

"Yep. It'll be a lot of work. Don't mean to pry, but I hope you folks don't scare easy."

"Sir?" Jew answered with a puzzled look.

"Hope you don't scare easy. There's them that say a ghost walks them woods out there."

"Clarence," Jeff interrupted, "you know that's a bunch of nonsense. Some old story someone started long ago and has been blown out of proportion over the years. Chances are some old boy high on moonshine saw a cow and thought he saw a ghost."

"No, sir, Jeff, there is a ghost out there." He turned to Jew. "How long you owned that place?"

"About five years now," Jew answered.

"Thought you said you just retired from the Army."

"Yes, sir, I did; but not the Army, the Marines. We bought the farm about five years ago and rented it out. Mr. Samuels at the real estate office handled it for us."

"Uh-huh. Have many renters in that five years?"

"Well, yeah. Several. Why?"

"They was scared off, bet you. That spook does funny things to folks, so they say."

"Well, maybe you're right, sir. But I'm not going to be

scared off. I've worked too hard, too long, for this and I'm staying. If there is a ghost, he's the one that'll have to leave." Jew turned to Jeff and winked.

"We'll see," the old man said as he turned and walked away.

After the old man was out of the store, Jeff turned to face Jew. "Don't worry about it. You know how people are in small towns. I suppose way back when, so little happened here they had to use their imaginations and one thing led to another."

"Sure, Jeff. One thing for sure I do know, is I had better get back and get this antenna put up or I'm in big trouble. Nice to have met you."

"My pleasure, Jew. You come back, hear?"

Jew left the store and drove slowly back toward the farm.

Clara was her usual organized self. She had Rhonda and Ronnie both picking up the loose items lying around outside the house. There was an old broken tricycle, several tires, plus all the cans and old boxes.

"What's going on, young'uns?" he called as he left the car.

"Hey, Dad, you get the TV antenna?" Ronnie asked.

"Yep. Come help me. We'll get this thing up in a jiffy."

The two of them set about their task and in about two hours had it completed.

"There you go, my love, soaps are in your life again."

"And none too soon," Clara responded.

28

Chapter 4

A few days later Jew was up and in the kitchen drinking coffee while he read the morning paper, when Clara came in.

"You're up bright and early this morning."

"Good morning, honey," Jew said as he got up and walked over to the stove and poured Clara a cup of coffee. "You sleep good last night?"

"I don't think I was awake when my head hit the pillow," she answered. "How about you?"

"Yeah, pretty good." He sat back down, lit a cigarette and sort of stared into his coffee cup.

"You know, Clara, there is something strange about this place."

"Strange? Like what?"

"I got up last night about two-thirty and had to go pee. In the still of the night, I could hear the crickets singing and some tree frogs down by the creek were really going to it.

As I stood there in the dark in the bathroom, I thought I heard someone out by the barn chopping wood, so I came downstairs and walked out on the porch." He paused. "The sound stopped, so I went back upstairs. As I lay in bed, I thought I heard it again, so I got up and slipped my pants and shoes on and went out to the barn. The sound stopped again when I got to the porch, so I went on down to the barn. A shutter was swinging in the breeze so I hooked it shut and came on back up to the house. I looked out there this morning and every damn window has the shutters open and the doors are wide open. There's nothing down there but that old lawn mower, so I know it's not someone trying to steal anything. It's just strange."

"I've heard that chopping before," Clara said. "Night before last I heard something out on the porch that sounded like a porch swing, too."

"Why didn't you say something about it?"

"Thought it was just the wind. These pines do whistle some, you know, when the wind is blowing. Remember I'm a city girl. I don't know what you hear in the country."

"Yeah, probably the wind. What else could it be?" Jew finished his coffee. "Think I'll go out and start working in the barn. I want to get a little shop set up. I can get a table saw from Jeff at the hardware store as cheap as I can from anyone. Maybe not as good, but for what I want it for, it'll be OK."

Jew poured another cup of coffee and stepped through the back door. He looked down the road and saw an old black man coming toward the house with a fishing pole on his shoulder. Jew walked out front toward the road and met the stranger at the front yard gate.

"Good morning," Jew greeted him.

"Morning, sir," the old man answered. "You live here now, do you?"

"Yes, sir," Jew replied and reaching his hand out said, "I'm Jew Williams."

"Pleased to meet you. I'm Daniel James Baker. Most folks call me Cigar. You say you're a Jew? Well, I'm a Baptist myself. Never knew me a Jew before. Funny you look black same as me."

"No. I'm not a Jew in that sense. My name is John Eric Williams, but my initials are J.E.W., so my friends call me Jew. We're Baptist, too. Didn't I see you at church last Sunday?"

"Yep. I saw you, too. Wondered why you said you were a Jew. Thought maybe you was one of them that only reads the old parts of the Bible. Someone told me once that's all them Jew people read. You reckon that's right?"

"Yes, sir, I reckon that's right. But tell me, what brings you up this way so early in the morning?"

"Well, I was going to yonder creek and catch me a catfish or two. Thought I'd ask if I could cut across your field. Been doing it for years, but thought I'd ask just the same."

"Sure. But how about a cup of coffee? Got plenty in the house."

"You sure you got plenty?"

"Yes, sir."

"Your missus ain't one to get upset if a stranger comes in, is she?"

"No. Why would she be?"

"Them last folks that lived here were sort of strange. I came up to ask about crossing the field and that lady 'bout jumped out of her skin. Never did know why for sure, but I always thought maybe she mistook me for ol' Isaac."

As they walked up to the house, Jew asked, "Who's ol' Isaac?"

"You ain't seen him?"

"No, sir, I don't think so. He live around here somewhere?"

The old man half laughed, half snickered. "Yep. You might say that. Ol' Isaac used to live right here. This was his place, or so they say. You mind if we just sit on the porch?" the old man asked.

"No. Not at all. Let me tell my wife and she'll get us some coffee."

Jew opened the door and called, "Honey, we have a neighbor out here. Will you bring us a cup of coffee out here on the porch? How you like yours, Cigar?" Jew asked.

"Just like I likes my women. Black and strong," he laughed.

Clara came out and handed Cigar his cup as Jew introduced them.

"Thank you, ma'am." He took a sip. "You sure know how to make a cup of coffee. Not like that sissy stuff you get in town. This reminds me of my second wife. Now there was a strong woman. Whip any two men in town." He laughed again.

"Tell me about old Isaac," Jew asked.

"Not too much to tell. Seems like a long time ago some old man named Isaac died here and his haint still comes back from time to time. He don't cotton much to folks living on his farm either."

"You ever see him?"

"Not me. I don't come down here much. 'Cept when I want a catfish and he ain't going to bother me. It's them that got his that he's going to bother. I ain't got nothing he wants."

Cigar reached in his shirt pocket and pulled out a stub of a cigar and lit it with a kitchen match he struck on the leg of his overalls. As he puffed on the small black cigar, he looked towards the woods.

"Them's his woods out there." He paused and exhaled a cloud of smoke. "That's why I cross over there and fish back up the creek by them blackjack trees over there. If them's his catfish down there, I don't want 'em. That's why I go up yonder."

"Well, Cigar, this is my place now. Bought and paid for and them's my catfish in that creek now and if you want to catch some, you go right ahead. If Isaac gives you any trouble, you send him to me and we'll get this problem straightened out in short order."

"Yes, sir. I'm obliged to you, but don't make no joke about ol' Isaac. I ain't going to screw with no haint. If he wants that piece of the creek, he can have it. I'll just go over yonder like always." He rose and started off, then stopped and turned. "Thank you, ma'am, for the coffee. I'll try to catch you a catfish while I'm at it."

"You're welcome, Mr. Baker, and a catfish would be something to look forward to."

"Mr. Baker. Ain't nobody called me that in twenty years." He chuckled as he walked toward the grove of blackjack trees. "Did you hear that? Mr. Baker." He chuckled and blew out a cloud of blue smoke from his cigar."

Clara sat down next to Jew on the steps. "What do you think of this Isaac person?" she asked. "And while you're at it, what do you think of Cigar Baker?"

"Shit, honey, he's just a superstitious old man. These people were filled so full of crap way back when, some of it has to have filtered down. It's a damn shame that old man has been walking a quarter of a mile farther than necessary all these years because he's afraid of some ghost from who knows where or when."

"Of course, you are right, John, but I guess if you believe in that sort of thing, it's real to you."

"Yeah. But that's the crime—to make people believe in that crap. Oh well, I can't change what's been going on for two hundred years and besides if he fishes down there, it means Ronnie and I'll fish up here where no one bothers the fish. In fact, ol' Uncle Lunk is probably living in a hole right over there somewhere and I am going to catch him one of these days. When I have time," he added. "But right now I'm going to get started on my shop."

Jew worked all morning in the barn getting the old collection of boards, wire and junk in general gathered up and carried outside where he put it in a pile.

Clara called to Jew that lunch was ready.

After lunch Clara told Jew she needed to go into town and do some shopping.

"Why don't you come on in with me and the kids? You can get that saw you want. Then when you get your shop ready, you'll have it," she said.

"That's a good idea. I'll get Jeff to bring it out in his pickup. That will give us a chance to get better acquainted. He seemed like a hell of a nice guy."

Clara dropped Jew and Ronnie off at the hardware. "Be back in about an hour," she said as she drove off.

"We've got to get us a pickup. We men have to have a truck, don't we?"

"You bet, Dad. A four-wheel drive."

"Well, I don't know about that, but one with four wheels to drive anyway." He chuckled as they went into the hardware.

"Hey, Jew, glad to see you. This your boy?" Jeff asked.

"Sure is. This is my son, Ronnie. Son, this is Mr. Sanders."

Ronnie extended his hand. Jeff took Ronnie's hand and shook it with vigor.

"You've got a good grip, son. You play football?"

"Yes, sir, I do."

"What position?"

"Well, I was a running back last season, but I played end on the defensive team year before last."

"Which did you like best?"

"Running back, I guess."

"Good. We can always use a good running back."

Jeff looked to Jew, "And what can I do for you gentlemen today?"

"I need to buy one of those table saws you have over there, except I've got a bit of a problem," Jew said.

"Tell me your problem, Jew. I bet we can solve it if you want to buy that saw over there."

"Well," Jew hesitated, "I need that saw; but, Jeff, I need you to deliver it for me. I don't think we could get it in the back of the station wagon."

"Jew, I thought you said you had a problem. The way I see it, you don't have a problem. You are just short $297.55, because you just bought yourself a saw." He laughed as he slapped Jew on the shoulder. "When do you want it?"

"In the next day or so will be fine."

"How about later this afternoon?"

"That's great. The girls will be back from the store in a few minutes and we'll be going on back to the farm. You wouldn't believe how much has to be done out there."

"Yeah I would too. I'll be out about three o'clock with your brand new saw."

"By the way, I met an old man this morning by the name of Cigar Baker. You know him?" Jew asked as he handed his check to Jeff.

"Yeah. Sure do. He's a good old man. Do anything for you. Used to work for old man Miller before he died. I think he was born in one of those old slave shacks on the Miller place. After Bert Miller died, his son came down from back east somewhere for a couple of months. But he went back. He probably sends a few dollars to the old man every now and then to keep him there looking after the place. I don't know why. Just kind of taking care of the old man, I guess. Where in the world would he go? He must be over seventy-five years old. Where did you meet him anyway? Out at your place?"

"Well, I saw him at church last Sunday, but this morning

he came by our place headed for a fishing hole down on the creek. He stopped in for a cup of coffee and told me some old story about a ghost named Isaac. Sort of adds to what that old gentleman was saying the other day, doesn't it?"

"Yeah. I've heard that old tale, too. The only ghosts I worry about, Jew, are the ones on the TV when I'm watching the news or a football game." Jeff laughed.

"Me, too, or when one shows up on Clara's soaps. Now, that's double bad."

Both men laughed. Clara had pulled up out front and Jew called to Ronnie who was looking at the saw his dad had just purchased.

"Let's go, son. We've got work to do."

"OK, Dad. Nice to have met you, Mr. Sanders."

"Nice to meet you, Ronnie, and I'm looking forward to seeing you on the field this fall, son."

"I'll sure make a try at it, sir. Thanks," Ronnie said as the door closed behind him.

On the way home, Ronnie remarked about how nice Jeff Sanders was. Not at all what he had expected.

Jew thought about that for a while, then asked, "How did you think he would be, Son?"

"I don't know, Dad. I just thought white people in the South wouldn't be very friendly to . . ." he paused, "you know what I mean."

"You mean because we are black. Is that what you mean?"

"Yes, sir. I guess so."

"Ronnie, son, whatever gave you that idea? These are people just like everybody else."

"I know, Dad. But the TV always shows how the whites sort of . . . well, don't want to have anything to do with the blacks."

"Most white people are the same as most black people. They judge you for what you are—good, bad, or indifferent.

You'll see, son, when you get in school this year and make the team. When you make a touchdown, they'll holler just as loud for you as they would for a white boy."

As they pulled into the driveway off the lane, Rhonda pointed toward the barn. "Look, Daddy. That old man just went in the barn."

"He did, Dad. I saw him, too," Ronnie said.

"OK. This is it. I'm going to go around to the back door. Ronnie, you take off and run over there." He pointed to the woods east of the barn. "Watch that side of the barn and if he comes out a side window, sing out. OK?"

"Right, Dad," he said as he started to run in the direction Jew had pointed.

"You girls stay here and watch this side and the front," Jew said as he broke into a trot toward the rear of the barn. As he approached the barn, he thought, "I'll bet we find old Cigar this time. No way can he get out without one of us seeing him."

Jew opened the rear door and stepped in. "Cigar, that you?" No reply came. "Hey, Cigar, the catfish, were they biting today and you ran out of worms?" Silence prevailed.

Jew walked to the front of the barn. He stepped out and waved at Clara. She waved back.

"Who was it, John?" she called.

"No one's here," he shouted back. Jew walked around the corner of the barn. There stood Ronnie right where he had a full view of the east side of the barn. "See anyone, son?" Jew called.

"Just you, Dad. No one came out over here."

"Son, you help Mom carry those groceries into the house. I'll be up in a few minutes."

"John," Clara said, "I know you love this place and that you have always wanted a farm, but this is too much. Never, not once in all our married years, have I made any real

37

demands on you. Not once. Have I?"

"No, you haven't and I've always . . ." Jew paused. "Hell, Clara, I've got some nut coming and going here like some kind of spook, a TV antenna to get up and now you. What the hell are you so up in the air about?"

"That's it, John Eric. You got that right. Mister, I am up in the air all right. I've got two kids to worry about, a husband who thinks he can fix anything and fears nothing. Well, I'm not that strong. I'm not strong at all," she sobbed. "I'm scared, John. I'm scared for the children and for myself and I'm scared for you." She began to shake.

"Hey. Cool it, honey. There isn't anything to be scared of. Come on. Calm down. All we have here is some old fool who is probably afraid to come up to the house and introduce himself. Hell, some of these country folks are just plain simple. You know that, don't you?"

"That's not it, John. This is more than just that. We have all seen this man several times now and not once, not one single time, have any of us seen him come out of this rundown heap of boards that was once a barn."

"Yeah, Daddy, that's right and I'm not going to come out here any more," Rhonda said.

"Hold on a minute, you two. All we have is some old nut who is probably twice as scared of you as you are of him. I'll get to the bottom of this. Now, don't try to read more into this than it really is. Come on, now."

Jew put his arm around Clara and patted Rhonda on the head. He knew they had good reason to be frightened. He was concerned too. It could be someone with a mental problem.

"Dad," Ronnie said, "I'm going to bring a baseball bat with me next time I come down here. I'll . . ."

Jew raised his hand. "I've heard about all this talk I'm going to hear. Now, listen to me and understand what I'm saying.

There is no reason to get all worked up. I'll get to the bottom of this." He paused. "Believe me, I will. Trust me, OK?"

"All right, John," Clara said. "We trust you, but I don't want to see him again. Not ever."

"OK, OK, you won't. Now, go on up to the house."

Clara turned and started toward the car. She stopped and half turned. Her arm was around Rhonda's shoulder.

"I mean it, John. I don't want to see that man in our yard again."

Jew shook his head in the affirmative. His mind was searching for an answer, but he could not come up with anything that was acceptable to him.

"Hell, this doesn't make any sense. None at all," he said half to himself.

Jew stood there looking first toward the stand of trees at the edge of his field, then turned back toward the barn. A chill seemed to sweep over him. He shook, then the thought came to him. It's almost 80° and these goose bumps came from a good cold weather chill. This is bull shit, plain old unadulterated bull shit. He walked into the barn. He looked up at the loft, then over toward the horse stalls. There were two. The top rail was eaten more than halfway through by horses probably many years ago. He moved over to what probably was a tack room. The door was gone and all that remained was a couple of shelves filled with dirt and cobwebs. An old bottle lay on its side. Jew walked over and picked up the bottle. He looked it over.

"Hmmm," he said as he tried to read the faded label. He could only make out a few letters. "Some kind of linament, I guess," he said as he put it to his nose. No odor remained of the former contents.

The wooden floor underfoot in this small area was old and creaked as he walked across it. Jew strolled back across the barn to the stalls. He leaned against one and placed a foot on the lower rail. He was in deep thought.

After a few moments, he began to speak. First as if to himself, but as he spoke his voice began to rise. He stopped, turned his head from side to side, and began to talk once again.

"OK, Cigar, Isaac, Bill, Henry or whatever your name is, hear me and hear me good. This crap can't, no—won't, go on. I'm tired of this shit, do you hear? OK, man, suppose you are a spook, or a haint, or whatever they call you. I don't give a shit. Understand? Maybe some time many years ago, this was your place. Maybe someone did you wrong. I'm sorry, but that's your problem. It wasn't me and it wasn't my family. You have upset my wife, got my kids half-ass scared to come out here and I, sir, am not going to stand for that. No way. Get this and get it straight, once and for all. I worked my ass off to get where I am. No one gave me nothing, you hear? I studied like hell to get my education. I worked my ass off to gain my wings. I never, not once, turned down an assignment. I flew missions when I should have, and could have, taken off; but, no, I didn't want anyone saying I was using the fact that I was black to get out of danger. Shit, I worked twice as hard as most.

"Clara and I bought this place with our money. Money we saved and money my grandmother left me. This is my place now. You had your turn. Maybe it didn't work out for you; but, friend, it's going to work out for me and I'll tell you why.

"Now, I don't believe in ghosts. Maybe I'm wrong. And if I am and you are a ghost, you had better listen to me. Some day, I'm going to die. And if you are a ghost, then someday I'll be one, too. Right? OK, then, if you hurt or cause anyone in my family to hurt themselves, I'll get you. I'll get you like no one has ever got anyone before. I have a lot of friends, some already dead, and I'll get those friends, and together we'll get your ass. Do you understand? We'll get your ass

40

good.

"Now, if you are someone here abouts and you think it cute to scare a woman and two kids to hell and back, I'll sooner or later catch you and then I'm going to kick your ass until your nose bleeds and after I do that I'm really going to get mad and hurt you bad. You got that mister, whoever you are?"

Jew shifted his weight. The lower rail supporting his foot broke, causing him to lose his balance. He fell backwards through the old stall. Its rotten boards gave way. As he fell Jew grabbed for an upright supporting the loft. It, too, gave way and came crashing down. Jew caught his balance and looked up to see the whole end of the loft coming down on top of him. It happened so quickly, he didn't have time to move.

Without effort he was jerked backwards, as if a hand had grabbed his shirt collar and thrown him clear. As he rolled toward the door, the loft crashed to the ground where a moment before he had stood. Jew rose to his feet in the cloud of dust and dusted off his trousers.

Clara and the kids had heard the noise and came running towards the barn. Clara cried out, "John! John! Are you all right? Oh, my God!" She gasped as she threw open the door. "What happened? Are you hurt?"

Jew stood there looking at the wreckage of the loft. "I don't know, honey. I'm OK. I'm OK," he said in a reassuring voice.

"You could have been killed," she said.

Jew could see she was shaken.

Rhonda hugged his waist. "Daddy, let's move away from here. I don't like it here anymore."

"It's OK, honey, it's OK." He paused. "No. We aren't going to move and I'll tell you why. This is our place, and we are not going to give it up, not for anything or anybody. It was just an accident. That old loft was being held up by old timbers, half rotten. When I grabbed one it broke. That's all."

"John," Clara interrupted, "your shirt is ripped out in the back. Are you sure you didn't get hit by a board or something?"

"Yeah. I'm sure. I was standing over there by the horse stalls when I fell through those old rotten boards and started this whole thing happening." He hesitated. "It was as if someone grabbed me by the back of my shirt and jerked me half way across the barn. No way could I have jumped clear. No, honey," he said to Clara, "I think we've got a friend. I don't know who or how, but there is an unseen friend here somewhere. I just know, or at least, I feel there is nothing to be afraid of. I don't understand it, but I really feel comfortable about it somehow. Know what I mean? It's just a feeling."

As Jew spoke Ronnie was moving a broken board from the floor. "Hey, Dad, look here. There's something down there under the boards."

"Let's see," Jew said as he grabbed one end and slid it to the side. Jew could see a box through the small space. "Looks like a hiding place of some kind. Son, run up to the house and get me that pry bar and a hammer off the back porch."

Ronnie took little time to make the round trip.

Jew took the pry bar and inserted it under one of the planks. As he put his weight on the bar, the leverage began to work. The old rusty nails slowly gave way. First one board, then another, until five or six were clear.

"Would you look at that" Jew stated.

"Treasure," Ronnie said.

"What is it, Daddy? Some old treasure box, do you think?"

"I don't know, but we are about to find out." Jew reached down into an area approximately three feet wide, three feet long and three feet deep. He took one of the side handles and pulled the box up.

It was dirty from years of being hidden under the old wooden flooring. The box reminded Jew of a homemade trunk. There were metal straps supporting the walls and top. It was plain to see that they had been hand forged and riveted to the native oak boards that were hand hewn. Jew pulled at the lock on the hasp. It held tight.

"Hand me that pry bar again, son."

Ronnie responded.

"John," Clara asked, "don't you think we ought to wait before we open it and see if anyone claims it?"

"Who's going to claim it? This is our place. What's on it is ours. Besides this old box has been in that hole for many years. If it belonged to anyone, they would have been back long ago for it. No, it's ours and whatever is in it is ours, too. Unless," he smiled, "it's trouble. Then we'll give it to someone else."

Jew had wedged the pry bar behind the hasp. He gave a quick pop. The lock held. He let up; then with a great deal of force popped the bar. The hasp broke. Jew slowly raised the top of the box. The hinges creaked from rust. He paused with the top about three inches open.

"Stand back. Dracula may fly out of this thing," he laughed.

"Daddy!" Rhonda screamed. "That's not funny."

Jew raised the lid. It stood by itself. The rusty hinges were stiff and the lid would not fall.

"What is it, Daddy?"

"Let me see," Ronnie said, pushing to get closer.

"Well, well, well. What have we here? Looks like an old uniform or what's left of it, anyway." Jew laid the bundle on the ground. "Would you look at that. I'll be damned!" Jew exclaimed.

"It's a gun," Clara said. "Maybe someone used it for something evil and then hid it there. Be careful with that thing, John."

"Maybe someone did do something with it, but I think it went with this old uniform. This is an old Colt, probably

43

a .45. This is the same type of handgun that won the West. It was used by the Army first, but like a lot of other things found its way into the hands of outlaws. Judging from the uniform, I'd say this was some old soldier's sidearm. Look at this," Jew said as he picked up a saber by its handle. He handed the revolver to Ronnie. "Be careful with that, son. I think it's loaded."

"John Eric, you put that thing on the ground until you are sure it's safe," Clara butted in.

"Aw, Mom, I'm no baby," Ronnie pleaded.

"Your Mom's right, son." He laid the sword down and opened the rear of the cylinder. With the push rod, he slowly pushed each cylinder clear of its loaded round. Six unfired cartridges lay on the ground.

"There," Jew said as he handed the gun to Ronnie. "We can't be too careful, son." His eyes went back to the saber. "My, my, look at this thing. I know they were almost twice this long. This blade has been broken and resharpened."

As Jew examined the blade, Clara looked into the box. She picked up a small leather bag.

"Look at this beadwork, John." She handed it to Jew.

"Indian, I'd say. Yep, that's Indian all right. God, this leather is still in good shape after all these years."

"What's in it, Daddy?" Rhonda said as she reached for the small pouch.

"Wait a minute, honey, let's take it easy and open it so we won't tear the leather. This thing is really old."

Jew slowly opened the top of the bag. The drawstring broke.

"Darn," Jew said. "Look at that, would you? Four pretty little ol' rocks," he said, looking at his hand.

"Wonder what they were for," Clara remarked.

"Who knows? Must have been important to someone." Jew laughed. "Could have been wish rocks."

"What's wish rocks?" Ronnie asked.

"You know, son, like some people carry a special coin or even a rabbit's foot for luck. That sort of thing. I never could understand it either. I knew a guy in Korea who had a rabbit's foot tied around his neck for luck. So one day, I asked him if he felt it was really working. He said, 'Sure, I'm still alive, ain't I?' Well, I looked him straight in the eye and said, 'Yep, you sure are, but the original owner ain't.' "

They all laughed.

"What's that package, Dad?" Ronnie asked.

Jew picked up a package. It had been tied with string, but there were just traces of that left. Jew examined it.

"Hmm," he remarked. "Looks like canvas packed with some kind of grease that is all dried out. Whoever did this wanted it to be water tight. Pretty clever, too."

He reached into his pocket and brought out his knife and opened the large blade and slid it along the folds in the canvas. Once this was completed, he folded the canvas back. The old dried grease cracked and fell to the floor. Jew was careful not to damage whatever was inside as he opened the package. Once open, he found a stack of hand-written pages.

"What's that say, Dad?" Ronnie asked.

"I don't know. Look at this, Clara. What do you think?"

"Spanish. It's written in Spanish." He handed it to her. Clara studied it for a second or two, then struggled through the inscription in large capital letters on the cover sheet.

"El Cuento de Mi Esposo."

"What's that mean, Mom?" Rhonda asked.

"I don't know for sure. Let me think." She reread it. "Yes, 'The Story of My . . .' " she paused, then repeated, " 'The Story of My . . .' " she hesitated, " 'Husband.' That's it. 'The Story of My Husband.' Some woman has written a story of her husband's life, I guess."

"This would really be interesting if we could read Spanish," Jew added.

"Someone can, Dad. Ask Mr. Sanders. He'll know who in town can read Spanish and here he comes up the lane now."

Jeff Sanders turned into the drive and saw Jew along with his family coming out of the barn. He pulled around the house and slowly drove toward the barn. Jeff stopped his truck and got out as Jew walked up.

"My goodness, man, what happened to you? Look at your shirt. Half ripped off and you're covered with dirt. You OK, Jew? You have an accident or something?"

"Yeah, something. Something for sure," Jew said. "But I'm OK. You wouldn't believe what happened. Come on up to the house and have a beer. I'll tell you about it."

"Don't care for a beer, but I'll sure do a number on a Coke or something cool."

Ronnie picked up the broken saber and bundle of old uniform. Jew handed the small leather bag to Clara. He carefully folded the cover over the writings and stood up.

"What you got there in the package, Jew?" Jeff asked.

"Oh, this. Some writing of some kind about some woman's husband. It's in Spanish. Jeff, you're not going to believe what I'm going to tell you. But man, this afternoon has been a day to remember."

Ronnie handed his dad the holster belt with the old gun in it.

"Look at this," he said as he handed it to Jeff.

Jeff pulled the handgun clear. "Colt .45, Army issue, I'd guess." He turned it over, studying. "Must be a hundred years old. Solid as a rock. Where did you get this thing?" he asked.

"Out there," Jew pointed toward the barn. "Jeff, let me tell you what happened. I don't believe it myself. So don't think I've lost my mind." Jew told the whole story to Jeff, who was very attentive.

After Jew had finished, Jeff said, "Jew, my wife taught Spanish in high school for about seven years. She could read that collection for you. Why don't you all come into town tomorrow night for dinner and let her take a look at it?"

"I don't want to be an imposition on you or your wife, Jeff."

Jew didn't finish his statement, when Jeff cut him off.

"Hell, man, no imposition at all. I'm going to barbecue some ribs. Y'all come in and take supper with us. Now help me unload that saw. You may have found a treasure, but I've got a sale."

Both men laughed and headed for the pickup.

"Let's put it in the barn," Jew said as he walked past the pickup toward the barn.

Chapter 5

Jew could see smoke from the barbecue pit coming up over the garage as he pulled into Jeff's driveway. The house was early American and it was obvious Jeff was a success. The yard was groomed and the hedge all trimmed with a neatness that required a yard man. No one working a retail store would have the time required to keep his yard this prim.

"Nice house," Clara remarked.

"Yep. Sure is, but wait until we have finished ours. It may even look something like this one someday."

"Even better, Daddy. It's on our farm, not in the middle of town," Rhonda added.

"Right on, honey," Jew commented.

Jeff came from around the garage with an apron on.

"Well. Look at you," Jew spread his arms out. "You look like King Bar-B-Q in person."

"Hey! The kids gave me this apron a couple of years ago

and I don't dare not wear it when I barbecue."

"Know what you mean, Jeff. There is wisdom in discretion."

"Come on in. Meet the family."

They went inside and Mrs. Sanders came in from the kitchen.

"Honey, I want you to meet the Williams, John, Clara and their children, Ronnie and Rhonda. Folks, this is my wife, Sara. Our daughter, Alice, should be back in a little while. She's at a music lesson. Our son, Harold, is working over in Savannah."

"I've heard a lot about you folks. You, John, made quite an impression on Jeff. Pleased to have you over for dinner, if Jeff doesn't burn our ribs." She turned to Jeff, "Why don't you men go on out and cook and let us women get acquainted. Go on, now. We have things to talk about." She waved her hands as if to shoo them out. As the men stepped out on the patio, Jeff turned back.

"Watch out, Clara. She'll have you in the Women's Club, Republican Women's group and lord knows what else."

"Hush yourself, Jeff, and cook," Sara replied.

When dinner was finished, the kids settled down to play video games in the den. Jew, Jeff, Clara and Sara retreated to the living room where Sara served coffee.

"John," Sara said, "Jeff told me about yesterday afternoon. That story is incredible."

"I think you are putting it mildly, Sara. I get the shakes when I think about it," Clara added.

"It's the strangest thing ever to happen to me, for sure," Jew said.

"About those papers," Sara inquired. "Jeff says they are written in Spanish."

"It looks like a book or at least a story of some kind. It's all written in long hand with a pen on some pages and a pencil on others. I suppose it took the author several years to do. Think you could interpret it, Sara?" Jew asked.

"I don't know. Let's take a look."

Jew excused himself and went out to the car. When he returned, he had the package. He put the package down on a coffee table and opened the wrapping.

"Interesting," Sara said.

"What's that, honey?" Jeff asked.

"That wrapping. They used to do that when important documents were being transported on old sailing ships. You know, government documents between the United States and England or France. It kept the moisture out when the ship was at sea."

"Well, it worked here. These pages are as clear and clean as the day they were written," Jew said as he handed the cover sheet to Sara.

"The Story of My Husband, by Maria Elena Estrada Pena Turner, the Wife of Isaac Turner. That's quite a title and name," Sara stated.

"What's it say, honey?" Jeff asked.

"Oh, this is going to take some time. It's in very old and proper Spanish. This lady was well educated, I'd say. Look at the punctuation she has used. This took more than just a knowledge of how to write. She knew the language. No question about that."

They settled back and Sara started to read, slowly at first. Then as she read, she began to put more and more feeling into it.

"My husband is unable to write or read but very little. He knows his numbers and can sign his name. Beyond that, he has no skills with the pen. I was educated in Mexico City and then studied in Spain for two years. My father is El Patron del Rancho de Cruz in Mexico, where I once lived until I was captured by Victorio, the Apache. Of this I will write later when it affects my husband's life. But the reader should know that my love and respect for the man, Isaac Turner, my husband, is stronger than the love for family or country. Only my love of God is greater. This I am sure is not clear to the reader now, but it will be when you have crossed the pages before you and learn about this man and his life. A man who started his life in bondage, a slave with no rights, not even a name. But through his pride and desire to better himself, he has achieved many things which I am very proud to record."

Chapter 6

Sara Sanders laid the manuscript down. "This is going to take some time to read. Why don't I get a friend of mine who also has taught Spanish and we could put it on a tape. That way we won't rush it and you'll have it like a record of the story."

"That sounds like a great idea to me, Sara. You sure you don't mind?" Jew asked.

"Not at all, but it'll probably take a couple of weeks."

"Fine. I know we'll all be anxious to hear what that lady wrote and maybe find out something about Isaac Turner. What time is it anyway?" Jew asked as he looked at his watch.

"Oh my gosh! Look at the time," Clara said. "It's almost eleven thirty. We didn't mean to keep you folks up half the night and on our first visit, too. I had no idea it had gotten so late, Sara."

"Don't worry about it. We all got so caught up in the events you experienced since you moved in and this story, time was the last thing we were thinking about. I am just really fascinated by this lady's use of the language. It's a very interestingly written form. Sometimes it's written in the first person, sometimes in the second and at other times as though by an observer. I think she just wanted to put it down as close as she could, just like it was given to her. Probably just like he told it to her or as close as she could anyway."

Jew stood up. "Sara, we really appreciate your doing this. Why don't you folks come out to the farm when you are finished with the translation? I'll cook and we'll have all afternoon to go over what you have been able to read. Let's make it, say Sunday after next. That sound OK or is that rushing you?"

"Sounds good to me," Jeff said. "How about it, honey? Can you get some of it read by then?" he asked Sara.

"I'll work on it every spare minute until I've got it all down. If I don't get it all read, I'll at least get most of it by Sunday after next, I'm sure."

On the way home, Jew and Clara talked about Isaac and speculated on what life must have been for a young slave boy just freed with no skills except farming and hard work.

They arrived home and the children went straight to bed. Clara changed and crawled in between the sheets. Jew was looking out the window of the bedroom.

"Come on to bed, honey," Clara said, as she shifted to get comfortable.

"Yeah, in a minute. I think I'll smoke a last cigarette first. I'm going down to the back porch. I'll be up in a minute."

"Oh, John, you have got to be given out."

"No. You go on to sleep. I'll be up in a couple of minutes." He turned and went out of the room. "Go on to sleep, honey. My mind is running forty miles to nothing. I've got to slow it down before I go to bed."

Jew opened the screen door. The outside light cast shadows over the yard. The barn could be seen in the dim light. He stood there and reached into his shirt pocket and pulled out the pack of cigarettes. "One left," he said as he took it from the package and crumpled the empty package in his hand. He reached into his trousers pocket with his free hand and came out with a lighter. He lit the cigarette and took a long pull on it. He glanced up and thought he saw a figure of someone standing by the barn.

Jew slowly raised his hand and gave a wave of a sort. The figure seemed to just disappear.

"Was he there?" Jew wondered. "We got your story, friend. Soon we'll know. Yeah, old friend, soon we'll know all about you." He hesitated. "Isaac, if you can hear me, thanks for pulling me out of the way out there when the loft came crashing down. I owe you, man, I owe you."

Jew crushed out his cigarette and returned to the house and to bed. As he settled down, he realized how tired he was. The next sound he heard was Clara shaking him and saying, "Come on, honey. It's almost 8:00. Time to get up."

Jew got up and for the next several days, with the help of Ronnie, worked in the barn getting the remains of the old loft down and the lumber stacked neatly outside.

From time to time, Jew would think about old Isaac and speculate about how life must have been back around the Civil War era for a black man.

Once as he and Ronnie sat resting, he told his son, "Back then, son, a man, if he were black, didn't even own his own life. I've read where a cruel or crazy white master could kill one of his slaves for whatever reason. It wasn't thought of any more than killing a hog or a chicken. God, it had to be really bad in some cases. However, I have also read that many of the white owners really cared about their slaves. After all, they were expensive and were needed to plant, care for and harvest the crops."

The Sunday morning came that Jew had been waiting for. His interest was growing like a field of weeds. The family was getting ready to go to church. Rhonda was at the kitchen sink getting a drink.

She looked out the window and without turning, she said, "Daddy, he's back."

"Who's back, honey?"

"That man. He's just standing there by the porch."

Jew walked over to the door and looked out. There, standing by the edge of the porch, was Cigar Baker.

"Morning," he greeted Jew.

"Well, morning, Cigar. What brings you up here so early, and on a Sunday, too?"

"Hoped you folks were going to church and thought maybe an old man could catch a ride."

"You bet. We'll be ready in a few minutes. How about a cup of coffee?" Jew asked.

"Don't mind if I do. I saw your little girl looking at me out of the window. Hope I didn't scare her."

"No, I don't think you did. She thought you were someone else for a minute."

"She seen that haint in the woods, has she?"

"I don't think so, Cigar. Hey, why don't you come on in and drink your coffee at the kitchen table while we finish getting dressed?"

"Nope." The old man sat down on the top step. "Just black and strong, like my women. Remember? I'll wait for you here. Don't like going in to people's houses. Some things best not done and believe me, mister, I ain't going in that house ever. You know it belonged to him a long time ago?"

"OK, Cigar. You sit there and we'll be ready in a jiffy." Jew gave the old man his coffee and then went back into the house.

56

"Golly, Daddy, that old man is strange, isn't he?" Rhonda asked.

"Don't worry about it, honey. Get finished dressing and let's go to church," Jew answered.

After church, Jew returned to the farm. Old Cigar had been very silent all the way to church and also on the return home. The family got out of the car and went inside. Clara asked Cigar if he would care to stay for lunch.

He studied the question over and after a few moments said, "No, ma'am. Thank you, but I think I'll just mosey on home and eat my fish. Jesus, he had friends who were fishermen, you know. Me, I'm a fisherman, too. That's the only reason that there old haint ain't bothered me all these years."

"OK, Mr. Baker, but you know that you are welcome any time." Clara disappeared through the door.

"Cigar," Jew said, "you have spoken about this haint several times now. Are you scared of him?"

"No, sir, I ain't scared of nothing. I can whup a truckload of anything and just begin to work up a sweat. I can pick a bale of cotton before noon and outrun any doggone white boy in the county. No, sir. I ain't scared. Just some things you don't crowd. Know what I mean?"

"Yeah. I know what you mean," Jew chuckled. He knew the old man had not been in a scrap for many years and all the cotton picked in the last fifteen or twenty years anywhere nearby had been picked with a machine. Furthermore, Jew doubted if old Cigar could do better than a quick walk. But if it made him feel good to think so, why not.

"Cigar," Jew continued, "You have spoken about this haint several times now. You ever really see him? I know you told me the other day you never did. But come on now, tell me the truth. Did you ever see him? I mean really see him up close, where you could tell what he looked like?"

"Yes, sir. I did once. Down by the creek over there." He

pointed toward the clump of oaks at the edge of the field. "I was fishing down there." He moved his arm and pointed toward the far end of the field. "I hadn't caught nothing, so I moved up the stream a bit. I started to get me a nibble when I feels someone watching me. I turns around slow, so as not to scare the fish, you know. Well, sir, up there on the bank was this man, about twenty feet from me. He was just looking; not moving, not talking, not anything. I doesn't know him, so I say 'howdy.' He don't say nothing, so I get up and he turns and walks away. I went back to fishing. 'Bout an hour later, I turns around again and there's this dude again. I say 'Can I help you, neighbor?' He don't talk. Man, I think this guy must be crazy. Crazy people some time don't talk. You know that?"

"That's what I've heard," Jew answered. "What was he wearing? I mean what did his clothes look like?"

"Well, sir, he had on blue pants. Had a yellow stripe on the leg; a blue shirt that had been washed a bunch of times. Was almost white from fading. He had on a hat like them pictures I is seen on them Yankees way back when."

"What are you saying, Cigar?" Jew asked. "He looked like a Yankee soldier?"

"Shoot, no. Everybody knows soldiers wear green or khaki. Everybody knows that."

"Yeah. Was he a white man?"

"Shoot, no, man. He was a black man. Light though. Like the whites call high yellow. But, man, he was big. 'Bout six foot, six inches, I'll bet. Mean eyes, too. His mouth, it weren't too big. His lips was skinny. You seen 'em like that, ain't you?"

"Yeah, sure. What happened then?" Jew probed the old man.

"Well, I got up and climbed the bank. I decided whatever the hell he was up to, I was going to find out. When I got to the top of the bank, he was gone. Man, just gone. There weren't no place to go, but he was gone. I knowed then and there I had seen a haint and no way was I going to fish his hole no more. From that day on, I fish way down there or over at Moss Phillips' place about a mile and a quarter up the creek. I never fished that hole again to this day. No, sir, and I ain't going to either."

"You ever see him again?"

"Nope. But folks living here have."

"What makes you think that?"

"I seen 'em move in here, stay a little while and leave. I knowed they seen him and he don't like nobody living here or fishing his hole either. No, sir, he don't like that!"

"You know who he's supposed to be?" Jew asked.

"Nope. I only heard him called Isaac. But my papa was borned about a mile over yonder way. I heard him tell about some man that got himself killed hereabouts. But 'fore he died, he told them that killed him he weren't going to leave his land."

"When was that, Cigar? A long time ago?"

"Sure 'nuf. Before my time, for sure."

"Your daddy ever see him?" Jew asked.

"Don't know. Got to go now. Thanks for the ride to church. Didn't catch but two little ol' catfish the other day. That's why I didn't bring you one." The old man turned to leave.

"Hold on a minute, Cigar," Jew said. Jew went into the house.

"Honey, that old man doesn't have any fish at home. He told me he only caught two the other day. Don't we have some of that ham left from the other night?"

"Sure, John. You think he'll take it?"

"He'll take it. Wrap it up for me, will you?"

Jew went back outside with a package. The old man had lit his stub of a black cigar and was puffing on it.

"Cigar, will you do me a favor?"

"Sure, Mr. Williams, but what can I do for you?"

"Well, the other night the wife cooked this ham. Now, I like ham all right, but, man, I've had ham sandwiches every day since. Do me a favor and take this ham so I won't have to eat it anymore."

The old man laughed. "I knows what you mean. My wife, God rest her soul, used to make me eat everything she cooked if it took a week."

"Then you know what I'm up against."

"Yep. Sure do. Much obliged. See you. And thank you, son. You're a good man."

"Hey, catch me a catfish next time, will you?"

The old man shook his head in the affirmative and turned and walked away. Jew could hear him humming as he went down the lane. He stopped about fifty yards away and turned. He raised his hand and shouted, "I'll catch you a fish so big you ain't got a pan it'll fit in." He laughed and turned back, continuing on his way home.

"You do that, you old rascal, you do that, and I'll cook it right here in the yard and make you stay and eat it with us," Jew said half to himself, half aloud.

Jew went in and changed clothes. As he came back downstairs, Clara met him at the foot of the stairs.

"Don't want to rush you, but you had better get a fire going in the barbecue. Jeff and Sara will be out any time."

"I'll have coals glowing in the pit before you can get that coffee pot to run through its cycle."

"Want some coffee, do you? Well, Mr. Smarty Pants, it's working right now, so you better get a move on."

"Woman, get out of my head. You can second guess me more than anybody ought to," Jew said shaking his head.

"No guessing to it, babe. This mama reads your mind like a book. So you had better watch what you think, my man."

Clara laughed.

Jew had his fire just where he wanted it when Jeff, Sara and their daughter, Alice, pulled into the driveway.

Sara greeted Jew with, "Wait until you hear this, John." She held up several tapes. "This is the most detailed, incredible story I've ever read."

"As good as we hoped for the other night?"

"Oh, yes. And the details ... This lady not only loved her husband very much, she was undoubtedly very proud of him."

"I gathered that the other night. I can't wait. Come on in. I'll get Clara and we'll start listening."

Alice and the Williams' children each grabbed a fishing pole and headed for the creek.

"You kids be careful down there, you hear," Jew called after them.

"Sure, Dad, don't worry. Old Cigar told me where to go today after church," Ronnie called over his shoulder.

Jeff moved over close to Jew and looking past him said in a quiet voice, "Jew, I know there are a lot of folks who wouldn't approve, but I have to ask you something."

"Sure, Jeff, what do you have on your mind?" he responded.

"Would you, by any chance, have a cold beer in that refrigerator out there in the kitchen?" Jeff asked in a very quiet voice.

"No, Jeff, I don't."

Jeff got a somewhat surprised look on his face.

"But, now, if we were to look in the one out on the back porch, we probably will find all the cold beer we can handle."

Both men laughed and moved toward the back door. Jeff slapped Jew on the back and draped his arm over his shoulder.

"Jew, I've known a lot of folks from California to Florida, Michigan to Texas and, by damn, I feel something when I'm around you." Both men took a beer and sat down in the chairs on the porch.

"I know what you are saying, Jeff. I've known a lot of people, too. And somehow I feel real relaxed around you. Where are you from? I mean really from. You weren't born around here, were you?"

"No. I was born in Ohio, a small town outside of Cleveland. But we had folks here long, long ago, before the Civil War. In fact, this place you bought once belonged to my great-great-grandfather."

Jew looked at him, "You don't mean you were related to old what's-his-name?"

"Yep. I'm the great-great-grandson of old Lucas James Willard himself. I often thought I would buy back some of this land myself, but it just doesn't ever seem to work out that way. I guess that's why I've gotten so hooked up in this story. That Sara won't tell me a thing about what she has been reading and recording. Says I'll just have to wait and hear it when the rest of you hear it." He sighed and took a long pull on his beer. "I guess if anyone had to buy this place besides me, I'm damn glad it's you. Know what I mean?"

"Yep, sure do. To tell the truth, I'm glad it's me, too," Jew answered.

They both laughed.

"What are you two up to?" Clara asked as she and Sara came out on the porch.

Sara stopped about two steps out of the door and placed both hands on her hips. "Jeff Sanders, what are you drinking? Is that a beer?" She seemed upset and both Jew and Clara felt a great strain to be placed in this position, especially if she really objected to drinking.

A smile crossed her lips. "I've always said some day our church is going to have an ecumenical council and the major decision will be to start drinking with each other," she laughed. "Suppose I could join you boys?"

They all laughed.

"I think I'll make mine white wine," Clara added.

They sat there enjoying the view. They could see the kids fishing about three hundred yards away. Several minutes went by with no one saying anything.

Then Jeff turned toward Jew and in a very sincere tone said, "Now this is how man is supposed to spend his time. With friends he enjoys and the joy of watching his offspring enjoy themselves. I wonder what the rest of the world is doing?" He did not really require an answer.

"Hey, babe, get the tapes. I've got to know what else was in that manuscript. It's been hard to get it off my mind," Jeff said. "How about you, Jew? I'll bet you have thought about it a time or two yourself, haven't you?"

"How about all the time?" Jew laughed.

Clara joined in, "Sara, I hope you didn't push yourself too hard on this. You've got to be busy."

She did not get to finish. Sara cut her off.

"This is the most exciting thing I've ever gotten into. I'll tell you what I did do, however. I knew I was going to be struggling in order to get finished for today, so I called a friend of mine, the one I mentioned the other night, Alicia Garcia. She is, in the true sense of the term, a master of the language. I called and asked her for help. She came over and we worked together. Otherwise, I would still be working on this narrative.

"Alicia took the last half of the work while I took the first half. We each worked at the same time, so no one has heard the whole story put together yet. I hope it's all right, if after we have heard it I can bring Alicia out, so she too can hear the story in its entirety."

"Well, you should have invited her out today," Clara said.

"I would have, Clara, but she and her husband had to leave last night to go somewhere up north on a business trip. I'll call you when she gets back and you all can meet her then."

"By all means," Jew said.

"From what I have read and put on tape, I know we are all going to be enchanted with this story." Sara set the tape down on a small table beside her chair.

"Before you start, Sara," Clara said, "Jew, why don't you put that brisket I've laid out on the drain board on the barbecue and it can be cooking while we listen."

"I thought we were going to have chicken," Jew said.

"We were, but Sara told me on the phone earlier this week that this tape would hold me to it better than one of my soaps, so I decided we would have brisket. Also, I've made some sandwiches and we can eat those and they will hold us over until supper."

"That's why I married her, Jeff. This here woman has always kept my stomach in mind," Jew said as he went into the kitchen. He returned with the meat.

"Now, that looks like good old southern vittles to me," Jeff remarked.

"You should know," Sara said as she patted Jeff in the mid-section.

Jew took a good long drink of his beer and lit a cigarette. "Now this is what I call entertainment."

They all laughed. The friendship being bound here would last for all the years the four of them would have. It was a good feeling, a feeling some people never have and others take for granted.

Sara picked up a tape marked No. 1 and turned it over in her hands, looking at it as if daydreaming.

"Come on, babe, put it in the machine," Jeff said.

She looked up, gave a slight turn of her head and placed the tape in the player. Her finger rested on the play button. Half to herself, half to the others, she said, "Like I've said several times, this lady was a very special, remarkable person. The details, the minute details, she has put down show how deep her love for this man really was." She paused for a second, smiled and pressed the button.

The tape started to turn.

Chapter 7

This is the story of my husband as he told it to me over the years of our marriage. I have tried to put it down as a record of his life.

I must first start with his mother, Iola, who played a strong part in the building of his character.

The spring of 1845 found Iola, a short, rather thin Negro slave girl about sixteen years old, on the block being sold at auction. The bidders were all white plantation owners looking for new stock to work in the fields and propagate their working stock.

"I'll give you $100 for that one," Lucas Willard called to the auctioneer as he pointed his riding crop at Iola.

"The gentleman says he'll give me $100 for this little plum. You have got to be out of your mind, sir. The bidding for this little jewel starts at $500."

A short, fat man sitting on a nail keg raised his hand. "You got $200 from me," he said in a hoarse, raspy voice.

"$250," Lucas said.

"$275," was the fat man's reply.

The bidding went back and forth between the two. Each bid was increased by $25. When the bid had reached $425, the auctioneer raised both of his fat hands, "Gentlemen, gentlemen, we are going to be here the rest of the day and half of the night. Which one of you wil give me $900?"

There was silence. After a few seconds, the auctioneer said, "Well, are you buying or do you just like to bid?"

"I'll give you $500 and that's my final offer," Lucas said.

"You just stole yourself a true black pearl nigger, friend," the fat man said as he stood up and walked off.

"Come on down here, girl," Lucas said. "Get over there with those others. I'll mate you with that big black on the end there. Now get." He kicked at her rear as she hastily moved over to where the other slaves stood huddled together.

The ride to the plantation took two days in the rear of the job wagon driven by a big, heavy set black man. The newly purchased slaves were not permitted to talk to one other. Every time one of them would speak, the driver would turn and strike out with a short whip.

"Shut yo' mouth, nigger," he would shout.

Lucas Willard rode out front on a big chestnut mare. Overseer, Clarence Haley, rode a gray.

"Well, Mr. Lucas, you done got yourself a fine bunch of darkies this trip."

"Yeah. I sure did. I want that last one I bought left alone, too. You hear?"

"Yes, sir. I never bother those darkies. You know that. Not once did I mess around with one of your blacks."

"Like hell you don't. What do you think I am? Blind? I know you've been breeding half of those mamas I got. But you keep your paws off that one. She'll work in the main house with old Lissy. That old woman is just going to up and die on me some day and my missus will kill me if I don't have a housekeeper and cook to take her place."

Iola could not believe the sight of the main house when the wagon pulled up in front of the plantation. Across the green field was a house so big, it looked like a whole village could live inside.

On her trip over on the ship chained in the hold where almost half of the captive slaves had died, she never expected to see anything like this. She could not have imagined anything so grand.

The months passed one day at a time and she was taught the duties of the housekeeper. Old Lissy showed her how to wash and iron. The task of making soap was now Iola's and the lye would eat at her hands on the day she would perform this task. Of all the jobs she hated, making soap was the worst.

Cooking came slowly. She had great difficulty understanding the necessity of measuring items that were to be mixed. Once this was understood, she became a very good cook.

Mrs. Willard, a frail small woman, told her one day, "Iola, you are the best cook in these parts. If the Jacksons knew about you, Mr. Willard couldn't afford to turn down the price you would bring. Lord knows, I hope they don't find out."

For several days, Iola felt sure she would be sold. How she hoped she wouldn't. She had grown to like the Willards and there was a big black named Henry she had been working on when she had the opportunity. She hoped Mr. Willard would mate her with him when the time came.

Iola had been at the Willard plantation a little over a year, when one night her bedroom door was thrown open. There, standing in the door with a lamp in his hand, was Lucas Willard, half drunk.

"Well, well, here you are in bed and ready for your master," he said as he set the lamp down and unhooked his belt.

Iola pulled the quilt covering her up to her neck. Her eyes were filled with fright. Lucas grabbed the quilt and ripped it away. Then he tore the gown from the trembling body of Iola. She tried to break free of his grasp, but he was too strong. He forced her back on the bed. His weight held her down. His big hands squeezed her breast as he held her tight.

She gave up the fight. It was in vain and she knew she could not escape. This was her lot in life and to fight could mean even worse punishment.

It was not long before Iola knew she was pregnant. She was surprised to learn that Mrs. Willard was also pregnant. The work was hard and her shame seemed to show at times when Lucas would come near her. The thing that she found hard to understand was not once did he say or act as if anything had taken place between them. The child she carried was his. "Surely he knows," she thought.

As the months went by, Mrs. Willard grew weaker. Her frail body seemed to waste away. Most of her meals were served in her room and she no longer moved about the house giving directions to the servants.

The spring of 1847, Iola went into labor and gave birth to a son. She called him Isaac after a preacher who had told the slaves about Christ. She felt he was a good man and very smart. Perhaps if she named her child after him, he too would be smart.

Three weeks later, Mrs. Willard gave birth to William Robert. It was a very difficult delivery and after the child was born, Mrs. Willard lived for only a few hours, then she died.

Lucas called Iola from the kitchen. She entered the study. Her head was bowed and she wept. Mrs. Willard had been kind to her these two years she had been in the house.

"You wanted me, sir?" she said as she sniffed to keep her nose from running.

"Yeah. I wanted you. Stop that snivelling, woman. I got a wet nurse job for you and I don't need any snivelling nigger doing it either."

"Yes, sir."

"My wife died, but she gave me a son. He'll be needing mother's milk. You came fresh when you had that pickaninny of yours. I want you to wet nurse my son. You know what that is, don't you girl?"

"Yes, sir."

"My boy sucks first, understand? Don't you give that pickaninny of yours a drop till my boy's had his fill. Your tits are big enough to feed half a dozen, so you got plenty. Now go upstairs and get my son. I've got business to take care of."

"Yes, sir," she answered and set about raising both children.

Besides taking care of the two boys, she had her regular work to do. There never seemed to be time to rest. At times she thought she would die from fatigue.

Iola's small frame had started to widen and her girlish figure was fast fading away. She knew she would soon be like most of the other blacks. Their bodies were much older than their age. They all seemed to grow old quickly and die. No one seemed to care. That's what bothered her most. No one seemed to care.

The winters came and went only to return after the harvest of the crops planted in the spring.

Isaac and William Robert grew in body and mind. Even though there was never any doubt about who was the slave and who was the master, the two boys were close friends.

Because of their friendship, Isaac was often left alone and did not receive the abuse the others got from the cruel overseer.

"Some day I'll break his neck," William Robert told Isaac one morning. "That fool hurts people just for the fun of it. When I'm master, I'll put his ass to outrunning my bird shot."

Isaac laughed. "He's bad, William Robert. Don't mess with him. Your Pa believes everything he tells him, too."

"I know, but my day is coming. Wait and see."

The years passed and the world stood still on the plantation.

Chapter 8

It was some time in the summer, 1861, before Isaac knew anything about a war between the States. He did not really understand just why they were at war. He knew it had to do with his freedom, but did not understand how that could be. He knew he belonged to Lucas Willard the same as his chestnut mare. He was property.

"William Robert, just why are they fighting a war anyway?"

"Hell, Isaac, it's like a fight between two darkies. You know, when they both want the same bitch."

"Oh yessuh, William Robert. I know. One's gonna kick the hell outta the other for a quick piece of tail. I knows about that all right, but who's the bitch?"

"I guess you are in a way, Isaac. The North says we ain't got no right to keep you on this plantation and the South is saying, 'Like hell we ain't. We bought and paid for our darkies. They are the same as our mules or cows. They are

73

ours.' Then they say it ain't right. We say, 'Why? We got a title to 'em.' They say, 'Because, just because.' So we're going to kick their ass. Not to worry. It'll all be over before fall, you'll see."

"I guess so, if you say so, William Robert. You got to own me. Where would I go if you didn't?"

"I told you, Isaac, don't worry about it."

Master Willard caught the two boys talking. "What you talking to that nigger about, son? He ain't got time to jaw with you. Now get up there and study your lessons. And you, nigger, get your black ass to work. You got a barn to clean."

"Yes, suh, Master Willard, yes, suh."

"You're just like your mama, boy. You'd screw off all day long if someone didn't keep on you all the time. You blacks are all alike. Them damn Yankees think we live like kings down here in Dixie. Lord, if they only knew how you blacks try a man's patience." He left grumbling to himself as Isaac finished cleaning up the barn and hauled the manure out to the pile at the edge of the field.

Fall came and went. The war went on. Mr. Willard spent more and more time in town. Each time he came home he was upset and cursed the blacks more each time. Then he would beat one of them for no real reason from time to time. He drank more and more.

"The war ain't going good, Isaac," William Robert told him one day. "I guess I'll be going soon. They need all the men they can get. There's just too many of those Yankees."

"William Robert, you ain't no man. You're a boy like me. You ain't no soldier. You couldn't kill nobody."

"I am a man, you dumb darkie. I'm fourteen years old and big for my age. I shoot as straight as any man in the county. Don't you tell me I'm not a man. I'll take a black snake to your back."

"William Robert, you and me, we been friends all our lives.

You sucked on one of my mammy's tits while I sucked on the other one at the same time. You couldn't take no whip to me no more than I could hurt you with a stick up side the head, even if you did need it. You know that, don't you?"

"I know that, Isaac, but I got to do something. Don't you see? We could lose everything. If them damn Yankees win this war, we're going to lose all our blackies. Who's going to work the field? We'll lose the plantation. It's been in my family since the war between us and them damn English people. What would we do if we lost this place?"

The next morning Isaac and four other slaves were sent up the river to cut wood for the coming winter. They were there three weeks. He wondered if William Robert was serious and would be gone to the war when he returned. He was pleased to see that he had not gone when they returned.

Food for the master's house and the darkies grew less and less each week until the hands began to eat wild onions and poke salad in season. Some gathered acorns and made a soup. It was bitter, but filled an empty stomach.

It was early spring when the first Federal troops came onto the plantation. The year was 1865. The flood of blue uniforms seemed to have no end. Master Willard ran out of the main house like a crazy man. He shouted and screamed. One of the soldiers rode up and hit him in the head with a rifle butt. They burned the fields and set the main house on fire. Then an officer had the blacks brought up to the main yard. They stood huddled together, scared of what would happen to them. They did not know who to trust, the master or the men in blue uniforms who destroyed the fields—fields they had worked, had cleared of trees and brush, plowed and planted. The soldiers acted as if they were crazy with whiskey—whooping and howling.

The officer in charge rode up on a large black gelding. He shouted some orders and the soldiers became very quiet. Isaac could hear the fire from the main house as it ate away at the once most beautiful house he had ever seen.

"You people," the officer shouted. "You people are free. This southern white trash doesn't own you any more. You don't need papers or permission to go You are free, so get the hell out of here."

They stood there not wanting to offend the officer, but not knowing what the master would do if they took off toward town. The officers horse turned around and reared, then stamped his front feet. The horse was frightened by the fire. The officer was getting madder at the darkies and his horse who kept on with his prancing and whirling.

"You damn black fools! Don't you understand? We have just set you free and all you do is stand there like a bunch of dummys. What the hell do you people have? Shit for brains? Get the hell out of here," he shouted. He was angry. The soldiers ran toward the blacks shouting, "Get out of here! Get the hell out of here!"

A black girl named Nellie about fifteen years old was there with the rest of the darkies. A big whiskered soldier half ran over and grabbed her by the arm and pulled her away as the soldiers crowded around.

Isaac stepped up and said, "That's my woman, master. Tell them to let her go." Isaac knew what they were going to do. They had been told by the master many times about these people.

The officer just looked at Isaac, then lifted his foot from the stirrups and kicked him in the chest, causing him to fall to the ground.

"That's a small price to pay for freedom, you black bastard. Now get the hell out of here or I'll take the whip to you."

Old One-eyed Sam grabbed Isaac by the arm and dragged him away toward the stable.

"Man," Isaac told him, "you know what they are going

to do to her. Let me go," Isaac begged.

"Don't be crazy, boy. You can't help her. Only get yourself killed. Ain't no sense in that, now, is they?"

Old One-eyed Sam was right and Isaac knew it, but it hurt to leave her. As they crossed the field, Isaac heard her scream once. He looked back and saw a soldier hit William Robert with a rifle butt as he tried to get her away from the soldier. He fell to the ground close to Master Willard.

Six of the freed slaves hid in the brush until dark. The soldiers had moved on down the road and set up a camp close to the creek. The main house burned all night.

Some time in the night, Isaac and two others crept back. William Robert and Master Willard were still lying on the ground. Isaac rolled William Robert over. His face was cut bad, but he was still alive.

Old One-eyed Sam whispered, "The Master's alive. Let's get 'em to the woods."

"He's alive, One-eye. He's alive." Isaac must have said it a dozen times. He was so glad they had not killed William Robert. Isaac really did not care too much about Master Willard, but William Robert was a different matter.

Isaac looked down toward the barn. One-eye knew what was in his mind.

"Don't even think about it, boy. They'll kill you if you go down there," he said.

"Maybe so. But I gots to go."

Isaac slipped down to the barn and peeked through a crack. Nellie was laying on the hay in the corner of a horse stall. Her clothes had been ripped off. She lay all spraddle-legged with one arm over her face. She was making a funny sound. Sort of crying, sort of moaning. One of the soldiers was sitting with his back to the wall. His pants were hanging on a nail by him and Isaac could see him drinking from a whiskey bottle. Isaac opened the door slowly, just wide enough to crawl in. He picked up a big rock and struck the soldier just above the ear with a crushing blow. He did not make a sound, except for the thud when the rock hit him. Isaac grabbed his trousers and helped Nellie put them on. He then helped her back to where One-eye was waiting with the Master and William Robert.

William Robert was about half awake but still groggy. One-Eyed Sam and Hickory Man carried the Master. Nellie followed behind. She never said a word. They spent the night in the woods with the soldiers about a quarter of a mile away.

The soldiers found the master's milk cow and killed her, then roasted her over a fire. That was the last of the livestock. The rest had been sold or eaten long ago. Isaac could see right now that the South was gone. The plantation was gone.

Isaac asked old One-eye, "What the hell we going to do now? We ain't got no place to go."

"I don't know, boy, but we can't stay here. They ain't nothing left."

When morning came, the soldiers left. Isaac saw two of them helping the one out of the barn laughing about how a nigger girl had bested him. William Robert was a bit better. Ole Annie had put a poultice on his cut face and around his eye. The eye was swollen shut, but she said he would not be blind like old One-Eye Sam. The master began to talk out of his head, ordering people long dead to plow the field and pull the corn. He started raving about some race horse his daddy had owned and lost when he was a boy. Old Annie said it was a fever and it would go away.

The group went back to the shacks about noon. The main house was still smoking. The master's second wife, Mabel Lea, and her two children, Beth Ann and Byron Louis, were gone to Charleston and had been gone for about two weeks. William Robert doubted if she would ever return when she heard about the fire and the Yankees running off the darkies. She was not one to stay where she did not have all the nice things in life. Even if she had been mistress for ten or twelve years, she probably would just stay on in Charleston.

Her father was a doctor and had property up north somewhere. William Robert told Isaac he had heard his father raise hell about that several times, calling her father a mugwumper. Isaac found out later that meant he could go with either the South or North, whoever won the war. Isaac had to agree with William Robert. She probably would not come back.

Three weeks passed and Master Willard was his old self, but even meaner. Old One-eye and Annie left to go up north. They took Nellie to the promised land as old One-eye called it. She was better now, but still in bad shape. He wanted Isaac to go with them, but Isaac told him he had heard some blacks talking about going West. Land out there was free for the taking. Somewhere out West, there was land no white man or black had set foot on. It was there for the taking. That was where Isaac would go.

"I'm going to get my own farm," Isaac told One-eye, "out there in the West."

Chapter 9

Winter was coming and Isaac knew he could not stay on. There was no work stock, no seed, and except for a rabbit or squirrel now and then, very little to eat. They ate the leaves off the grape vines and wild onions most of the time.

Isaac decided he would leave, but did not want to tell William Robert goodby. He started to just walk away. He took an old butcher knife so he would have some kind of weapon, just in case he needed it along his way. People were crazy with hunger and just plain mad at the world most of the time. Isaac knew he had to defend himself. He knew he would be all alone once he left the plantation.

It was just after daylight when Isaac got up and started to leave. He was half way across the old front field, when he heard William Robert calling. Isaac stopped and turned around. William Robert was running across the field. He caught up to Isaac. Out of wind, he leaned over and placed both hands on his knees, his breath coming in gasps.

When he caught his breath, he straightened up and asked, "Where the hell are you going?"

"William Robert, I got to go. We are going to starve to death here. Come on and go with me. We'll get us a farm out west. It's free land out there. I heard 'em talking in town about it."

"Isaac, that's bull shit. There's no free land anywhere and, sure as hell not out west. There's Indians out there. Man, they'll cut your peter off. Those are bad people out there. They hate the whites. I mean really hate them."

"But, William Robert, I ain't white."

"Makes no difference, man. They'll hate you, too."

"Well, I'm going. You coming?"

"No. I'll stay here. This is where I belong and so do you."

"No, sir, I have got to go. My mind is made up. Don't try to change it."

They looked at each other for a few minutes, knowing full well they may never see one another again, not in this lifetime anyway.

"William Robert," Isaac said, "before I leave there's something I got to tell you."

"What is it, Isaac? What you got to tell me?" he replied in a mocking manner.

"William Robert, you know you sucked on one of my mama's tits while I sucked on the other, don't you?"

"Of course. You told me enough times. So what? She was the wet nurse when I was born."

"Yeah, she was. Your mama died giving you life and my mama had me about three weeks before. So your daddy put you on her tits. But, William Robert, there's more to it than that."

"Yeah, like what?" WIlliam Robert asked.

"Well," Isaac sat down on his haunches. William Robert

followed. "Mammy told me when your daddy married Miss Mabel she had one child, Beth Ann. Later they had Byron Louis."

William Robert interrupted, "That lazy little fart."

"Yeah, I know. But he is what my mammy called your half brother. Your daddy and his daddy is Master Willard. Right?"

"So what?"

"So my mammy told me on her deathbed that one night after the chicken fights over at the Willow Springs plantation, your daddy came home drunk. Your mammy was upstairs asleep. Well, he come into my mammy's room and he . . ."

"He what, Isaac, screwed her? Hell! He screwed all his darkies at one time or another. Everybody knows that. So what?"

"Yeah, William Robert, he screwed her and it's the only time anyone did that to her. I mean ever."

"What are you saying, nigger? What the hell are you saying?"

William Robert stood up and clutched his fist.

Isaac looked up into his eyes and slowly stood up. Their eyes were locked to one another.

"William Robert, we have been close all these years. There wasn't nothing I wouldn't do for you, you know that, and you kept me from being whipped several times when the Master was really mad at me. That's true as sin and you know it. The reason is, we got the same daddy. We is brothers, or like they say half brothers."

William Robert turned white and got weak kneed. His face turned red. "Me? I'm half brother to a nigger?"

"No, William Robert, not to a nigger. To me, Isaac. Hey, I didn't do it. Your daddy did. Why you think I'm a high yellow? You know how black my mammy was. Hell, I just wanted you to know why I've loved you all these years, that's all. I didn't even know why until she told me. Ain't no one going to know 'cept you and me. But I'll think about you from time to time. I'd be proud if you'd do the same. Say when the catfish are biting or the squirrels are jumping all over the trees again."

A tear rolled down William Robert's cheek. "Hell, Isaac, I'm going to miss you. You be safe, you hear." William Robert stuck out his hand. "Come back, you crazy nigger." He gulped and cleared his throat. "Come back rich and buy this damn place. It'll be your turn.

"And something else, Isaac, I've known for a long time we had the same daddy. I was just putting you on. Your mama was a special lady to me, you know that. Well, one day about two or three years ago, she told me the same story, but asked me not to tell you. I promised her I wouldn't, so I never did. She had my word on it. You understand?"

The two boys shook hands, then grabbed each other and hugged one another. They both understood.

Lucas Willard came out to the edge of the field. He shouted, "Billy Bob, what you and Isaac doing down there?"

"Nothing, Daddy. Isaac is leaving. I'm just saying goodbye."

Master Willard put his head down and taking long strides came straight over to them. When he got there, he grabbed William Robert by the elbow and pulled him back.

"Where you going, nigger?" he asked.

"Out west, sir. Out west to get me some land of my own."

"You niggers are all alike. I raise you, feed you, clothe you, call the doctor when you are sick, and when I need you, where the hell are you?" In a mocking voice, he added, "I'm going out west, sir, to get me some land. You ungrateful bastard, get your ass off my land. Get." He drew his hand back to strike Isaac, when William Robert stepped in between them.

"Don't hit him, Daddy. We've been like brothers. If he

wants to go west, he's got his reasons. We can't keep him here any more. He's free to do what he wants. That's the law."

"It may be the law, but it ain't right."

"But it's the law," William Robert said.

The old man shrugged his shoulders and turned to walk away. He took a couple of steps and stopped. He half turned and spoke to the ground.

"I hope you'll look after yourself and remember us sometime and how it used to be here before the Yankees came. Your mama, she was a good woman. You remember that. Will you do that, boy?"

"Yes, sir, I'll never forget this place or the people that made it what it was and thank you for saying that about my mama."

The old man, with stooped shoulders, turned and walked toward the burned out main house.

"Damn," Jew said. "Life had to be hard then. Can you imagine how it must have been? God, their whole way of life changed."

"It had to be hard at first, John," Clara remarked, "but after all, it was bound to happen sooner or later. You can't keep people like cattle and expect it to last forever."

"I know, honey, I know; but we are looking at it from today's point of view, too."

"You both are right, of course," Jeff added. "However, the one thing that really stands out to me in the story thus far is the way no one really cared about anyone except himself. Did you notice how the Yankee officer acted? He really didn't care about the slaves. His main goal was to impress them and his men with his authority."

"Yeah, I've known a few of those myself," Jew chuckled.

Sara had stopped the tape as the others talked.

"Start it up," Jeff requested.

Chapter 10

The years to follow were very different ones for Isaac. He worked when and where he could find employment. He chopped wood at farms many times for just a little to eat.

In the town of Indianola, Texas, he found steady work in the wagon yard. Here he repaired the freight wagons and took care of the livestock.

One of the owners of the wagon yard was a man named Eric Van Pelt, a Dutchman from Amsterdam, Holland. He had worked his way over to the United States on a ship that had brought immigrants to the Indianola port, a growing town on the Mexican Gulf in South Texas.

Van Pelt jumped ship and stayed on. He met a man named Johnson, who was old but had money. Johnson took a liking to Van Pelt and set him up in business. With Van Pelt working the business and Johnson with the money, they had become very succcessful in the freight business.

Isaac liked working for Van Pelt and seldom saw Johnson, as he was old and his bad leg kept him away from the wagon yard.

Isaac knew this job was too good to last. He felt somehow he would not grow old here. He did not know why, but he had loved the plantation in Georgia and now he had grown to love it here in Indianola. The good things just seemed to give him a taste, but not a full meal. Isaac was strong, however, and accepted this as his plight, but he still wanted to own his own farm. It was his dream and he never stopped thinking of it. But for some reason, he knew he would be forced to leave some day.

His fears came true in September of 1875. He was never sure of the date because of the pain and confusion that followed the worst storm he had ever seen.

It was early in the morning and he was working at the forge repairing a wheel. He had replaced several spokes and was fitting the metal rim. Old man Johnson had come down to the yard on one of his rare visits and was sitting on a barrel talking to Van Pelt. The storm seemed to be getting worse. Isaac remembered old man Johnson saying to him, "You had better watch this one, boy. It's going to be one to tell your young'uns about." Van Pelt agreed. He had never seen a storm building like this one.

The wind hit like a wall. It came in from the sea and buildings collapsed like wheat being mowed in the field. A board came flying through the barn door and hit Mr. Johnson, sending the old man flying across the barn. Isaac grabbed Van Pelt and threw him to the corner of the barn and fell on top of him just when what seemed like a bomb went off. The entire barn exploded right over them. Then the water came. A huge wave seemed to have raised up and swept the little town away.

Isaac was never sure what happened next. When he regained consciousness, he was lying on a little grassy knoll. His head was cut and his leg felt like it was on fire. He was lucky, however; he had no broken bones. His body did feel like it had been beaten with a big stick. He made his way back to where he thought the wagon barn had been. Nothing was left. He never knew what became of Van Pelt or Johnson. They must have been washed out to sea with about three-fourths of the town.

Isaac thought to himself, "Just like when the Yankees came. There ain't nothing left, nothing at all."

He started north on foot. He travelled north following the dirt road for two days. No travellers passed him in either direction. He felt sure someone would come by and he would catch a ride. Half starved and totally worn out, he would rest along the roadside hoping for someone, anyone, to come by.

The morning of the third day he came up on two mules. He recognized them as being from Van Pelt's line.

"They must have been washed up this way."

He caught one. It had a bad leg, but with it he was able to lure the other one close enough to catch it. The animal was sound, except for a few minor cuts. The animal turned out to be a godsend. The mule still had its halter on and Isaac made a rein with his belt. This permitted him to ride the mule with no problem.

Several days after finding the mules, Isaac rode into a town called Six Gun Junction. It did not take long to find out why the town had such a name. He went to the first stable he saw and asked for work. The man he talked to was a bear of a man. His beard was wild and he smelled worse than the stable. As Isaac went into the barnyard to speak to the owner, whose name was Willie Davis, he had no problem in knowing that Davis was not a pleasant man.

"What the hell you want, nigger? And where did you get that mule?"

"I'm looking for work, sir, and this here mule, he belongs to Mr. Van Pelt. I'm taking him to San Antone for him, sir."

Isaac had learned a long time ago if he used a lot of "sirs" and kept his head bowed as if in submission to authority, he would be more quickly accepted as no threat.

"What the hell can you do that I can't do myself?"

"Well, sir, I could clean this stable up to where it shines like a new double eagle," Isaac told him.

"Yeah? Well, I'll give you four bits and a bowl of chili if you can get this lot clean before the sun sets. That's just like one of them damn foreign Dutchmen to send a nigger off with no money. I ain't seen one yet that wasn't so tight he squeaked when he walked," Davis said as he walked away.

"Yes, sir, I can do it." Isaac was without a penny to his name and his stomach was beginning to think his throat had been cut.

Isaac had just started to work when two men came out of the bar next door shouting and cursing each other. They reached the street and one of the men reached for his sidearm. Before it was out of its holster, the other man shot him dead with a small gun he had in his coat pocket. As he stood over the man on the ground, he fired another shot into the man's head. The small gun held two shots and both were now spent. As he opened the gun to replace the spent shells, another man came out onto the porch of the bar with a shot gun. He yelled at the man in the street. As he looked up, the man on the porch shot both barrels, cutting the other one almost in half.

Two men came from across the street and dragged the two dead men over to the side of the building. Isaac watched them go through their pockets, then put the bodies in a wagon and drive out toward the cemetery.

"What them fellas going to do with them dead people, Mr. Davis?" he asked.

"They're going to plant 'em, that's what. You'll be lucky if they don't plant you, nigger, if you hang around this damn town too long. These damn people here are half crazy."

Isaac went back to work and two hours later, he saw the wagon coming back down the hill. The two men in it were laughing. As they drove past the lot, Davis walked out to the street.

"What's so funny, Jack?" he asked the driver.

"That damn Billy Joe we just put in the ground up there. Well, a couple of days ago, he cheated me out of old Sally. He knowed I don't have no gun, so he run me off when I was just about to get me a little. Well, I got even, I did. I planted him head first in that hole. I wanted him to get a head start for hell." They all laughed.

Isaac could see life, anyone's life, did not have much meaning to these people. He knew he would move on as soon as he could. Maybe he could find a job on one of the ranches around.

The next day he asked around, but times were hard. None of the ranches were hiring, so he left on his mule before daylight and headed for the big city to the north, San Antonio.

Sometime in the night he had heard gun shots again. As he rode out of town, he saw a body lying in the wagon that had been used to carry the other two to the cemetery. This is an evil town, he thought, as he shifted his weight on the back of the mule. He reached down and felt the handle of the knife he had in his boot.

"Hope I never have to use this," he said to his mule. "But if we do, we will. Ain't nobody going to do me in. Not like that. When we get to San Antonio, I'm going to get me a job and buy me a gun."

Isaac reached San Antonio in a slow steady rain. The streets were a mire from the mud. He saw a wagon stuck down to the axle. The team had been unhitched and the owner just left it until the weather would permit him to return and get it out of the mud.

Isaac saw an old Mexican man carrying an armload of wood. The old man slipped and fell. Isaac tied his mule and helped the old man up and picked up his wood, which was soaked.

"Where are you going?" he asked the old man.

The old man said something in Spanish, but Isaac did not understand. The old man pointed down the street. Isaac followed him carrying the wood. The old man led the mule. They came to an old stucco shack and the old man tied the mule to the side of the house. Both men went inside. An old woman was there cooking something on an open fire. She scooped some up in a bowl and handed it to Isaac. He did not know what it was, but it was good. The peppers in it warmed his stomach and caused him to gasp. The old man laughed and handed Isaac a dipper of water. It felt cool and was badly needed. His tongue felt scorched, but his empty stomach took over and he finished the bowl of food.

"You speak Spanish?" a voice asked him from a darkened corner of the room.

Isaac turned to see a boy of about ten years of age. He had not seen the boy and his actions showed he was surprised. The lad stepped out of the shadows and asked again, "You speak Spanish, black one?"

Isaac looked the boy over. He was barefooted and the shirt he was wearing was worse than the slaves wore back in Georgia. His pants were patched on top of patches and were held to his skinny waist by a small rope.

"No, I don't. But you speak English?"

"Si. Some. Not too much."

"What's your name, boy?" Isaac asked.

"Jose," the boy answered. "And you? How are you called?"

"I'm Isaac. This here town. Is it San Antonio?"

92

"Si. Where you from?" The boy was taken by Isaac's size and color.

"You ever see a black man before, boy?"

"Si. But not close." The boy reached out and drug a finger down Isaac's arm as if to wipe off the black.

Isaac chuckled. "It stays on, boy," he said as the boy looked at his finger.

The old man had gotten a bottle and poured a cupful for Isaac. He handed it to Isaac who smelled it. It had a sweet smell, but Isaac could tell it was strong.

"Tequila," the boy said. "Make you warm inside."

Isaac took a sip. It tasted awful, but he felt he had to drink it or insult the old man. So he downed it in one gulp. The old woman made a sound and put her hand to her mouth. She said something in Spanish and the old man and boy laughed. Isaac thought he would lose his breath.

"Damn, that's bad," he said as he ran to the water bucket. He poured a dipper full of water down his throat. Some of it ran down the front of his shirt. The old man handed the bottle to Isaac.

"No, sir, I don't think I'll go for seconds on that stuff. What did you call it, Jose?"

"Tequila. It's a Mexican, how you say?" he paused, "whiskey. Plenty strong."

"Yeah, that I've found out for myself."

The old lady had made a pallet in the corner and said something to Isaac, then pointed toward the pallet. He understood and lay down. This was the best night's rest he had had in a very long time and he slept soundly all night.

When he awoke in the morning, the rain had stopped. The old woman was making tortillas and cooking them on the open fire. They ate without talking.

After they had finished, the boy asked, "You going to stay here with us?"

"No. I have to find a job somewhere."

"No jobs here, unless you're in the Army. You going to be in the Army?" the boy asked.

"Never thought of it. Maybe. Yeah, maybe I will join the Army."

The idea appealed to Isaac.

"Where do they join the Army around here, Jose?"

"Fort Sam, I guess," he answered.

"Fort Sam? Never heard of it. Where is it? Is it close by?"

"Si. Over there," he pointed, "about four blocks. They got a big rock gate."

Isaac walked up to Fort Sam Houston and Jose followed along. Once there, Isaac asked a trooper what you had to do to join the Army.

"The first thing you have to do is be crazy," the soldier told him. "And if you are crazy enough, go over there to that building, the one with the clock tower. Ask for the enlistment officer. They'll help you." He laughed and went on his way shaking his head.

Isaac found the sergeant and asked him about joining the Army. The sergeant was a bull of a man.

He listened to Isaac, then in a husky voice, he asked, "You ever been in the Army before, boy? You ever fight with them people in the Confederacy? You ever been in prison? You on the run or something?"

"No, sir," he answered. "I ain't never done none of them things. I just need a job and three square meals a day. I thought maybe I could find that in the Army."

"OK. Sign here," the sergeant told him.

"Can't write my name, sir," Isaac informed him.

"Hell, I'm not surprised. Make your mark," he pointed, "right there."

Isaac placed his mark on the paper. "Now what do I do?" he asked.

"Raise your right hand." Isaac obeyed. "Repeat after me." The sergeant went slow and Isaac repeated the words as the sergeant said them. Isaac later understood it was called a swearing in, but at the same time he did not have any idea what he was doing.

As Isaac came out of the headquarters building, he saw the small Mexican boy, Jose, standing by the gate. The boy waved and shouted, "Good luck, Senor Isaac." Isaac waved back.

"Move out, boy. You got work to do in this man's Army," the sergeant barked.

Isaac was assigned to a stable detail right away and worked in the barns. He had never seen so many good horses in one herd before. They had plenty of hay and oats. Isaac soon found out that regular details were sent out to load feed purchased from the farms and stored at Fort Sam.

He liked the work and was sure he had found a home.

The days of drill found Isaac trying hard to enjoy the Army. He had trouble from the start and the sergeant in charge would not let up on him. Every mistake he made, and there were plenty, the sergeant would shout and curse him. There seemed to be no satisfying this man. He had a dislike for all black people, but Isaac really drew his hatred.

The situation was reaching a climax, when one day Isaac was loading a wagon with flour and beans at the Quartermaster's storage barn when Sgt. Kirkland came up.

"Watch what you are doing, nigger. Don't you break one of those sacks or I'll kick your ass from here to the guardhouse." He laughed.

His friend, Corp. Jones, chimed in, "Yeah, nigger, we'll kick your black ass up between your shoulders. Might improve your marching." They both laughed.

As Isaac walked past them with a hundred pound sack of flour on his shoulder, the sergeant stuck his foot out and tripped Isaac. He fell and the flour sack broke. Flour went everywhere in a cloud of white dust.

"You dumb nigger. I told you not to break them sacks. Now get up and get your black ass over to the guardhouse," he shouted.

As Isaac got up, he tried hard to contain himself. "Sergeant, you tripped me on purpose," he said.

"I what!" said the sergeant. He reached out and slapped Isaac across the face with the riding crop he was carrying. "Don't talk back to me, nigger," he shouted as he pointed to his sleeve. "I'm a sergeant."

The anger exploded in Isaac. His fist moved like lightening. As he buried his left one deep in the stomach, the sergeant doubled over and a knee caught him in the face sending him flying backwards. The corporal jumped on Isaac's back, but found himself caught by a strong black arm. Isaac bent forward and threw the corporal over his shoulder right on top of Sgt. Kirkland, who was trying to get up. Both men lay in a heap. Isaac hit the half raised Kirkland on the jaw which sent him sprawling.

Isaac was ready for either man to regain his balance. He knew by now he was in trouble, so he might as well do it right. He squared off, ready to hit the first one to get up.

The command of "Attention!" almost went unheard because of the excitement running through Isaac.

"I said 'Attention!', soldier, and all I want to hear is your eyeballs snap, mister," the voice commanded.

Isaac froze. The sergeant and the corporal both struggled to their feet. The sergeant tried to salute, but stuck his thumb in his eye. Isaac wanted to laugh out loud.

"What the hell's going on here?" the officer said as he stepped past Isaac and faced the sergeant. Isaac could see he was a high ranking officer; but with the flour and sweat in his eyes, he could not tell what rank he was, plus he really did not know one from the other at this point. He just knew he was a boss of some sort.

"This black here, sir," the sergeant said. "He's a bad egg. He attacked the corporal and me for no reason. I was in the process of whipping his ass and teaching him a lesson in discipline, sir."

"I saw the lesson you were teaching him, Sergeant," another man said as he stepped past the first officer. "You were beating hell out of his hands with your face." He stepped over to the sergeant and ripped his chevrons off his arm. Next he tore the stripes from the corporal. He turned to Isaac and handed him the corporal's stripes.

"Here, Corporal. Now get these two privates busy and finish loading up this wagon. Can you handle that? When you finish here, report to me at HQ. I'm Col. Benjamin Grierson. You'll be assigned to my unit. Can you ride a horse?"

"Yes, sir," Isaac answered.

"Good. I need good fighting men who can ride. You better be good, too, or you won't make it. We'll be going to hell before we get back."

"But, sir," the sergeant said.

The colonel raised his hand, "Boy, I saw the whole thing that happened here. This man whipped you fair and square. Then you lied to me. I hate a liar almost as bad as I hate a yellow belly. Now you get busy and finish this loading. Then if you are smart, you will report to your CO and tell him Col. Grierson would like to see him at HQ. Can you remember that, Private?"

"Yes, sir," the former sergeant answered.

The colonel left. Isaac stood over the two men until the loading was completed. He then ordered the two men to take the load to the cook tent. As he turned to walk away, he heard Kirkland say, "Watch your back, blackie."

Isaac stopped and turned around. He pointed his finger at Kirkland. "Watch your mouth, whitie. You call me Corporal

Turner or I'll have your white ass in that guardhouse you've been bragging about." He smiled and headed for headquarters.

"Hot damn," Jew exclaimed. "Old Isaac is coming into his own. He's a hell of a man. He has realized he is a free man. Better than that, he has learned to strike back."

Jeff looked at Jew and smiled. "He'll make a hell of a soldier," Jeff said. As the tape continued to turn, their attention was once again drawn to the words being spoken.

Chapter 11

Isaac was in the Army almost a year and except for the short time at Fort Sam, he had been with Col. Grierson the whole time. He liked the colonel even though he was rough and spoke in a very demanding way. He was always barking orders, but he was fair and Isaac felt the man really cared for his men.

The men of the 9th Cavalry were all black. Only the officers were white. Most of the men had been slaves before the war and had worked on farms or plantations in the South. One of the corporals had lived with an Indian tribe along the Rio Grande and the colonel used him as a scout.

His name was Otis White. He did not talk much and that suited Isaac fine, as he was also quiet. He did not talk to the troops, except when he had a detail. But he could talk to Otis about things he would need to know when they went west on the Indian campaign they all knew was coming. Isaac learned fast and remembered everything Otis told him. Isaac felt he and Otis were becoming very close friends.

It was a hot Saturday afternoon. Isaac and Otis were returning from the river, where Otis had been showing Isaac how to track a person who goes into a river or stream in an effort to lose his trackers. As the two men approached the porch of their barracks, four troopers were coming out.

"Hey, why don't you two corporals come on and go to town with us? We are going to get us some girls and have us a party," one of them said.

Another chimed in, "Hell, yeah. Come on, Otis. You and . . ."

Before he could finish, Otis grabbed him and threw him up against the wall. His eyes were cold as ice, his lips tight, and the muscles in his jaw rippled. He held the trooper tight and without opening his mouth, he spoke through his teeth, "Don't you ever call me Otis. I'm a corporal, mister, and don't you ever forget it." He released his grip.

"He didn't mean anything, Corporal. Just trying to be friendly," one of the men said.

"I ain't got no friends. Now get the hell out of here." He shoved the trooper into the other three. They left mumbling to themselves.

Isaac walked into the barracks. Otis followed.

"Isaac," he said, "what I said out there about me not having any friends . . ."

"It's OK, Otis, I understand," Isaac answered.

"I don't think you do. I've been in this man's Army a lot longer than you. When you get in a fight with them red devils and you got to leave somebody for whatever reason, you don't want to have any friends. When you come up on one of our troops who got caught and they have worked on him two or three days, you don't want any friends."

He walked to the door and looked out, then turned back,

"I had a friend once, two of them, Shorty Sam and Water Man. We were like brothers. We drank, chased women and cleaned out a bar a week over there on Snake Hill. Shit, we could whip a dozen troopers without working up a sweat. Then one day, we went on a patrol out by Fort Clark. We ran into about fifty of them red devils. We had us a little fight. Killed maybe six or seven. The rest hightailed it toward the Mexican border."

"So," Isaac said, "we can't cross the border. I'd head for it, too."

"Yeah, that's what we thought, so we pulled back. That night we camped on a creek. The captain felt sure they'd come back for their dead. He sent out scouts. He sent out Shorty Sam and Water Man to the west where we knew about a crossing. They were to get back if they saw anything. Me and a big black, I mean a mountain of a man named Jake, we went on downstream about three or four miles. We were to watch that crossing. Morning came and we ain't seen or heard a damn thing, except a couple of coyotes, so we rode back to camp. We waited about an hour and the captain gave the order to mount up. We rode out toward where Shorty and Water Man were supposed to be. When we got there, they weren't nowhere around. We seen the tracks—had to be fifty or sixty of 'em, I'd guess. They went into Mexico. I wanted to go after them."

He took a deep breath and wiped his cheek. "Shit, man, they were like brothers to me. But the captain, he said no way were we going to go across that river and he would personally shoot the first man who tried. He would, too. You damn right he would. Well, we rode on patrol for two days following the damn river and then we turned north to swing back to Fort Clark. It was about midday and them devils had circled ahead of us and staked out Shorty and Water Man. They knew damn well we'd find them. Man, you ain't never seen nothing like it. What they did to them. I've wished a hundred times I would have gone on across that river and took a chance the captain would have missed."

"Man, what could you have done against fifty or sixty of 'em, huh? What could you have done?" Isaac asked.

"I could have tried, man. I could have tried. Hell, man, they cut off their ears, they cut off their noses. They even cut off their . . ." he gasped. "Them damn bastards cut off their man parts and stuffed them in their mouths. They cut open Water Man's guts and put a big rock where his stomach was."

The silence that followed was deafening. Neither man spoke. Otis was lost in remembering this terrible event. Isaac was too shaken to respond. Isaac had been sitting on his bunk. He rose and walked to the door and leaned against it.

"Why you telling me this, Otis? You got a message or something you trying to tell me?" Isaac asked.

"Yeah, man, I got a message. Don't make friends. You got no friends, you got no fears. Out there, friend, you don't need any fears. If you got 'em, you are good as dead.

"Man, I'll tell you what. The next five of them devils I killed, I cut off their ears, their noses and their damn tallywhackers, then I stuffed 'em in their damn mouths. But I did one thing more, I stuck sticks in their eyes, just so they couldn't see in the hereafter. What I'm trying to say is, I took chances to get even that could have got me killed. That's stupid. A good trooper ain't stupid. He stays alive to kill those devils. That's what I'm telling you. Having friends can make you stupid—and dead."

Isaac understood why Otis was advising him about becoming too close to other troopers. It was for his own good. Otis knew Isaac was a very sentimental person. His sentimentality could get him and possibly others killed.

The next few days were very busy. The units were preparing to head west. This would be Isaac's first real patrol. He had been out by Fort Mason once and once south of San Antonio toward Laredo, but they had not found any hostiles.

This was different. They had all heard of an Apache named Victorio. He was said to be the half brother to the devil himself. His band of cutthroats had killed fifteen men from Carrizal when they went looking for him. Another group went looking for the fifteen when they did not return. They found the bodies and set out to bury them. Victorio attacked this party, too. When Victorio was finished, another fifteen men lay dead on the hot sands of West Texas.

This aroused the government and made the command at Fort Davis look bad. Back at Fort Sam Houston, Col. Grierson had asked for and been given more troops. He would "rid the world of this murdering animal." That is what Isaac had heard the colonel tell his officers at a meeting, while he stood guard one afternoon.

It was early September when the troops rode out of Fort Sam Houston headed west. As the long column rode toward Commerce Street, people stood to watch as if a parade was passing by.

Isaac saw a boy. He recognized him as Jose. The boy saw Isaac and waved. Isaac tipped his head and smiled. The boy placed two fingers on his arm just above his elbow in recognition of Isaac's stripes. Isaac was filled with pride. He had never had anyone show pride for him before. He never saw Jose again, but often remembered the night he spent in the tiny shack and his experience with the tequila and the hot peppers.

Chapter 12

The troops rode for four days through the white brush, pear thickets and scattered mesquite trees. Isaac had heard that everything west of San Antonio was unfriendly. It either stuck you, bit you or stung you.

The afternoon found the troops approaching Fort Clark, where they would bivouac until the following Monday. This would give them three days to ready themselves for a long, dry march to what many called the end of the world, Fort Davis. This would be the last chance for rest and most of the men knew there was no picnic ahead of them. The days would be suffocating from the heat and dust and the nights would be bone chilling. Several of the men in Isaac's company had pulled duty at Fort Davis before. Some of the stories they told were hard for Isaac to believe and he passed them off as typical troop trash.

Sunday was a day to remember. Isaac went to the post

chapel and after church went swimming in a creek that ran through the post. The commander of Fort Clark had the Quartermaster collect enough unbranded beef from the surrounding area for the entire 9th Cavalry and a barbecue was held on the banks of the creek.

Isaac watched the fires that had burned all night. He had never seen so much go into one meal. He found out later that the commander of Fort Clark was Col. Grierson's cousin and he wanted to make the colonel feel that the welcome shown was for the service that he and his troops were about to face and that it was, indeed, appreciated.

The local ranchers were more than happy to help. These troops meant safety for them and their families.

After lunch that Sunday Isaac, like the rest of the men, just laid around and did nothing special except rest.

Long before daylight the following Monday, the men were awakened and after the usual roll call, camp was broken and they moved out. When the sun came over the eastern ridge, Fort Clark was nowhere in sight.

The column moved west for six days. Each night, sentries were posted and the closer to the mountains the troops were, the more sentries were used.

It was the fifth day and Isaac was sent out on scout to look for signs. The colonel felt sure they were being followed by the Indians. Isaac was to ride ahead and off the southern point about two or three miles ahead of the main column. He could see them from time to time when he topped a ridge. The first day he saw a few signs, but they were old and he reported his findings to the sergeant.

The second day he was out, he came up on fresh tracks of a single pony riding fast toward the Mexican border. Isaac followed with caution, knowing full well an ambush could be awaiting him just around every turn. As he topped a rocky knoll, he saw a pony lying on its side and what looked like a rider pinned under him.

Isaac circled the area looking for signs and taking care to watch for anything out of place that would indicate an ambush.

"This location's not one you'd pick for an ambush," he thought to himself. Two sides had openings to an open plain and the hill to the south would not support anyone hiding. There were no boulders or tall grass. It took over half an hour, but Isaac was sure there was not an ambush waiting for him. He dismounted and closed in on the fallen pony.

His observations were right. The pony had fallen and pinned the leg of its rider under it. Isaac had his rifle ready. The rider was an Indian boy of about 14 or 15 years of age. He was conscious and alert. Except for his leg, he seemed unhurt. His eyes were cold and they did not miss a move Isaac made. There was fear there, but strength, too.

Isaac spoke to him in English. The boy did not respond. He then tried some of the Spanish he had managed to learn. The boy told him to go ahead and kill him. He was not afraid. Isaac told him he was not going to kill him. That he would help him get free. But if he tried to attack him or made any moves toward him, he would kill him on the spot.

Isaac then went back to where he had left his horse and got a rope. He placed the rope around the neck of the dead pony and pulled him off the boy's leg. The lad tried to get up, but fell back to the ground. His leg was not broken, but was badly skinned and swollen.

Isaac asked him how long he had been there and the boy told him he had seen one night come and go. Isaac went to his saddle bags where he kept his water and dried jerky. He handed the water to the boy. He would not take it. Isaac thought he may fear it was poison, so he took a bite of the meat and a drink of the water, then handed them to the boy. He took them and drank the water. Isaac pulled the canteen away from him so he would not drink it too fast. The boy then ate a bite of the jerky. He said something Isaac did not understand.

The boy repeated it and pointed toward the south. Isaac thought maybe that was where he had come from.

"What do I do with you, boy?" he said speaking in English. "If I take you back with me, you're a dead Indian. If I take you to your village, I'm a dead trooper. Boy, we got us a problem."

They looked at each other without talking for several minutes. Then Isaac spoke to him in his broken Spanish, "I leave you here, OK?"

"Si. You leave me," the boy responded.

Isaac picked up some twigs and a few pieces of wood. He pulled up some green weeds and laid them close to the dead pony. He reached into his shirt pocket and brought out several matches.

He asked the boy, "You know what these are?"

"Si. Fire sticks," he answered.

"You know how to use fire sticks?"

"Si."

"OK. I'm going to leave you with these fire sticks." He counted out five of the matches. "Come high sun," he pointed overhead, "the troops will be long gone. You light a signal fire and make smoke. Maybe your people will find you. More than that, I can't help you. You understand?"

"I understand," the boy answered.

Isaac reached into his saddle bags and pulled out another chunk of jerky and tossed it to the boy.

"That'll hold you for a while," he said.

The boy caught the jerky and laid it down beside him. He untied a small sack tied to his waistband and pitched it to Isaac.

"This good medicine. Keep you safe. My medicine bag be good for you, black one. You ride with both eyes open, you live long time."

The tape came to its end and as Sara ejected it and started to place a new cassette in the machine, Clara heard Jew's stomach growl.

She turned to face Sara and said, "Girl, there's no way we are going to hear what is on that tape with John's stomach growling like that. Why don't we go out and fill a plate, then come back in here to eat while we listen?"

"Sounds like a great idea," Jeff agreed.

The conversation centered around the story as each one filled his plate.

"Most folks probably would have sent that boy to the happy hunting ground, don't you think, Jew?" Jeff asked.

"Probably so, but Isaac doesn't seem to be like most. Look how he took to that Mexican boy in San Antonio. Nope, this man likes people. I've seen his kind before. He'll have to see death before he can dish it out, but he will be hell when he gets started. That type always is. It's hard to hold them back."

They settled back with TV trays in front of them and Sara started the tape . . .

Isaac placed the small skin bag in his shirt and touched his cap in a half salute. He mounted his horse and took a glance over his shoulder at the boy. Knowing he could do no more, he set the spurs to his horse and headed over the ridge. He did not look back, but rode straight to the rendezvous point.

The troops were setting up tents when he rode up. He went straight to the sergeant and reported. He advised the sergeant that he had found the tracks of one horse and that he believed them to be two, maybe three days, old. He made no mention of the boy he found. The sergeant was satisfied and dismissed him.

Isaac met Otis at the picket line. "You find any Indians today?" Isaac asked Otis.

"Nope. A few signs but they were old. How about you?"

"Naw. Ain't no Indians around here."

"The hell they ain't. This is their land. Them red devils are here all right. When they want to be found, you'll know it. You best hope you see 'em first or you ain't going to see nothing.

"We been deep in Apache land for two days. You keep a keen eye, Isaac. I've been here before. Tomorrow we will be in some big hills and a lot of boulders they can hide behind. They'll sure ambush your ass if given half a chance." Otis was sincere. He knew his business and Isaac knew it. This warning was not taken lightly.

"I'll keep my eye peeled, Otis. You take care of yourself. I heard the lieutenant telling Col. Grierson a trader was found dead up on the Devil's River. They believe he was running rifles and whiskey."

"Damn fool got what he deserved," Otis commented.

"No doubt about that, but some of them have rifles. You be careful. That's up where you been scouting."

"Yeah, I'll be careful all right. Don't worry about me. I got too much whiskey to drink and too many women to run to let any Apache get my pretty hair."

Both men laughed and headed for the mess tent.

Morning came early, but Isaac did not mind. As a scout, he did not have to pull guard duty and could get a good night's rest. Besides he had risen early every morning of his life.

The morning air was damp. It felt like it might rain as he mounted up and rode out on his day's duty of scouting the trail the troops were to follow.

Otis rode up along side of him and looking straight ahead said in a very matter of fact manner, "Watch yourself out there today. I feel 'em in my bones. They are watching us. Have been for a couple of days. My guess is it's ol' Victorio himself. He'll be feeling real cocky by now. He took them thirty

Mexicans out with very little effort. He'll be feeling his medicine is very strong and he can't be hurt. So you watch out, hear?"

"I'll be especially careful. You might do the same and don't worry about me," Isaac told him.

Otis' head was still straight forward. "I don't worry about nobody except Otis. You're a good scout and I don't want to have to do both our jobs. So don't get your hair lifted." He did not wait for a response, but put his heels to his mount and galloped off to the northwest.

Isaac rode to the southwest and found himself about two miles from the column when he rode up on a deep gully. There was no place to cross, so he decided to swing south and follow the gully until he could cut across it. He would have to ride hard to make up for lost time, he knew; but to cut back toward the column may put him in too close if an ambush was set. He would not have time to warn the troops. South was his best bet, so he pushed his horse for about an hour and found a break in the sheer walls. He crossed with no problem and was up the other side in short order.

He could not use the sun for direction nor time as the clouds were heavy and the rain was sure to start any time. It was early afternoon when he spotted the column in the distance and he felt somewhat safer. There were a few times he had felt that he may have been lost, but the rain had not come and the clouds were breaking up. This enabled him to follow the map he had and to see the distance points to which he could ride. These reference points were all he really had to go by, but they worked out very well. The lack of trees permitted him to see great distances when on top of a hill or even a large knoll.

Isaac stopped and tended to his mount. He needed rest and so did Isaac. While the mount grazed the clumps of grass, Isaac ate a piece of jerky and a biscuit. He wondered if the

Indian boy was able to get a fire going and whether or not his people found him. He reached into his shirt and pulled out the small sack the boy had given him.

He untied the drawstring. He poured out the contents into his hand. There were four stones. One was a blue green, one was like a little piece of iron ore, the third was round and was brown in color and the fourth was a piece of flint that had been chipped into a small square cube.

"Some medicine," Isaac said. "Must have been important to that boy."

His mount rested, Isaac took to the saddle once again. He had covered about five miles when he pulled his horse to a stop and looked across a valley. Approximately four hundred yards up the valley from where he had stopped was a sight that sent chills up his spine.

Stretched out spread eagle and staked to the ground was someone. It looked like a woman. Her dress was torn and Isaac could see bare legs.

"Oh, shit. Now what do I do? I hate to see a woman all cut to hell like Otis told me they do." He drew his rifle and checked his load. He eased down the slope and started up the valley. As he approached he could hear the woman moaning and trying to pull out the stakes that held her. He was close enough now to see that she was tied down at the edge of a very big red ant bed.

He put the steel to his horse and raced up to her. Before the horse was stopped, he was down and running to her side, his knife in one hand, his rifle in the other. The blade was sharp and the leather thongs were no problem as he cut them away.

The woman tried to get up, but was weak from the sun and the bites that covered her body. Isaac grabbed her arm and half drug, half carried her to where the horse had stopped. He laid his rifle down and began to wipe the remaining ants off the girl, who by now was sobbing almost uncontrollably.

"It's OK," he said. "I'm an American."

"American?" she asked.

"Yeah. I'll get you to the doctor back with the column."

She screamed and covered her face, as Isaac heard the yell from behind him. He turned and grabbed for his rifle. Before he could get it in his grip, he felt the loud crack of something hitting him in the head. He fell forward and, though dazed, tried to rise again. He felt the sharp sting of yet another blow in the middle of his back. The coolness of unconsciousness swept over his body.

It was dark when Isaac regained consciousness. He opened his eyes very slowly and looked around him. He was now lying as he had found the girl, except he was not in the ant bed. He turned his head. There were four or five Indians squatting by a small fire eating something. They noticed he was awake and one of them walked over to him and stood staring down.

In Spanish he said to Isaac, "You know who I am, black one?"

Isaac replied, "No."

The Indian seemed disappointed. He kicked Isaac in the side. After a minute or two he said, "You with the hair of the buffalo, you come to my land with many buffalo soldiers to kill my people, but we will kill you." He reached down and grabbed Isaac by the hair.

"Me," he thumped his chest with his free hand, "I am Victorio. This is my land, not yours. I would kill you now and cut you up, but you saved my son when his pony fell on him." He shoved Isaac's head down and held up the medicine bag. "For this, I spare your life. If the sun kills you, it is the way of the great spirit. If I see you again, I will kill you. You understand?" He threw the small bag down on Isaac's chest.

"Yeah, I understand. So cut me loose," Isaac answered.

113

"I will not cut you loose, but then I will not cut your throat either." He laughed and stood up. The others at the fire also laughed.

Victorio walked to his horse and said something to the others. They stood up and walked toward their horses. One of them stopped and turned back. He walked over to Isaac with a limp and stood over him looking down.

Isaac recognized him as the boy he had helped. One of the Indians in the background yelled something and the boy moved his loin cloth to the side and held up his penis as if to relieve himself. The others laughed.

With his back toward the others who were now mounted, he started to urinate on Isaac, or so it appeared to the others. What he really did was to relieve himself on the area of the stake holding Isaac's right hand.

"It will help," he said in a quiet voice. Then loud enough for the others to hear, he said, "We are even, buffalo hair. My father gave you your life back. Now I piss on you. I hope some day, we meet again. I will kill you."

The boy swung up onto his pony and rode through the others. They gave a yell and rode off following him and laughing.

Isaac worked the stake the boy had urinated on and he could feel it giving to his pull. The leather cut into his wrist. He knew he could not waste time. The rawhide would shrink as it dried. Out here moisture did not take long to evaporate, so he worked harder until he felt the stake start to pull out. Once his hand was free, he quickly freed himself from the other stakes.

He went over by the fire. It was cold now, but something caught his eye by a rock. He reached down and picked up a piece of dried meat and dusted it off.

"Now we're even, lad," he said.

Isaac climbed to the top of the rim and took a look. He

had lost his bearings and was not sure which way the column would have gone. The clouds had moved in again and it had begun to drizzle. He decided he would walk in the direction he felt the column would have gone.

He walked all day. Thirst had his lips cracked and his throat felt like it was a dust bowl. The blood on his head where he had been hit had dried and caked and, from time to time, he felt he would pass out. After a short rest he would feel better and push on. It was nearly dark and he had sat down to rest when he spotted a rattlesnake hiding under a rocky ledge.

Isaac picked up a rock and threw it at the snake, striking it right behind the head. The snake crawled out and tried to coil, but Isaac hit it again and crushed its head with a big rock.

The Indians had taken his pistol and rifle, but his boot knife was still inside his boot. He skinned the snake and ate it raw, saving some of it for later. The moisture from the meat felt good to his throat and the meat satisfied the gnawing he had felt in his stomach.

The next morning Isaac continued walking toward what he thought was northwest. It had rained during the night. The clouds still lingered. He had found shelter under a rock ledge during the heavy rain, but he had still gotten soaked to the bone. Now besides being hungry, he was cold.

Each time he topped a hill, he could only see another one that he would have to climb and in the distance he could see the mountains.

"What will I do when I get there?" he said to himself. "I don't even remember seeing any mountains on my map."

For the first time, he knew he was lost and fear grabbed him. He turned cold and began to sweat as if he were in the fields working. He wanted to run and scream, but caught hold of himself.

"Where are you going to run, you fool? Scream your head

off. The only thing to hear you is a snake or two or maybe a red devil. That's just what you need, boy. A red devil to know you are here."

He sat down feeling totally alone.

"Now think about this thing," he said aloud. "You are out here and on foot. The troop's somewhere out there. Otis will find you, so stay calm. Just keep on walking toward them mountains. Otis said Fort Davis was set in some mountains. Maybe that's them. That's got to be them. So take it easy. Don't get all worked up." He paused. "Look at me talking to myself like I lost my sense. Hell, ain't nothing to it. I'll walk out of here and when I do, I'm going to find that red devil and dry his mean hide on a barn door somewhere."

He ate the rest of the snake he had killed and walked until after dark. Before dark, he climbed to the top of a hill.

"This will be a good place to watch for a camp fire, if I'm close to the main column. They always have six or seven fires going at night," he thought.

The night was dark and clear. The rain had stopped about midday. The moon would not be up until early in the morning and he could see a long way from the top of the hill.

At first when Isaac saw the glow in the distance, he was not sure if it was a fire burning or if he just wanted it to be one so bad he was imagining it to be there. After watching in the direction for a long time, he was convinced it was a fire. He could see the stars and he knew the fire was south. That would take him away from where he thought the column would be, but he had been travelling for several days now, living on roots and berries. He had chewed cactus for moisture and he was totally lost. He could have wandered to the north of the column. He had no way of knowing how, but he was not thinking any too clearly.

He worked his way down the hill and in the direction where he had seen the fire. Most of the night he stumbled through the prairie. Shortly before daylight, he came up on the camp he had seen.

It was what he had feared most. It was a camp all right, but an Indian camp. He counted six men standing around the fire.

Daylight came and Isaac concealed himself in the rocks. He watched as four of the men rode off. He recognized Victorio's palamino horse as one of those leaving. They were no more out of sight when one of the remaining Indians went into a leanto type tent and drug out the Mexican girl. He proceded to rape her. She was in no shape to fight off the attack. Once he had finished, the other one took his turn. Both satisfied, they stretched out on the ground laughing as the girl lay in a heap.

Isaac watched them for close to half an hour. The girl never moved. One of the bucks finally got up and went over to her and kicked her in the ribs. She moaned and rolled over on her side. He reached down and got her by the waist and pulled her into position, where he mounted her again.

"Animals," Isaac thought. "They even screw like dogs." The anger he felt rose up in his throat. He began to crawl toward the camp.

The Indians had a bottle that looked like whiskey and they began taking turns drinking from it. When they seemed to be half drunk, Isaac had worked to within ten yards of where they sat. His knife was in his hand, when he leaped to his feet taking both men by complete surprise. The knife struck out at one and almost decapitated him. The other felt the toe of a cavalry boot smash in his groin. Isaac then rammed the knife deep into his chest, withdrew it and drove it into him again. The girl had risen to a sitting position and was crying.

"Are there others?" he asked her in Spanish.

"Just the ones that left, but they'll be back. Gone to meet others," she sobbed.

"Where the hell did these bastards put their horses?" Isaac demanded.

"Over there." She pointed toward a box canyon.

Isaac grabbed a chunk of meat by the fire and took a bite as he started for the horses. He found them hobbled behind a boulder grazing. Three fine ponies. He took all three and went back to the girl.

"Can you ride?" he asked.

"Si. I can ride. You let me see your knife?" she asked.

"What?"

"You let me have your knife."

Isaac handed her the knife and watched her. She went over to the two dead Indians and cut their penises off, then kicked them.

"Bastards," she said. "I hope you rot in hell."

She handed Isaac the knife. One of the dead Indians had a Colt .45 stuck in his waistband. Isaac took the gun and stuck it in his belt. He then helped the girl up on one of the horses. He swung up on the largest one and leading the third, they rode off in the opposite direction as the four had riden earlier. He did not want to run into them now. The gun in his belt did give him a feeling of confidence. He pulled it out and checked to make sure it was loaded. The cylinder was full, six rounds. The feeling of having a loaded handgun brought a smile to his lips.

They rode for the rest of the day and rested that night without a fire. The girl had brought along a water bag and a slab of dried meat. After their cold meal, they both settled down and tried to sleep.

Even though Isaac was bone weary, he found sleep only teased him. He would doze only to be awakened by far off sounds. Once he lay still with his gun in his hand for the better part of an hour listening for what he thought was someone out there in the darkness. He finally accepted the thought that it was some animal about his night hunt and not an Indian. The night was almost over before he fell into a deep slumber.

Maria shook him hard by the shoulder when the first rays of light streaked the eastern sky.

"What?" Isaac said as he sat up with his gun ready.

"Ssh! Don't make so much noise," she cautioned him.

A quick meal of the dried meat and the two of them were ready to ride. They had to get more distance between them and Victorio. Isaac knew the Apache would be wanting the girl back and his hide would be hung to dry, if they were caught. Their only hope was to find the troops.

As the day passed, they rode along the edge of the mountains and found fresh water from a spring. The girl washed her body as best she could and Isaac finally got the rest of the dried blood out of his hair.

It was almost dark when they came up on the main body of the troop. Isaac rode in and was met by several soldiers.

"We gave you up for dead!" he heard someone say. He recognized the voice. It was Otis.

"I thought you'd find me, Otis. Where the hell were you?"

"I tried to, but it rained too hard. I lost your tracks."

"He looked for two days, Isaac, and the lieutenant made him give up the search," a soldier added.

"Who's the girl?" a trooper asked.

"Get the doctor. She needs help," Isaac said.

The colonel had come out of his tent. "Well, Corporal, I see you decided to join us again," he said.

"Yes, Sir. Didn't mean to get caught, but I did, Sir."

"You OK, boy?" he asked.

"Yes, Sir. A bit hungry and wore thin, but I'm OK and ready to ride at sunup."

"You'll ride in the column tomorrow. Now get a bite to eat and report back here."

"Yes, Sir," Isaac responded and saluted.

Col. Grierson returned the salute and barked, "Get this girl to the doctor and get her something to eat and then something to wear in that order and make it quick."

The girl was led to the doctor. After Isaac had eaten, he returned to the colonel's tent. The sentry told him to go on in, that Col. Grierson was waiting.

Isaac stepped through the tent flap and stood at attention.

"Corporal Turner reporting, Sir," he said.

"Do you know who that girl is?" the colonel asked Isaac.

"Yes, Sir, she told me her name was Maria something and she is from Mexico. Her family owns a ranch or something down there," Isaac responded.

"You're damn right they own a ranch. It's about 200,000 acres. It's one of the biggest in Mexico. Her papa is very strong and has a lot of influence on both sides of the border. He'll be happy you brought his daughter back alive," the lieutenant said as he stood and walked over to Isaac.

"Now, we want to know what happened out there. Where did you lose your horse, soldier?" Col. Grierson asked.

Isaac told them the whole story, except he did not tell them about the boy. He felt the small pouch of rocks in his waist. "Maybe this is good medicine," he thought. "I'm still alive."

Chapter 13

Fort Davis was not at all what Isaac had expected. The mountains were huge, barren rocky formations. These formations had been a haven for the Apache and they had launched attacks on the fort almost at will. The reinforcement of Col. Grierson and the 9th was to ward off the attacks and keep the Indians in check.

The 9th was at Fort Davis less than a week when Isaac was ordered to accompany a lieutenant in a detail of five enlisted men to Mexico where Maria's family owned their ranch. She was escorted by these six brave men. Her heart felt like it would burst. She was happy to be returning home at last.

Isaac could see her excitement and said to her, "Well, senorita, soon you will be home and you can pick up the pieces of your life and get on with it."

"You are right, Senor Turner. I was to be married this fall. I thank you again for saving my life. Manuel will thank you, too. You will see."

They did not speak too much the rest of the trip as Isaac was always ahead of the small party scouting for any trouble.

The ride would have taken several days to reach the ranch of Maria's father. They had ridden three days when they crossed the Rio Grande. Word of their coming had already reached the rancho and they were met by a group of Maria's father's vaqueros. They rode up and blocked the way. The lieutenant rode out and told them who they were. Maria recognized several of the men and noticed as they spoke with the lieutenant that none would look directly at her, but stole a glimpse from time to time. A strange feeling came over her and somehow she felt very alone.

Isaac pulled his horse up close to Maria. He sensed her fears.

"You know what's going on here?" he asked.

"No, I don't understand. Those are men from my father's rancho, but they are not happy to see me. I don't understand."

The lieutenant reined his horse and came back to the small detail.

"I have some bad news," he said.

"My father and mother, are they dead?"

"Yes, I'm afraid so. Victorio raided the rancho three weeks ago and killed everybody at the rancho. These vaqueros were away and were spared. They now claim ownership to the rancho. They asked that we take you back."

"I won't go back. That rancho belongs to my family. I have a right to it."

The lieutenant interrupted, "I think it best if we go back. I have my doubts if Victorio was the one who killed your parents. I heard two different stories from them. I suspect they are the killers. We'll have to let the Mexican government take care of this problem. For now, let's go back to Fort Davis. We'll get a message off to Mexico City, as soon as we get back."

The lieutenant moved out toward the Rio Grande. The detail, along with Maria, followed. The vaqueros turned and rode back into Mexico. Maria knew she would not see her home again and her heart almost burst with sadness for her mother, her father and her home. They were all gone—maybe forever.

"Don't worry, little one," Isaac said. "The colonel will get to the bottom of this for you. If anyone can get your ranch back, he can. I'm sorry about your mama and papa, but you know they both have gone to a better place than this. You know that, don't you?"

"Si, but what about Manuel? Why did he not come with those vaqueros?"

"I don't know," Isaac answered. "I'll ask the lieutenant." Isaac rode ahead to the lieutenant.

"Sir, did those fellows say anything about the man she is supposed to marry? Some guy named Manuel?"

"Yeah, they told me that he is the one they worked for now and that he was the one who owned the ranch. I asked them about the girl and was told in no uncertain terms that Manuel did not want a used woman for a wife."

"That bastard," Jeff blurted out. "Doesn't he know what that lady's been through?"

"Be still, dear," Sara said, "and watch your language." She hesitated, then added, "Even if he was a bastard."

The lieutenant continued, "They went on to tell me that he was close friends with high members of the Mexican government and any effort to regain the rancho would only make our two governments grow farther apart. I can tell you now, Isaac, we won't get much help from Washington, not with the Indian problems we are having. We need their help to squash the Apache. We've got to get permission to cross that damn river and go after them. You know that as well

123

as I, but I don't want to tell that to that girl back there. She's got all the trouble she needs right now."

"Yes, Sir." Isaac rode back and reined in next to Maria. Both were silent for a while.

"He did not know why Manuel wasn't there," Isaac finally said.

"I know why. He is a big man in Mexico. Very rich, very important. His family is very important. His uncle is in Mexico City and in the government. He didn't come because he knew I was used by the Apaches. The big man couldn't stand that. I know why. You know that, too." She looked at Isaac. He looked away.

"Does it bother you that the Apaches used me?" she asked.

"It wasn't your doing. I saw how those bastards treated you. You don't need to remember it. Think of something else," Isaac told her in a reassuring voice.

"You did not answer my question," she snapped.

"No. Hell, no. It don't bother me," he snapped back. "I'll tell you what bothers me. That bastard back there. He doesn't know that you saw the inside of hell. He don't know the abuse you took. He don't know how you struggled just to keep yourself alive. He don't know any of that and what's more, he don't give a damn either. That's what bothers me. You asked me and I told you. Now I ain't going to talk about it no more."

Isaac looked straight into her eyes. "I've been there, girl. I know what you are going through. It ain't pleasant. It's almost unbearable, I know. But it'll pass. All things pass. We got a chance at tomorrow. That's more than a lot of people have. We are lucky to be alive, you and me. That's enough for me. Let it be enough for you."

She wiped a tear from her cheek and rode in silence. That night as they camped, Maria walked over to Isaac.

"It's enough," she said.

"What? What you say, girl?"

"I said, it's enough, and I wish you would improve your Spanish. I have to struggle to understand you."

"What's enough?" Isaac asked.

"Life. What you said. To have my life, that's enough. Besides I never did love that bastard, Manuel."

"Well, that's a comfort," Isaac told her. "I don't love him either." He laughed and she joined him.

As the small group rode into the fort, it was plain to see that the troops had been busy. Tents were set up and rocks outlined the walkways. The group rode straight to headquarters. The lieutenant told the detail to dismount and wait. He then changed his mind and ordered Isaac to stay with Maria. The others were to stable and care for the horses. He went inside and reported to Col. Grierson.

Isaac and Maria waited what seemed like hours. A clerk came out and asked her to come in. He told Isaac he could go to his company and he was dismissed. Maria was feeling very alone as she went into the colonel's office.

Col. Grierson asked her to sit. She did. "The lieutenant told me what happened. I'm sorry about your parents and the man you were to marry." The colonel was having difficulty finding the words he wanted to use.

"It's all right, Colonel. I understand. But what's to become of me now? I have no where to go." She began to sob.

"Don't do that. Please don't cry," the colonel said. "I can't stand to see a woman cry." He walked over and placed a hand on her shoulder. "Look, you are an educated woman. Have you ever been around a hospital? Do you know anything about nursing?"

"No. But I can learn," she said.

"Fine. I'll talk to the doctor and you can work in the field hospital until you have decided what you want to do. Does that sound OK to you?"

Chapter 14

The weeks that followed were somewhat routine. The patrols went out and came back with very little to report. The Indian problem seemed to have quieted down.

"Maybe they have accepted us," Isaac told Otis one day.

"You believe that and you'll lose your hair for sure," Otis answered. "These devils ain't accepting nothing except that we all either get the hell out of here or die. That's all they'll ever accept. You can bet your jack-knife on that."

"Well, I hope something happens soon. I need to see some action," Isaac said as he curried his horse.

"You'll see it soon enough. Be patient. When it comes, it'll be like a storm at the end of a drought. You want it to come, but you'll be double glad when it's over." Otis went back to rubbing his saddle with oil.

There was silence for several minutes. Then Otis stopped moving his hand back and forth working the leather to a fine shine.

"Isaac," he said. "I've got to ask you something. I know it ain't none of my business and I've whipped men for less, but I got to ask you anyway."

"What's on your mind, Otis? I ain't got no secrets from you, man. You're like a brother to me," Isaac told him.

"Don't think of me like a brother, Isaac. I'm just another trooper. Thinking like that can get you killed out here. I told you that."

Isaac interrupted him, "Man, don't put that crap on me. I know what you are trying to say, but it don't work that way and you know it. So come on. Get off that trash with me. Look, this is Isaac, not some raw recruit you can bullshit. Tell me the truth. If you saw me in a fix and you thought you could save me, wouldn't you try, even if it meant you might get killed in the effort?"

The two men looked eye to eye. Otis took a deep breath.

"Hell, no," he said, "not if I thought I'd get killed." He paused. "Now, I might if I thought I wouldn't get killed." They both laughed.

"Now, what's on your mind that you want to ask me that might get you whipped?" Isaac asked.

"Well, man, I seen you sneaking around that hospital. I know you been meeting that Mexican girl. What are you trying to do, get your black ass hung?" Otis asked.

"I ain't been sneaking. I've gone straight there. I ain't trying to hide nothing. I like her, that's all."

"Yeah. A lot of these horny troopers like her."

"Horny ain't got nothing to do with it and talk like that about her will get your ass whipped, friend or not."

Otis could tell he had touched a nerve.

"Hey, man, I don't mean to get your feathers ruffled. I just know there's been some talk around and I don't want you getting all messed up," Otis defended himself.

"What kind of talk you mean? You trying to say somebody's making smart ass remarks about Maria and me? Is that what you mean?" Isaac was showing more interest than Otis had ever seen in him.

"Look, man, you love her?" Otis asked.

"Yeah, I love her and she loves me. We are going to get married when my hitch is up. We are saving our money and we are going back to Hazel, Georgia, where I come from and I'm going to buy a piece of that plantation where my mama was a slave and I was a slave. I'm going to own me a chunk of that land that we cleared and planted. I earned it and I'm going to get it." Isaac had determination in his voice.

"Sounds good, Isaac, but what do you think those white people will do when you show up with a white woman for a wife? Man, you're looking to get yourself killed for sure." Otis shook his head. "But if that's what you want, I'd go for it, man. You're big enough to take your licks and maybe even deal out some if you got to."

"You bet, Otis. If anybody screws with me or her, I'm going to kick ass like you never saw it kicked before."

The bugle sounded assembly. Both men dropped what they were doing and ran to the parade field. Once in formation, the colonel and his staff came out on the porch of the Headquarters building. They walked to the designated place and the colonel barked, "Report!"

Each squad was checked by the platoon sergeant and he in turn reported to the company commander. The company commanders then began their reports to the adjutant. The men in each company were present or accounted for.

The report was given to the colonel, "All companies present or accounted for, Sir." The adjutant saluted the colonel.

The colonel returned the salute and gave the order, "At ease."

This order was relayed in military fashion to the companies. The men of the 9th Cavalry were well disciplined and well trained. When they responded to the command of "at ease," they went to parade rest, legs approximately a shoulder's width apart, hands clamped in front of them resting on their waist. This movement was done with such crispness, the colonel heard only one loud snap.

"You men have been itching for some action. Well the old Apache is about to scratch that itch. He's on the move. We have word that a large number of hostile Apaches have been gathering on the Mexican side of the Rio Grande River and getting ready to paint this part of the world red with blood, anyone's blood they come across. They would love to spread your blood across Texas. I don't think we'll stand by and let them do that. I think the 9th will just ride down there and kill those red savages. Does that sound OK to you men?" He paused.

"Yes, Sir!" The answer was in unison. It echoed through the canyon.

"OK then. Company commanders, get your companies ready to march. We will leave at first light tomorrow. Company A and Company C will remain at the Post."

The colonel stepped back and gave the order to his adjutant, "Dismiss the troops."

The adjutant turned to the field, "Troops, attention!" Again one big snap. "Dismissed."

The men broke and ran toward their tents. Those barracksed in the newly erected long barracks headed for them. The rest of the day was spent getting ready to move out. Field equipment had to be packed and each man had to report to the armory for his ration of ammunition, both for rifle and sidearm. Each trooper would carry three days' dry rations consisting of biscuits and dried meat.

Isaac managed to go by the hospital on his way to his company's magazine. He stopped by the porch where Maria was waiting for him.

"Don't worry," he told her. "We'll be back in a week or two. I've got six months to go on this enlistment and we'll head for Georgia."

"Isaac, you be careful out there. That Victorio is really mean. Remember, he's not just a dumb Indian. He has the cunning of a Mexican and the bravery of an Apache. He was captured by the Apaches when he was a little boy and raised as one of them. The test he was given to prove he was Apache through and through when he was becoming a warrior speaks for itself. He was taken back to his village and told to murder his own mother and father. He did it with joy. He's plenty bad. It's said he's half crazy and does not know the meaning of the word danger. He thinks his medicine is strong and will keep him from being killed or even hurt. You watch behind every rock and bush."

"Don't worry. I'll be all right. Remember I've got his son's medicine bag." He patted his belt where the small skin bag hung. "This medicine kept me safe more than once now. No reason to believe it won't this time. Besides I've got too much to live for to let some red devil do me in." His voice was reassuring.

She smiled and raised her hand as he started to leave. "Vaya con Dios," she said.

Isaac turned his head. "Two weeks, maybe sooner," he said and continued toward his barracks.

The morning came early. The bugle sounded and the men hurried to roll their beds. There would be no time to see Maria this morning and Isaac knew that the scout detail would be out before the column.

After breakfast, he drew his ration of jerky and hard tack, enough to last four days. The scouts carried four days' supply of water also. This precaution was taken just in case they were cut off from the main column. The scouts often stayed on the move and came to the main unit only to report findings of the enemy or to replenish supplies.

The first day went as expected. No hostiles were seen. The absence of signs made both Isaac and Otis wonder if maybe they were not moving in the wrong direction. They discussed what they had not found and decided to talk it over with the lieutenant.

Lt. Hood was young, perhaps twenty-four, no more than twenty-five, and had not been out west long. But unlike most young officers out of West Point, he would listen to the more experienced non-coms before making a snap decision. Both Isaac and Otis found him to be a very bright young man with an unusual amount of common sense for what they called a "green Johnnie."

"Lieutenant," Otis said as they approached him. "Could we talk to you, Sir?"

"Corporal, what do you two have on your mind?"

"Sir, we've been talking and none of our people have picked up any signs. Seems to me if old Victorio was coming across the Rio, he would have scouts out himself. And we, well to tell the truth, Sir, haven't picked up one sign that would say any scouts have been this way. Seems funny, that's all, Sir."

"Well, I think from the information that Col. Grierson had, you can expect to find signs tomorrow. This Victorio is a cocky one. He thinks he is beyond our reach. What he doesn't know is that we are going to crush his red ass when we find him. We have a column marching in from Fort Quitman. We'll trap him between us. We also have those two 12 pounders back there. We are going to blow his red ass plumb off this world, when we find him. Don't worry about signs. Like I said, you'll probably start seeing them tomorrow or the next day for sure. Now get some rest and keep your powder dry." He chuckled and entered his tent.

"Damn sure hope he's right," Isaac said. "I want to be the one that catches that bastard. I owe him something for Maria."

Otis was sincere as he said, "Tell you what, old friend, if I find him, I'll make sure word gets to you and I'll give you the pleasure of doing him in."

"I'd be much obliged, Otis. I truly would. I got me plans for that one, I truly do."

Isaac slept lightly that night. He was awakened four or five times with bad dreams and morning came none too soon to suit him.

After a quick breakfast, he went straight to the picket line and saddled his horse. He would have four scouts working with him. As he buckled the girth on his saddle, the sergeant came up with Isaac's detail.

"Isaac, you know Green and Johnson, but these two Apaches will be working with you, too. The old man says it takes an Apache to track one. He's probably right, too."

"You know these Apaches?" Isaac asked.

"Naw. I don't know 'em, but Captain Roth does. He brought 'em in yesterday when his company joined up with the column. Don't worry about 'em. They're supposed to be good, real good, and besides they got their own reasons for wanting ol' Victorio dead," the sergeant said.

Isaac finished with his mount and swung into the saddle. He turned to the older Apache who was already mounted.

"How are you called?" Isaac asked.

The Apache responded with his Apache name which was almost a sentence.

"That's too damn hard for me to remember. What's it mean?" Isaac asked.

"In white man's tongue, it means 'the man turkey that flys'," the Apache said.

"OK," Isaac said. "How's about I just call you Tom?"

"Tum? You call me Tum?" the Apache asked.

133

"Yeah, I'll call you Tom. How about him? What's his name mean in white man's tongue?"

The Indian thought for a second and said something to the younger Apache. They passed a few words back and forth, then the younger one nudged his pony forward a few steps.

"I am called the man deer with many horns," he told Isaac in fairly good Spanish.

"You don't say? Many horns, huh?" Isaac responded.

"Yes, Man Deer with Many Horns. Big, powerful, smart, like me. Me smart. Me speak Spanish, some English, and me track better than any buffalo soldier."

"OK, Many Horns. I'll call you Buck. You got that? To me, your name's Buck," Isaac said with little humor in his voice. He did not like the cockiness of this young Apache. Isaac made up his mind he was not going to trust him as completely as the sergeant said. Captain Roth said they could be trusted. Isaac would see.

"No, sir, you ain't going to get on my blind side or behind me. You'll stay where I know where you are at all times," Isaac thought.

"Well, if you're such a good tracker, let's get out there and find your old friend, Victorio."

"Victorio, he not my friend. He my enemy. I kill him if I find him. I cut his head off and spit in the hole." He spit on the ground.

Isaac laughed. "Then, let's go get him."

They rode out in a group and stayed together for about an hour when they fanned out looking for signs of riders. Shortly after the noon break, when their horses were rested, one of the Apaches signaled to Isaac. He rode over and Tom pointed to the ground and held up four fingers and made the sign that four riders had passed not more than two hours before.

"This is what we've been looking for," he said. He had gotten down to examine the tracks closer. He felt that Tom was right, but he really knew that even before he looked. The Apache was seldom wrong. He raised up, holding his horse by the reins and looked over his saddle.

"Victorio?" he asked.

The Apache scout nodded his head. "Scouts for Victorio," he said in broken English.

Isaac smiled. The Apache smiled back. Something they did not do too often.

As the day wore on, Isaac found more and more signs. He knew that this could mean only one thing. The main body of Indians was close by. "They could be in any of these hidden canyons," Isaac thought as he entered into an area where the hills began to get higher and the ravines were unseen until one rode up on them.

The scouts were working back and forth when Isaac heard a quick whistle. He looked toward the sound and saw Buck make a sign for him to come over to where he had gotten off his pony and was kneeling down.

Isaac pulled his horse up and started toward the Indian thinking, "What's he found he wants me to see?" Isaac stopped his horse and leaned over its neck and looked at the ground. He did not see anything. There was no sign he could read.

"What do you see there? I don't see nothing," Isaac said.

"Apache see signs. I told you me good tracker," Buck said looking up at Isaac. "Look here. Apache been here on foot, not horse. Maybe last night, maybe this morning."

"Where?" Isaac asked, getting down from his horse.

"There," Buck said as he pointed at a rock that had been turned over on its side. Isaac bent down to take a look.

For some reason, he had a strange feeling. Just about the same time a shadow moved, he jumped to the side and came up with his pistol in hand and cocked as the Apache stone club whisked by his head and barely caught his hat, knocking it off.

"Well, you little bastard," Isaac shouted as he fired his handgun almost point blank into the Apache's chest, blowing him backwards. Green and Johnson both heard the shot and came riding toward it from their points at a full gallop. They both rode up at about the same time from different directions. They saw Isaac standing over the dead scout's body.

Green was off his mount before it stopped. "What the hell?" he said trailing off the question.

"This here bastard tried to smash in my head with that damn war club there." Isaac looked around. As he jumped into the saddle, he said, "Where the hell is the other one?"

"I saw him over there," Johnson said as he put the heels of his boots to his horse. All three men started for the direction, when over a rise came the Indian Isaac had named Tom. He saw the three troopers coming and reined in his pony so hard his rear end almost touched the ground. A cloud of dust covered him and for a split second he was engulfed and almost hidden from sight.

When the dust cloud cleared, he was sitting his pony, both hands up in the air, almost as if to say, "don't shoot." The three men surrounded the scout.

"You know what that bastard friend of yours tried to do?" Isaac shouted.

"Me no friends with him," he said.

"The hell you ain't. You rode in with him. I ought to blow your damn head off right here and now." Isaac pointed his revolver at the Indian's face.

"Me, Tum, rode in with Captain Roth. Him not with me." The Indian had lowered his hands slowly to his horse's back. "Me ride with Captain Roth two, maybe three winters. Me save his hair in raid by Mangus Colorado. Him know me good Apache, not hurt buffalo soldier."

"Well, maybe so, but I'm not taking any chances. Green,

tie his hands and get his weapons. We'll just take him back and hear what Captain Roth has to say about this. I don't cotton to getting my brains knocked out of my head by no damn Apache who's supposed to be working with us."

Isaac had settled down, but he recalled a lesson Otis had told him, "Never trust anyone your first sense tells you not to. In fact, don't trust nobody that's not dead and you're less likely to be disappointed or killed."

Isaac told Green, "You keep your gun on him. If he even looks like he's going to do anything, shoot him."

"Right, Corporal," Green responded. "I'll blow the son-of-a-bitch plumb off his horse."

The day was just about over, so the four of them headed back to where they would meet up with the main column.

Capt. Roth was talking to Col. Grierson when the detail rode up. They saw Tom riding in between Green and Johnson. Isaac was to the rear with his pistol drawn and pointed at Tom. The two officers watched as they dismounted. Isaac reported, as was expected.

"Why the hell do you have my best scout's hands tied behind his back and you riding in here with your sidearm cocked and ready to blow him to the happy hunting grounds, Corporal?"

"Sir, I don't mean no disrespect, but your other scout, that young one, he tried to crack my skull this afternoon. I don't know how you feel about that sort of thing," he paused but a second and continued, "Sir," he paused again, "but I just don't cotton to that sort of thing myself. Not when I got to trust those I'm scouting with, Sir."

Captain Roth stepped to the Apache and they spoke in the Apache tongue. After they had talked for several minutes, the captain took his knife from its sheath and cut the rope holding the Apache's hands.

"What's this all about, Captain?" Col. Grierson asked. "I

don't need my scouts distrusting each other. I sure as hell don't need them killing each other."

"Yes, Sir," the captain answered. "Sir, we have a very serious matter here, but we can clear it up."

"I hope so, Captain," the colonel remarked.

"Sir, that young Apache joined up with us back at the water tank on our march to meet up with the 9th. A couple of the other Apache scouts knew him and told me his family had been killed by Victorio and his followers. His sisters were raped and then torn apart by tying their legs to two horses when the braves rode in separate directions. He and a brother were left for dead after being forced to watch. His brother did die, but he managed to live and wanted only a chance to kill Victorio."

"Where are these other scouts now?" the colonel asked.

"They rode out with our second detail," the captain answered.

"They went out with Otis?" Isaac butted in.

The colonel looked straight into Isaac's eyes, "Soldier, you don't interrupt two officers when they are talking. Do you understand?" His lips were tight and his voice firm.

"Yes, Sir. I'm sorry, Sir," Isaac said. "But Corporal White and me, we been through some hard times together, and Sir, if he's out there with them other two Apaches, then Otis might well be in trouble. Sir, I was thinking maybe me and these two," he pointed to Green and Johnson, "could go out and make sure he's OK, Sir."

The colonel was not angry, but he was firm and straight-forward. "Corporal, you are not paid to think about anything but scouting. That's all, do you understand? You are not to worry about Corporal White. He's been a scout long before you even knew what a scout was. If anybody in this man's army can take care of himself, it's White. I'd put him up against any ten Apaches and give you fifty to one odds. The whole time I'd feel guilty taking your dollar. Now get your horses taken care of. You've got to ride tomorrow and those mounts cost the taxpayer fourteen dollars a piece. Now, you and your details are dismissed."

"Yes, Sir," Isaac said. He saluted and turned. On the way to the picket line, Isaac told Green and Johnson, "If Otis doesn't come in tonight, I'm going out there and look for him tomorrow. You coming?"

"I'm a soldier, Corporal. I go where I'm ordered to go. If the colonel tells me to go to hell, I'd look for the door, but I ain't going to go against the colonel, not for Otis, not for you, not for myself. So don't ask me. This here army is the first place I ever had in my whole life where I could act like a man. You come from a fine plantation. Me, I come from a dirt farm where we never had enough to eat and the master, he felt he had to whip us most every day. No, sir, I ain't going to do nothing the colonel don't want."

Green went back to rubbing his horse down. When he finished he went toward the mess tent. Johnson never said a word, but followed Green.

"I'll go by myself," Isaac thought. "I ain't going to leave him out there. Not without looking for him. He came after me that time I was out there. I owe him."

Sara pushed the stop button on the tape player. "You all will just have to wait on me, but I have got to make a trip to the powder room," she said.

"I'll bet Isaac goes after Otis," Jeff said.

"I wouldn't be a bit surprised," Jew agreed.

"Military life had to be hard back then. I mean really hard." Jeff's statement had the tone of a question in it.

"It was," Jew agreed. "I was involved in a very extensive research program a few years ago while I was taking some classes at the academy. I was amazed at the number of Medals of Honor the early black soldiers won fighting in the Indian wars."

"Really?" Sara said as she returned to her chair.

"They sure did. They made great soldiers. I suppose they were a natural for military duty."

"Why is that?"

"Well," Jew continued, "being raised as slaves, they were accustomed to taking orders without question for one thing. Probably the most significant reason was they didn't expect much. By that, I mean that if the flour had weevils in it, so what? That was more than likely all they ever saw back home. Since none of them ever had a horse of their own, the ones assigned to them were treated special. There was a great deal of pride in those men. The most important thing I found was they had complete and absolute respect for their officers. I would go so far as to say if this Grierson told Isaac or Otis to jump off a cliff, they would do it without hesitation."

Jew stood up. "Before you start the tape, let me get Jeff and me a fresh beer." He went out into the kitchen. When he returned he handed Jeff his beer and sat down. He pointed a finger toward Sara. That ever present, pleasant smile was on his face as he said, "Roll 'em."

Chapter 15

When reveille sounded, Isaac was already up. His horse was saddled and he had gone by the mess tent. One of the cooks was a friend and he fed Isaac and wrapped five biscuits and a piece of dried meat in a rag for his lunch.

At roll call, the sergeant gave the troops their instructions for the day's march. He dismissed the platoon except for Isaac, Green and Johnson. They were to remain for special orders.

"You three buckaroos got yourselves a little special assignment," the sergeant said, half smiling.

"You are to work the north side of the column today. You are also to work wider than you have been. We'll have another detail of scouts inside between you and the column. The lieutenant says to keep an extra sharp eye. He also said it might be smart to swing back some and make sure we ain't got nobody on our tails that we don't know about. Now get out there."

Isaac smiled. He knew the lieutenant was saying "go find Otis, but not officially."

"We'll keep an extra sharp eye, Sergeant, you can bet on that."

The three men rode north for about an hour and turned back east. Here they began their crisscross search. They had ridden most of the morning when Isaac heard their signal whistle.

He stopped his horse and listened. He heard it again and rode toward the sound. Just over the next hill, he saw Green and rode toward him.

"Find something?" he shouted as he rode up.

"Yep. A set of tracks. Looks like Otis. See, this horse has been shod," Green said, pointing at a track.

"Looks like I owe you a drink," Isaac said. "Now let's find out why the hell he didn't come in last night."

Johnson was sitting his horse on top of a hill about a quarter of a mile away watching them. Isaac raised his hand and formed a circle, then pointed to the northeast. Johnson raised his arm and made the same sign. The three then moved off in that direction. Green swung to the right of Isaac and Johnson stayed on the left.

Isaac kept on the trail Otis had cut. His eyes never left the tracks and signs he could read.

They had ridden no more than an hour, when Johnson started working toward Isaac. He could tell he was going to join the trail Isaac was following. Green at the same time was moving in, also towards Otis' trail. Both men had cut trails and were following them. The trails they were on were of unshod Indian ponies.

It was clear to all three scouts that the two Indian ponies were behind the shod horse. They topped a ridge and halted their horses. There lay Otis and the two Indians he had in his detail. Isaac knew they were dead. Green started to go in.

142

"Hold it there, mister," Isaac said. "We are going to be sure before we go in. Green, you circle to the left and come in from the north. Johnson, you circle the right and come in there. I'll cover this end and we'll move in. Now, get. Watch yourselves. It could be an ambush."

The minutes seemed like hours as Isaac waited; then he waited some more. Then he saw Green. He was leading the horse Otis had ridden. He mounted up and slowly started down. His Springfield carbine was at the ready. He stopped his horse about fifteen yards away from the three bodies and slid to the ground. He walked over to one of the Apaches and rolled him over with his foot and stepped back, ready. The Indian had Otis' knife still in his chest. The other one had been shot. The bullet had exited out his back. Otis lay face down. He had one of the Indian's knives stuck in his back. Isaac laid his rifle down. Johnson and Green were both on the ground and watching the top of the surrounding hills for any attack that might come. Isaac slowly turned Otis over. He was limp. He felt his neck for a pulse.

"Well, kiss my ass. He's alive," Isaac said.

Otis picked up his head and opened one eye. "Isaac, that you?" he asked.

"Damn right, it's me," Isaac answered.

"What took you so long?" He sighed and passed out.

Isaac remembered passing a grove of cottonwood trees a couple of miles back. He sent both Green and Johnson to cut a couple of limbs that would let them make a travois. They were gone about an hour and returned with two long straight poles, plus the two Indian ponies. They still had the blanket saddles the Apaches rode.

Isaac took the blankets off the Indian ponies and used them for the center of the travois. Otis would be carried back on the travois as he was much too weak to ride. Isaac thought about removing the knife, but was afraid Otis might start bleeding. The three of them talked it over. To leave it in could be worse. The moving could cause the knife blade to cut something it had not up to now.

Isaac told Green to build a fire with dry wood, so as not to make too much smoke. He did and Isaac put his knife into the fire.

"When that's hot, I'm going to pull this damn devil's knife out. Stick that on the wound, hear?" he told Johnson.

"I hear you. Just tell me when."

The time seemed to drag. Otis remained unconscious.

"This thing's hot," Johnson told Isaac.

"OK, Green," Isaac ordered. "Hold him tight. He may try to move and I don't want him to move a muscle. You get that blade over here, Johnson," he said as he pulled the Apache's knife out of Otis' shoulder. The blood ran freely. "Slap that steel to the hole," Isaac shouted.

The cooking of flesh filled the air. Otis jerked and went limp. The bleeding stopped.

"Looks good, Isaac," Green said.

"Looks like shit," Isaac told him. "We need to get him back to the doctor. He ain't got a lot of time. Hell, man, he's got a lump on his head the size of your foot. Those bastards tried to smack his head like they did mine. They were going to kill us off one at a time. If that skunk would have got me yesterday, he'd have come after you one at a time. But all they got was dead."

The three of them picked Otis up, still face down.

"Leave him on his stomach. He'll ride OK like that. Tie him to the travois so he won't slip."

As Green and Johnson tied Otis to the travois, Isaac walked over to the two dead Indians and took his knife to them.

"This ought to tell Victorio we ain't so soft as he thinks." He then pulled his pistol and pointed it at the ponies standing close by.

"Don't shoot that gun, Corporal," Green said.

"What?" Isaac demanded.

"Those bastards knew what they were doing. I'm betting they got friends not too far away. You shoot that gun and they are going to know where we are. I looked at that one Otis shot. The muzzle had to be up against him when he shot. Had to muffle the sound. I'll bet they don't know their boys are found out yet and they're probably up by the main body of our troops."

Isaac lowered his handgun. "You're right, but we can't leave these ponies out here for them to use and I don't plan on taking 'em back."

"No need to take 'em back." Green picked up a hoof and drove his knife deep into the soft part of the hoof. He then stepped to the other pony and repeated the action.

"Ain't nobody going to ride these ponies for a long time."

Isaac returned his pistol to its holster. "Guess you ain't such a dumb nigger as I thought you was."

The three of them headed for camp. Johnson rode out front as scout. Green led Otis' horse with the travois and Isaac rode to the side of his friend, keeping an eye on the back trail. From time to time, Isaac remembered Otis was the best friend he had had since William Robert.

How he wished William Robert could see him now. A corporal in the United States Cavalry. He thought about that then said, half out loud, "Hell, I wouldn't want him to see me in no Yankee uniform, not after what those Yankees did back there in Georgia."

After they had travelled for a while, they stopped and Isaac checked Otis. He seemed to be OK, still unconscious. He had lost a lot of blood and for the first time, Isaac felt his friend might not make it.

"Green," he barked, "you get yourself back to the column and tell the lieutenant what happened out here. We'll travel slow and hope we don't do anymore harm to Otis. Ask the lieutenant to send the doc out to meet us. I don't think Otis will make it all the way in." He placed his hand on Otis' head. "He's burning up with fever. Get going, man. Don't waste any time."

Green dug his spurs into the side of his horse and rode straight for the main column.

The hours seemed to drag by as Isaac slowly made his way toward help.

"Where the hell are they?"

"I don't know, Corporal. Maybe the captain wouldn't let the lieutenant send the doctor."

The sun was almost set when they saw riders coming their way. Isaac recognized Green out front. He lowered his rifle and halted the horses. Green rode up and dismounted.

"Doc couldn't come, Corporal, but Private Morris knows how to treat the injured."

"Shit. He needs a doctor," Isaac shouted.

Morris felt Otis' neck for a pulse. "No sir, Corporal, this trooper, he don't need anything."

"What you saying, man? Get out of my way." Isaac shoved the private back.

Slowly he turned Otis' head. He could tell he was dead.

"No! No!" he shouted. "Not this one, God! He ain't supposed to die. Not like this. Not at the hands of them damn red bastards."

He felt himself start to sob down deep, but caught hold of his feelings. "Can't show these boneheads any soft part," his mind seemed to say. "Got to show strength. No place for weakness. Not out here." He pulled the blanket up over Otis' head.

"You're right, Private. He don't need anything anymore. But I damn well promise you them red devils are going to need something when I find 'em. It ain't going to stop with them two Otis' took out. No sir. They'll pay a hell of a price for this, I promise you that." He patted Otis' back.

"OK, men, let's get to camp. We got a hell of a trooper to put to rest."

Otis was buried just outside of camp the following morning. As the bugles blew taps, Isaac could feel a tear roll down his cheek.

"So long, good friend. You rest in peace," he whispered to himself. "I don't know how, but somewhere we'll meet again."

The command to move out was given and the column began to move. Isaac took a long look at the surroundings.

"I'll remember this valley. Someday I'll get back here and mark that grave."

"Corporal, get your butt out there," came the order from the first sergeant. "We ain't got any time to waste in this man's army."

Isaac put the steel to his horse and headed to his assigned point.

Chapter 16

The search for Victorio and his followers had been in progress for two weeks and as yet, no sign of them had been found. Isaac and the scouts were out each day looking. The colonel had set up a temporary camp and from this point, they would strike when word was returned of Victorio's whereabouts.

The scouts would stay out from three to four days before returning.

They were into the sixteenth day when Isaac struck a trail of what looked like fifty or sixty horses.

"Best get word back to the colonel. This looks like he may be going to work pretty soon."

He then rode to a hilltop and spotted two of his detail and signaled them to come. After they saw the tracks, Isaac explained that he wanted them to get back to the camp and advise Col. Grierson that he and the remaining scouts would follow the trail.

It was late afternoon when Isaac and the other two scouts came to a water hole fed by a small spring. They were in the process of filling their canteens when four Apaches rode up on them. Both parties were taken by surprise.

As Isaac pulled his revolver from its holster, one of the Indians tried to ride him down with his horse. Isaac jumped to the side, as the Indian and horse plunged into the water hole. The Apache fell from the horse as it lost its balance and tumbled into the water. The other three Apaches all gave shouts and screams as they followed the first one's lead. The scouts had their side arms ready and when the smoke cleared, all four Apaches lay dead.

"Let's get the hell out of here," one of the scouts shouted.

"You don't have to say that twice," another one answered.

The three men mounted and headed for the column as fast as their horses would carry them. They rode for a little over an hour and slowed to a walk in order to save the horses in case they found themselves being pursued.

Their fears were well founded. Looking back, they could see a dust cloud in the distance. That meant only one thing. They were now the main topic of Apache interest.

Isaac thought he would confuse them by cutting across the rocky flats. This would take a little longer in the route to the unit, but he knew that help would be on its way. If he could stall the Indians and draw them out onto the open plains, the soldiers would have a much better chance.

Isaac turned to Johnson, "Get back to the column and bring them on the double. Green and I will head for the open plains." Isaac stopped at one point and looked over his back trail. He could see the dust cloud following and gaining ground.

"They are still coming," he said as he put the heels of his boots to the flank of his horse. "Don't fail me now," he said to the big bay.

Isaac and Green had covered about another mile and a half, when the front horse ridden by Green stepped in a hole and went down. Isaac, riding close behind, did not have a chance to pull his horse up and it fell over the top of the downed animal. Both riders were unhurt except for bumps and bruises. Green's horse had a broken leg and Isaac's had broken its neck and lay dead.

"What the hell are we going to do, Isaac?" Green said as he stripped his canteen and saddle bags from the downed horse's saddle.

Isaac had hurt his leg and knew he was not going to go too far, so he looked around for some high ground they could defend themselves from.

"Over there," he pointed toward a pile of large boulders. "We'll hole up there and hope Johnson gets back with help in time. If he don't, I plan on taking just as many of those devils with me as I can." He pulled his rifle and saber from his dead horse.

The two made it to the rocks. They were well hidden when the war party arrived. They hooped and howled. Several shot arrows into the body of Isaac's horse. One jumped down and cut the throat of Green's horse.

One of the braves pointed toward the rocks and they all started for the two scouts. When they were within 150 feet, Isaac opened up with his carbine. Green followed and two warriors were knocked from their ponies. The others turned and dashed for cover. Isaac pulled his saber from its sheath and laid it on the rock next to him.

"I'll shoot till I'm dry, then I'll hack if I have to," he said to Green.

"Here they come," Green shouted.

The fight was short as the black powder filled the air with smoke. Twice the Indians rushed them. Each time Isaac and

Green drove them back and caused them to lose three or four warriors. Isaac knew they could not hold out for long. He was down to five rounds for his carbine and his revolver was empty.

"How many rounds you got left?" he asked Green.

"Four for my carbine and one left in my revolver. I ain't going to let 'em take me alive, Isaac. I just ain't going to let 'em do to me what I've seen them do to others. No sir, I ain't."

"Shut your mouth about that crap. Me, I'm going out fishing and I'll take as many of them bastards as I can."

As he talked, Isaac was trying to work out a plan and was watching the flat ground between him and the Indians.

"Hell, Green. I'm going to shoot until I run plumb out, then I'm going to take this here saber and hack my way."

Isaac had laid his carbine down and picked up his saber. Holding it in his right hand and point it up, he looked at the edge and said, "Yep. I'll hack my way all the way back to Georgia if I have to."

Several pieces of gravel rolled down behind him. He looked up to see an Indian standing on the rocks overhead with a war club in his hand. The Indian jumped and screamed. Isaac threw up his left arm to protect himself and at the same time pointed the saber toward the Indian coming down on him.

Isaac felt the blade as it went through the Indian's body. The war club cracked down. Isaac tried to get out of the way, but the club caught him a glancing blow to the side of the head and left shoulder. The weight of the Indian as he fell broke the blade on Isaac's saber.

When Isaac came to, he could feel the wagon bouncing. He opened his eyes.

"Well, did you decide to join us, Corporal?" he heard someone say.

"Where am I?" he said with a groan. His head felt like it would burst and his shoulder hurt like it had been crushed.

"God, am I dead?"

The voice laughed. "Hell no, you ain't dead. That damn fool Indian hit you in the head." The man talking moved over and placed his hand on Isaac's shoulder. "You took a hell of a lick, soldier, but you'll be OK. I'm Lieutenant James and I'm a field doctor. Your head is all bandaged because of the lick you took. Your shoulder will be stiff for a few days, too. But you'll be OK with some rest."

"What about Green? Is he OK?"

"Yeah. He took a couple of shots, but I think he'll make it," the doctor said reassuringly.

"How in the world did you find us in time?" Isaac asked.

"Look, don't talk so much. I'll tell you this much, then try to rest." The lieutenant settled down next to Isaac. "They heard your shooting. The lieutenant felt he had better hurry. So he split the column into two troops and came in from the east and the north side of you. The Indians were so intent on doing you two in that he moved in and cut them to pieces." He paused. "There were about seventy of them. Did you know that?"

"No, Sir, I just knew it was a bunch. A hell of a bunch," Isaac answered.

"Well, you killed the big boy. Did you know that?" the doctor asked. "Old Victorio himself," he said reaching back behind him. "Here's your saber for what it's worth. The other scout told the lieutenant you would want it. That you had a special reason to keep it, so the lieutenant said to make sure you got it."

Isaac felt the hilt and held it up. He was having a hard time seeing. "Is it broken?" he asked.

"Yeah. He must have fallen on the blade and broke it, but you did him in. There was a price on his head, too. Over a thousand dollars and it was for anyone who killed him. Unusual, too. Most of the time those rewards don't apply to soldiers or lawmen, but this one does. You're a rich, man, Corporal. What are you going to do with all that money anyway?"

"Oh, it'll get spent, Lieutenant. It'll get spent." Isaac closed his eyes and faded off to sleep.

"I knew it! Somehow I knew he would catch up to and do away with that red devil," Jew said.

Clara looked toward Sara as she spoke, "As John stated earlier, he was involved in a research program." She turned to Jew, "Would you say Maria has accurately described the times, John, according to what you have read?"

"As a matter of fact, she has," Jew agreed. "I would even go so far as to say that her narrative is better since it is to the point and doesn't ponder or belabor an insignificant event as often as the historians like to do. I have read accounts that could have been written in a couple of pages that were dragged out to what seemed like infinity."

"I know what you mean," Jeff said. "I've had to struggle through that type of writing a time or two myself." He paused, then added, "A thousand dollars . . ."

Sara interrupted, "Over a thousand, dear."

"Yeah, that's right. Over a thousand," Jeff said. "Can you imagine what that could have purchased then?"

"A lot," Jew said. "Now I know why the broken saber. In fact, a lot of light is being shed on the contents of that box we found."

Jeff glanced at the saber hanging on the wall. "Get that tape to rolling again, Sara. I've got to know what happens next."

Chapter 17

Maria saw the dust rising long before she saw the troops as they returned to Fort Davis. She was beside herself. She walked back and forth on the long porch that ran the full length of the hospital.

"Don't fret so, girl. They'll be here in an hour or so. That man of yours is too damn mean to be hurt, so calm down," the doctor told her as he stepped out on the porch to watch the troops returning from their engagement.

"It's been five weeks," she said. "It was supposed to take only a couple."

"Sometimes these things just don't fit our schedule. We have to be patient," the doctor said in his Texas drawl.

As the troops came into the fort, Maria searched each face looking for Isaac. Most of the men were covered with white caliche dust. The further back in the column, the whiter the troops were. She did not see Isaac and started to walk toward the troops, when they assembled on the parade ground.

"Hold on, girl," the doctor said. "I know you want to find that man of yours, but we are going to have work here in just a few minutes. That ambulance wagon headed this way means we got some injured coming in and I'll need all the help I've got. So don't go wandering off until we get finished."

She knew the doctor was right and stepped back onto the porch.

"Maybe I should get the operating room ready, doctor," she said.

"Maybe. But why don't we wait and see first." The doctor's calm voice had a settling effect on her.

The wagon pulled up, followed by two others.

"How many?" the doctor asked.

"Six you can do something about," the driver of the first wagon said.

"How many dead?" the doctor asked.

"Four," the driver answered. "About as many Apache scouts, but they don't count."

"Get 'em in here and we'll get ready." The doctor turned to Maria. "OK, girl, let's get cleaned up. Time for us to go to work." He went inside and Maria followed, looking over her shoulder for Isaac, but not seeing him anywhere.

The doctor had to amputate the first soldier's right arm. Maria wondered if he would make it. He had lost a lot of blood and he was on the edge of shock. She covered him with two blankets and put two hot water bottles in next to him in an effort to ward off shock, which she knew would kill him.

Maria returned to the operating room and began to prepare bandages. She took a tray filled with folded ones to the table next to the operating table that Dr. Davis was working on. She looked at the patient. He was covered with dust and dried blood from a head wound. She cut away the bandage and saw it was Isaac. She gasped and both hands flew up to her own face.

"Oh, my God!" she said. The blood rushed out of her head and she felt she would faint. Her blood pressure went up and in a flash she thought her head would explode.

The doctor saw her reaction and without seeming too excited said, "Hold on, girl. What's wrong with you? Can't you see he's been hit in the head? Ain't no Apache born can really hurt one of our buffalo soldiers by hitting him in the head. Hell, I've seen worse than this come out of the bar in town on any given Saturday night and the trooper would be in a work detail Monday morning." He glanced at her and smiled. "Now, I don't think he'll be in a work detail Monday, but he'll be OK. Besides I'll bet he'll get some pretty good nursing while he's here, too."

"Is he going to be all right, Doctor? I mean is he really going to be all right?" she asked in a pleading voice.

"I'll be better than OK," Isaac said as he opened his eyes. "We got us a thousand dollars, maybe more, to take us to Georgia."

"What are you talking about, you big nut? We have a thousand dollars? That red devil knock all the sense out of your head?" she said with a sound of relief in her voice.

"It's true," a soldier lying across the room said.

"What are you saying?" she asked.

"He killed ol' Victorio himself. Yes, ma'am. He stuck that red devil through and through with his saber. Sent him to the happy hunting grounds, he did. Yes, ma'am, he done won the thousand dollar bounty on that red man's head." The soldier had raised up on an elbow while he spoke. After he finished, he laid back down and said, "What I couldn't do with me a thousand dollars. Lordy, lordy, them girls in town would line up for me and I'd try 'em all," he laughed.

"You be still or you aren't going to try anybody," the doctor said to him.

Col. Grierson came into the operating room. No one stopped working. He looked over Maria's shoulder.

"How's he doing?" he asked.

"The doctor said he'll be OK, Colonel, but he's going to have a sore head and shoulder for a couple of weeks," Maria said.

"Good. Put this up somewhere for him." He handed her the broken saber. "Make sure it does not get lost."

"What is this? It's broken," she said.

"Yep. It's broken, but it did its job. I know he will want it. This is the blade he used to kill Victorio."

"He really did kill Victorio and with this saber?" she asked.

"Sure did. I'm damn proud of him, too. I knew in San Antonio he would make a hell of a soldier. Knew it right off. I can always pick a fighting man. Always could."

The colonel turned to the doctor. "Take care of my people, Doc. They are a bunch of brave men. The United States needs men like these. I'm ordering you not to lose one of them either."

"Do my best, Sir," the doctor answered.

"Can't ask for more," the colonel said and turned and left.

The weeks passed slowly for Isaac in the hospital. Only having Maria close made it tolerable. He was not one to lie around and when the doctor let him start moving out on the front porch, he felt much better.

"Well," he told Maria one day. "Only three more weeks and my enlistment will be up. We got to get someone to marry us before we head for Georgia."

"Isaac," she said. "I spoke to the padre in town. He said he will marry us if you will join the church."

"What do I have to do? I'm already a Baptist. I was baptized when I was a boy back home by old Brother Henry."

"Well, you'll have to go for instructions from the priest. It won't be hard. He promised you would not have any problems remembering the few things required. He won't marry us if you don't join the church." She was almost apologizing in the way she told him of the terms of the priest.

"Don't fret about it. I'll join. When can I start?"

She sat up. Her eyes seemed to light up and a sparkle could be heard in her voice. "Thursday. He starts classes Thursday." The excitement in her voice was genuine. "I'll go tell him now. Isaac, I'm so happy. I was afraid you would not do it. Especially with the priest saying you had to. I'm so happy. I truly love you so much." She leaned over and kissed his cheek.

"Hey, girl, none of that. Not here. Those troops out there won't let me hear the end of it if they see you do that." He laughed as she hurried off to tell the priest he was about to have a convert.

Chapter 18

"What do you call that thing that priest gave you? Tell me one more time. I promise not to forget this time." Isaac asked as the team pulled their small wagon into the outskirts of San Antonio.

"It's called a crucifix. I'm going to place it over our bed when we get a home. It will bless our house and we will have many children."

"That's what we are going to need, girl. Lots and lots of children," Isaac laughed. "And I'm going to enjoy building a great big family. Yes, ma'am. I'm really going to enjoy that, for sure."

She pinched him in the arm and he winced. His arm was still tender. She put her hand to her mouth. "I did not mean to hurt you," she said.

"You didn't hurt me a bit. I just wanted you to feel sorry for me. That way you've got to make up to me later." He laughed again.

They stayed only a couple of days in San Antonio. Just long enough to get supplies and let the team of mules rest before moving on. Isaac thought of trying to find the old man who befriended him when he first came to town several years before, but time just would not allow it. He had one thing on his mind. He had to get back to Georgia and get him some land, good black land, and get his crop in the ground.

Each day's travel which took them closer to Georgia seemed to take longer and longer. Isaac could hardly wait. He told Maria the same stories over and over so many times she was starting to feel like she had lived there when she had been a young girl instead of Mexico.

As the wagon pulled into Hazel, the first person who saw them stopped and watched.

"You know him?" Maria asked.

"I don't think so, but it's been a long time. I was in the Army for almost five years and I left here four or five years before that. Folks change."

Several children pointed as the wagon rolled through town.

"Not what I remember," Isaac remarked. "It used to be bigger."

He looked down each side street. There was an old black man sitting on the porch of a run down shack. Isaac pulled the team up.

"Howdy," Isaac said.

"Howdy, yourself, stranger," the old man replied.

"Tell me, sir, where could a fellow feed his mules around here?" Isaac asked.

"Livery, I guess," he paused and then added, "Mr. Winn's going to want cash. You ain't going to get no credit."

"I got cash," Isaac answered.

"Going to cost two dollars."

"That's OK. I got it. Where is this Mr. Winn's place?"

"Down there by the creek," the old man pointed. He looked closer and raised up from his stool. "Do I know you?"

"Maybe. My name's Isaac. Took the last name of Turner. Used to belong to the Willard Plantation before the war."

"Lordy, lordy, Isaac. I'll be damned. I'm old Snowball Jones. You remember me, don't you? I used to belong to Master Willard, too. I knowed you even before you was borned. I mean I knowed your mama," the old man chuckled. "Tie them mules up and come on in this house, boy. I got to see you closer. Got some coffee on the stove." He turned his head and yelled into the house. "Woman, get that coffee on the stove. We got us some visitors."

"I really need to take care of my team," Isaac told him.

"Looky yonder," the old man said, pointing down the street.

Isaac saw a man coming out of the general store. He had one arm and was carrying a small sack of groceries.

"You wait right there. Don't move," the old man said as he hurried off toward the store. He met the white man and they talked for a few seconds. Isaac could see the old man pointing toward them.

"Who do you suppose that is?" Maria asked.

"Beats me. Don't remember any one-armed fellow when I was here."

The two men came across the street.

"Isaac," the one-armed man said about halfway across the dirt street. "Isaac, is that really you? By damn, it is. I don't believe this. You came back home like I always knew you would."

"Well, bless my bones, if it ain't William Robert," Isaac said with a feeling of joy he had not felt for a long, long time. He jumped to the ground and grabbed William Robert by the shoulders.

(As Clara spoke very softly, one could hear the compassion in her voice, "I knew they would get together again

163

somehow.")

William Robert pulled Isaac closer, then he stepped back. "God, it's good to see you. I was afraid you might be dead." A tear swelled up in his eye. "Where you been? What you been doing?" he asked.

"Hey. Hold on a minute," Isaac said. "We got about seven or eight years to catch up on, but first I want you to meet my wife." Isaac turned to Maria, still sitting in the wagon. "Honey, this here is William Robert, the one I told you about."

"This is your wife, Isaac?" William Robert asked.

Isaac could see the startled look on his face, and for the first time really realized she would be considered white.

"Yep. It's a long story. I'll tell you all about it later. Right now, I've got to find a place to spend the night and take care of my mules."

"Isaac, I didn't mean nothing by that dumb question. Sorry, ma'am. Pleased to meet you. You got yourself quite a man. Him and me, we go way back." He was stumbling and Maria could see the difficulty he was having.

"Si. My husband has told me about you. I am pleased to meet you. I have heard many stories, some of which I don't really know if I should believe or not. Maybe you will tell me the whole truth, not only the good parts." Her smile was gentle. There was a sweetness in her expression and William Robert could feel it in her voice.

"I sure will, ma'am. I'll tell you what a rascal he really was. Now, about tonight, come on down to my place. It ain't much but it's mine." He looked at Isaac and sadness filled his eyes. "I lost the plantation right before Papa died. I'll always think that's what really killed him. To see them damn carpetbaggers move in and take it all. Damn shame. Hey! Let's not talk about that now. Got to get you settled. Plenty of time for all that later." He was already leading the team as he finished his statement.

The house William Robert had was little more than a shack, but it did have a small barn and a pen for the mules. After the team was taken care of, William Robert told Isaac he would be back in a minute, to make himself and Maria at home.

He returned in about ten minutes with a little heavy set black woman.

"Isaac, this is Aunt Hattie." He turned to Maria. "Aunt Hattie is Isaac's aunt. Her sister was Isaac's mother."

"This here is little Isaac?" she said. "My, my, but you sure did turn out to be a fine looking man. Who's this pretty thing?" She turned to Maria.

"This is my wife, Maria, Aunt Hattie."

"Your wife? My, my, ain't she fair."

"Yes, ma'am. She's Mexican."

"I've heard of them Mexicans. Didn't know they were so pretty."

"Aunt Hattie has a job with old Doc Flowers. She'll be leaving in the morning for the North."

"Yes, sir, Isaac, I got me a job with him right after you left. Been with him ever since. Right here in Hazel. Now you come back and I got to leave. The doctor, he's got a job in a hospital up north in Ohio state. He's taking me along as his housekeeper. I gots to go. There just ain't no jobs here for an old woman any more."

"You wait right here a minute, Aunt Hattie. I got something for you in a trunk out there in the wagon."

Isaac went to a box and got out a tintype picture of him in uniform.

"Here, Aunt Hattie, I want you to have this. I had it taken at Fort Davis when a traveling man came to camp taking pictures. See me there. I was a corporal."

"You was in the Army? My goodness. I sure am proud of

you. You growed up to make your mama proud. You sure 'nuff did. I'll keep this picture all my days, I will."

They visited for about an hour and Aunt Hattie asked to be excused. She had work to do and the family she worked for would be needing her as they were to leave in the morning. Isaac kissed her and she left.

"That's a fine woman," William Robert said. "Wish I could afford to keep her. I would, I sure would. But she's got a good job with a good family. They treat her like one of the family, too."

"I'm glad I got to see her one more time," Isaac said.

They sat down to eat. After a meal of beans, sow belly and cornbread, they moved into the small living room by the fireplace. William Robert went out back and returned with a jug. He gave Isaac a tin cup.

"How about you, Maria? Would you join us? It ain't champagne, but the effect's just the same," he smiled.

"Yes, I think I could use a little pick me up. Thank you," she responded.

"Well, Isaac, like I said, I lost the place," William Robert started. "Then I lost my damn arm."

"How did you do that, William Robert?" Isaac said as he nodded toward the shoulder without an arm.

"Damn yellow legs did it. I'll bet you weren't gone a year when several of those bastards came riding in across the field. I had a garden growing. They rode right through it. One of them took his horse and started making it back up, then he rode forward until he had my garden almost all stomped down. I got so damn mad I grabbed a pitchfork and made a run at him. One of them pulled a gun and shot me through the arm. I don't know what kind of gun he had, but it damn near blew my arm off. Well, ol' Sally Jane was still with us. She had been taking care of Papa. She came running and I guess they would have killed me if she hadn't of covered me up with her body. They just laughed and rode off. She sent little Rabbit John," he paused. "Remember Rabbit John?"

Isaac nodded his head indicating he remembered.

"Well," William Robert continued, "he ran all the way to town and got old Doc Evans. He came on down and they put me on the kitchen table and finished cutting my arm off."

"Who were those men that shot you? Did you know them?" Isaac asked.

"Never saw them before in my life. Somebody said they were just some Yankee soldiers mustered out and heading home, back up north, I guess." He looked down, then he raised his head and looked Isaac straight in the face. "Wish I knew where their home was. I'd get 'em for sure. I truly would."

"Well, we don't or I would help you," Isaac told him.

"Aw, that's enough about me. Tell me about you, Isaac. You have to have some interesting stories to tell."

"Well, I managed to stay alive and to some point made a little money. I'm looking to buy a little piece of the old place. Think I can get the owner to sell?"

"There's a piece about 35 acres for sale now. Down there at the old creek. You know where that big redheaded overseer used to live. What was his name? Oh, yeah, Clarence Ridgewright. God, he was a mean one. He got killed in a bar by a Yankee." His mind seemed to wander and his voice trailed off.

"You say there's about 35 acres?" Isaac asked.

"Yeah, and what's left of the house and barn, too." William Robert's eyes sparkled. The thought of Isaac buying part of the old home place pleased him.

"How much you think they want for it?" Isaac asked.

"I think they are asking $600. You got that much, Isaac?" William Robert asked.

"Yep. I think we can scrape up $600. It'll be hard, but we

can do it, I'm sure."

"Good. We'll go look at it tomorrow." He stood up and crossed the room. He filled his cup and turned to Isaac. "More?"

"Nope. That's strong stuff. You better take it easy yourself."

"Yeah, I better." He set the cup down and turned to face Isaac. "Isaac," he said looking down, "don't take this the wrong way, but there's something you better understand." He hesitated.

"What do you have on your mind, man? Speak up." Isaac could see that William Robert was having trouble finding the right words.

"Well, Isaac, you're a black man. Your wife is white. There are some here abouts ain't going to take kindly to that. If you show up with six hundred dollars and want to buy a farm, some just ain't going to sell no matter how bad they need to. They just ain't. Do you understand what I'm saying?" he asked.

"I think so, but what the hell am I going to do? I want a farm. I earned the money. I was a soldier for the U.S. Army and served my time. I got the paper saying I'm a full blooded American. What the hell am I to do? I can't change my color and I'm going to have my farm. I earned that right. Man, I got cuts, scars and pain right here in this body that say I earned that right. No damn bastard is going to keep that from me." Isaac was getting mad and the more he talked the madder he was becoming.

William Robert raised his hand. "Hold on there, you hot headed burrhead. You always did get worked up too damn fast. What if you and I go look at the property? If you like it, we'll go to the owner and I'll deal with him. He won't know I don't have six hundred dollars. Folks here about still think we had money hid out. We didn't, but they think we might. So I'll close the deal right up to the point of signing. You act like my pet nigger and when it comes time to sign, I'll sign as a witness. You can sign your name, can't you?"

"Sure I can sign my name," Isaac responded.

"OK, then, most of these quick deeds have the buyer's signature on a line and right under it a place for the witness to sign. I'll sign it first in the witness blank. You sign right above me and you'll be signing on the buyer's line. I'll bet they won't even notice until they file the deed and it'll be too late then, because that damn courthouse is filled with Yankees. They'll make sure you get your farm."

Isaac laughed. "By damn, you think it'll work?"

"It's got to work. It's your only chance."

The next morning the two men rode out and looked at the land and the buildings.

"They are in pretty sad shape," Isaac remarked.

"Sure they are, but I'll help you. We can fix it up. Hell, it ain't so bad. That field over there—you remember when it used to grow cotton like crazy? You had to stand up to pick a bough to wipe your butt with. Remember?"

Both men laughed.

"That is a good field," Isaac agreed. "That's good bottom land. Let's go do it." He reached into his pocket and pulled out the money and the small medicine bag.

"What's that, boy?" William Robert asked, pointing at the old Indian charm.

"That is my luck. It's got a charm to it you wouldn't believe. Saved my life three times for sure, maybe more I don't know about." He put the small bag back in his pocket. Isaac counted out six hundred dollars and handed it to William Robert. "You try to get it for less now. Don't be too easy with my money, hear?"

William Robert put the money into his shirt pocket and buttoned the flap. "I'm going to spend every penny," he said as he winked at Isaac.

The deal was made in town and like William Robert had predicted, no one noticed that Isaac was the true purchaser. In fact, they joked about William Robert having a darkie for a witness.

("By God, they pulled it off," Jew stated.)

The next day when the real estate agent recorded the sale, he was told Mr. Turner could expect his clear title in about three weeks. It did not take long for the agent to realize what had taken place. He came down the dusty street in his buckboard and pulled his horse up right at the edge of William Robert's porch.

"That's a real smart thing you did, Billy Bob. You and that nigger. You really screwed me up. Ain't no one this side of Atlanta going to let me handle their property from here on out. If this was before the war and the South was what it was, I'd blow your ass away and your nigger's along with it."

William Robert stepped out on the porch. "Well, well, well, Mr. Reed, you got some more land you want to sell or you just riding around town shooting off your fat mouth?"

"Billy Bob, you did it this time, boy," he said.

Isaac pushed past William Robert. "You got something to say, friend, why not say it to me?" he said.

"You're damn right I got something to say, nigger. But I don't talk to the likes of you, so just shut your mouth," he demanded.

Isaac stepped off the porch and walked up to Reed. Before Reed knew it, Isaac's hands had him by the front of his coat. He yanked him off the wagon and threw him up against the house.

"Just who do you think you are calling nigger, you white scum?" Isaac said. His eyes had narrowed and his anger was at the breaking point. "You can call me Isaac, or you can call me Turner. You can even call me Mr. Turner, but don't you ever call me nigger again or I'll break every bone in your stupid head."

Maria had come out on the porch. She rushed to Isaac's side and grabbed his right arm, thus preventing him from hitting Reed.

"He's not worth it. Don't give them any reason to cause us trouble," she pleaded.

"You're right. The likes of him ain't worth it. You leave us alone, you hear. We don't want any trouble, but we ain't running from it neither," Isaac said as he released Reed's collar and stepped back.

Reed straightened his coat. "Hmmm," he said, " 'we', you said, 'we'. That mean this is your woman?"

"That's right. This is my wife. So what?" Isaac stepped toward him.

Reed raised his arm to protect himself.

"Don't do it, Isaac," William Robert said. "Maria's right. This kind of trash ain't worth it. He's all mouth. Always has been, always will be. Now get your fat ass out of here, Reed, before my friend here gets really mad and kicks it up around your shoulder blades."

Reed climbed back on to his buckboard and turned his horse around. As he cleared the yard and was in the street, he pulled up on the reins and turned. "You ain't heard the last of this," he said.

Isaac took a step toward him and he popped the horse's rump with the reins and drove away in such a hurry his hat flew off and landed in the street. Isaac walked over and picked it up. He held the brim. Reed looked back to see him punch his fist through the crown and throw it to the side of the street.

Back on the porch, William Robert said, "He's right, Isaac. We ain't heard the last of it, I'm afraid. It'll be all over town before dark you got yourself a white wife.'

Chapter 19

Isaac had heard a few sly remarks in town about him and Maria, but he tried to ignore them and went about his business of getting his farm in shape. He decided he did not have time to fight the war all over again. He was free and he had a good wife.

"If they want to waste their time worrying over things they can't do anything about, that's their problem. Me, I got to worry about getting a crop in the ground before the rains come," he told Maria.

They had been on the farm for a little over six months. Isaac had his field planted in corn. That would be his first crop. It would be his crop and the money the crop brought in would be his. For the first time in his life, he could feel the joy of being a free man. To make things even better, he was doing what he really loved—farming.

Each day Isaac spent chopping the weeds that seemed to

grow overnight and would overtake the small corn plants. The field was clean and Isaac knew he would turn a few dollars come fall.

Each time he went to the field or even looked at it from afar, his feeling of pride would overwhelm him.

The night was warm and the tree frogs were in great harmony as their songs filled the still night air.

Isaac rose from the table and picked up his coffee cup, leaned down and kissed Maria on the back of the neck.

"Let's sit on the porch a spell and enjoy the peace and quiet of our farm," he said.

As he walked toward the front door, he stopped and picked up his pipe, filled it, struck a match and took a deep puff.

"If you are going to smoke that stinking thing, you had better get yourself out on that porch," Maria said as she pushed him through the doorway.

They sat there on the porch for a quarter of an hour. Neither said anything. They just enjoyed their surroundings.

Finally Isaac said almost to himself, "Yep, come fall I'll get that crop sold. Then I'm buying me a new pair of them boots I saw at the store in town." He paused. "I'm going to get you, my sweet thing, a brand new one of them really good iron cook stoves that has the oven on it. Then, I'm going . . ." His voice stopped. He cocked his head first to one side and then to the other.

"What do you hear?" Maria asked.

He raised his hand. "Wait," he replied, still straining to hear something.

Isaac rose to his feet and turned toward the front door. "Get in the house and get that shotgun ready. There's a rider coming hell bent for election down the road."

Isaac reached inside and picked up his rifle and returned to his chair on the porch.

"You going to stay out there?" Maria asked.

"Yeah. You stay out of the light and watch from the window. It's only one rider. Don't you hear him?"

"I do now," she replied.

Isaac sat with his eyes fixed on the lane that ran to the main road. His wait was short. A rider in a cloud of dust was headed straight for the house. Isaac could see with the moonlight there was only one. He stood and stepped to the edge of the porch next to one of the supporting posts. If he needed cover, this was his only chance.

The rider rode up to the house and hit the ground running. He fell down and Isaac saw it was William Robert. He jumped from the porch and ran to him. As Isaac helped him up, he saw that William Robert's face was covered with blood.

"What the hell?" Isaac said.

"They are coming, Isaac! That bunch of dumb rednecks are coming! They're going to hang you! Get Maria and get the hell out of here! Now!" he pleaded.

"Who's coming? We ain't done nothing to nobody," Isaac told him.

"Makes no difference. They're coming, I tell you. It's them damn rednecks in town. They're coming and they plan on hanging you, man. Hell, some of them may be out there in the brush now for all I know."

"Like hell I'll git. I'll blow me a hole in that trash if they show up here. Maria, get him in the house," he demanded.

Isaac grabbed a handful of rifle shells and shoved them into his pocket. "I'm better in the open, so I'm staying outside. Honey, you get that shotgun and if one of those bastards come through that door, blow him back in the yard," he told her. "William Robert, you stay here with her and don't let anybody get in here, you hear."

"I hear, Isaac. Don't worry. I won't let anyone in."

Isaac could see William Robert would not be much help. He had taken what looked like a bullet that had creased his scalp just above his ear.

"Maria, see if you can stop his bleeding," Isaac said, pointing toward William Robert's head.

"I'm all right. They missed me. The damn bullet sang right past me. My ears ring like hell but I'm OK. Now get out there, man. I mean they were right behind me."

Isaac jumped off the porch and headed for the brush across the yard. As he reached the brush, a shot rang out. Maria blew out the lamp and waited. She did not hear anything for a long time. Then several horses could be heard and voices somewhere in the brushy area by the field.

She called out into the darkness, "Isaac, you OK?"

No answer came back.

"Isaac?" she shouted. "Are you OK?" She spoke in Spanish this time.

William Robert staggered to the doorway. "They got him. I know they have." His voice was cut short by another shot. William Robert fell back into the house face up and Maria could see from the moonlight that he landed in that his face was covered with blood.

"My God," she said. "What's going on here?"

"We got your nigger. Now you little brown honey, I'm going to show you how a white man can take care of a woman. You spent too much time with the likes of that darkie."

A figure appeared in the doorway. It was a man. Maria thought it was Reed. Without hesitation, she pulled the trigger on the old shotgun and the man's body flew back into the yard. She heard someone drag him off.

"You bitch," someone shouted. "You killed him."

"You bastard. You killed William Robert. Where is my husband? Leave us alone. We haven't done anything to you. Why are you doing this to us anyway?"

"We got your husband all right, just like we got that nigger lover Willard. You look down at the creek and you'll see that damn nigger of yours."

She raised up in time to see the fire start. It burned up slowly until it reached its full height. There in the glare of the blaze, she could see five or six men. They mounted their horses and rode away. She clasped both hands to her mouth.

Isaac was hanging from an oak tree. Without caring what happened to her, she raced through the field and reached the once brave soldier who was now dead at the hands of unknown enemies for no reason that would ever make sense.

I cut my husband down and laid him next to an oak tree. I then returned to the house and dragged William Robert across the field where I had left Isaac.

My grief was beyond my ability to describe, seeing those two men lying there. But I knew they had to be buried. The rest of the night, I dug in the ground. Just before sunrise I finished and placed Isaac in the grave. Next to him I laid William Robert. On Isaac's chest I placed the holy crucifix given to us on our wedding day by Father Lopez.

I have hurriedly finished these last pages, for I fear for my life. Those animals that killed my man and his half brother are sure to return.

I will go now back to Mexico where there have been some changes in the government. Perhaps I will be able to reclaim my rancho. Perhaps some day I will return and give these two fine men a proper grave marker.

I may never return, but the love I have known from this man, Isaac, will live with me until the end of my days.

Maria Elena Estrada Pena Turner
Wife of Isaac Turner, a Freed
Slave and a Great Soldier in the
United States 9th Cavalry
1882

Chapter 20

Jeff reached over and turned the tape player off. No one said anything for a few minutes.

"Can you believe that?" Jeff asked. "They just came in here and killed him. They killed William Robert, too. Two men killed for what?" He did not expect an answer.

"For prejudice, Jeff," Jew answered. "For pure old prejudice. No other reason was needed then and life was treated cheaply."

"It's a shame. What a waste," Jeff said. "You know, Jew, I'm from that Willard family. I guess William Robert would be my great, great, great uncle. I never knew he was killed out here. I vaguely remember a story about him being shot, but never knew where. I thought it was during the war somewhere a long way off."

"Funny. Here we sit, a black family and a white family enjoying a common friendship. How small those people were.

Some still are," Sara said.

"Hey, it's late. We've got to get home. Those kids will never get up tomorrow," Jeff said, looking at his watch.

Jew was deep in thought.

"What you thinking about so hard, honey?" Clara asked.

"I don't know for sure," he said and shook his head. "Just some crazy thoughts running through my head. Guess I got caught up in the story."

"I know what you mean, Jew. Come on in tomorrow and have lunch with me in town," Jeff said as they made ready to leave.

"I might do that. I might just do that," Jew responded.

As they started out to the car, Jew called out, "Sara."

"Yes?"

"You did a beautiful job. You both did. Thank you, and don't forget, we want to have Alicia out when she gets back."

"It was our pleasure, John. This story needed to be told. Everyone really should know about Isaac and Maria and William Robert. It was people like them who made this a decent place for us to live. Maybe we should try to condense it and put it in the paper. On second thought, let's put the whole story in the paper."

"Maybe. Let's talk about it later."

"See you tomorrow for lunch," Jeff said as he closed the car door.

Jeff was putting stock up from a newly received shipment when Jew came into the store the next morning.

"Well, how are things today?" Jeff asked.

"Fine. Hey, Jeff, you have a metal detector here in the store?"

"No, but I have one at home. What's up?"

"Remember Maria said she placed a metal crucifix on Isaac's chest?"

"Yeah, but it would be rusted to nothing by now, wouldn't

it?"

"I don't know. It wouldn't take but a small bit of it to set off a detector, would it?"

"Sure. I've found bottle caps five or six inches deep. Why not? It's worth a try anyway."

The two men left for lunch and discussed the story over the table. Both were deeply taken by the woman's story.

On the way back to the store Jew said to Jeff, "I've been thinking if we find the graves and even if we don't, I'm going to have a headstone made and put it out there by that grove of oaks."

"Good idea. I'll have one made for William Robert, too. I think they would both like that, don't you?" Jeff said.

"Sure do, but why do you suppose," Jew looked around to make sure no one could overhear him, "Isaac keeps coming back? Man, I know I'm not supposed to believe in ghosts, but by god, I've seen him. Not once, but several times. In fact, he's the reason I didn't get hurt when that old hay loft fell. I'm sure of it now. Why would he keep coming back? I just don't understand it."

"What all did you find in that box, Jew? I remember the saber and the gun, plus the story, but what else was in the box you found?"

Jew thought for a minute. "Hell, that's it," he said.

"What? What's it?"

"The medicine bag. He wants his medicine bag. I'll bet he didn't have it with him the night he died and he wants his charm."

"I'll bet you're right. That charm was that important to him. He was sure it had saved him when he was fighting Indians, remember? We've got to find that grave and get it to him, so the man can find his peace. I'll have Jim Oates work for me tomorrow and I'll be out with the metal detector. We'll look until we find it." Jeff's excitement was obvious.

Jew returned home with a feeling of excitement himself. On the way home, he stopped off at a monument company and ordered two stones. One would be for Isaac and the other for William Robert. The dates he chose were as close as he could surmise to be correct from the data available. "Born 1847. Died 1882." These dates would be placed on each stone. Only the inscription would be different. On Isaac's stone he ordered the following epitaph: "Corp. Isaac Turner, Scout for the United States Cavalry, 9th Regiment. It was by efforts like his that the West was opened to all Americans." On William Robert's stone, he had the epitaph "From birth to the grave, no man could want a better friend or brother."

As Jew drove home, he thought, "I think they'll both like that. After all these years, they deserve at least that much."

Clara was in the garden when she heard Jew coming up the lane. She stopped her work and walked toward the house. She knew he would want to talk. A lot had happened that was strange and unusual these last few days. Clara knew Jew and how sensitive he was. The thought of Isaac being hung for no real reason would be bothering him. She went into the house and put the coffee pot on the stove. Jew did not like his coffee to be run through the new drip pot. He really liked it boiled on top of the stove.

Clara had the pot on and the water was about to boil when Jew came in the back door.

"What took you so long to get in from the car?" she asked.

"You won't believe what I just saw," he said as he pulled out a chair and sat down at the breakfast table.

"You saw our friendly ghost, didn't you?"

"Yeah, how did you know?"

"I saw him earlier this morning."

"Out by the barn?" Jew asked.

"Yes, as a matter of fact; but he went into the woods."

"That's what he did just now. Every time we have seen him

before, he walked from the woods to the barn. Now he has changed and goes from the barn to the woods. If someone told me this was happening, I would think him crazy."

They were both silent for a few moments.

"God, sometimes I think I am crazy. Am I really seeing something that isn't there? How can I see a man that's been dead for over one hundred years?"

"John," Clara said, placing her hand on his, resting on the table. "You know as well as I that we have all seen him, not once but several times. Right? We are educated and wise enough with just plain old common sense to know that we do not know everything about everything. In fact, about some things, we know very little."

"That's what scares me sometimes," Jew confessed.

"What? That we don't know everything?"

"No. Not that. That about some things, we, you and me, Jeff, everybody, hell, we don't know anything, anything at all."

"John," she said in a quiet but firm voice, "are you scared of Isaac out there?"

Jew looked up and thought for a few moments. "No, I'm not. I'm really not. In fact, for some reason, I feel a closeness to him. It's hard to put my finger on why, but I really kind of like him. I know I respect him and admire what he did." Jew stood up and walked to the window. He stood there looking out without saying a word, just looking at nothing, yet seeing everything in sight.

He turned after his mind seemed to stop its racing. So many thoughts seemed to rush into his brain he had difficulty putting them into order. He sat back down and sipped on his coffee.

"You know," he started, then hesitated.

"Do I know what?" Clara asked.

"It's really hard to imagine what life had to be like back

then. We sit here in our own kitchen talking and drinking coffee with not a single worry. We have my retirement check, the house and land is paid for and we don't lay awake at night waiting for a group of wild men to come in and drag me out to a tree and hang me, just because I'm black. God knows what Isaac could have done if he had been born white."

Silence again filled the room, except for the hum of the refrigerator.

Clara shifted in her chair. "William Robert was white. What did it get him? He lost everything. The plantation, his friends, even his life and for what? A lost cause and a friend. I would even go so far as to say both of those men, as hard as it was, would not have changed it if they could."

"You don't think so?" Jew asked.

"No, I don't," she said matter-of-factly. "I believe those two men both had their turn at life. The fact that times were different and hard, even unbearable at times I suppose, who's to say that a hundred years from now someone may not say the same about us."

"But they were killed and so young, too."

Clara interrupted Jew, "That's true; but except for the grace of God, you could have died a very young man yourself, John Williams, in some hot, muggy jungle so far away from your home. They did die on their land at home, on the land they loved, probably as much as life itself. Now, I think you have thought of this long enough in a negative sense. Try thinking of it in a positive sense."

"And how's that, my love? You give me so much pleasure. Did I ever tell you that before?"

She smiled as Jew leaned over and kissed her on the cheek.

"Well," he said. "Tell me something positive."

"OK. I'll tell you something positive, but don't think me crazy. You promise?"

"I promise," Jew said in a serous manner.

"Look out there." She pointed toward the oak grove. "Some of those trees are a hundred and fifty or more years old. Right?"

"Sure. I suppose so, but what's that got to do with anything?" Jew asked. He could not see her point or where she was going with her analysis.

"So," she continued, "suppose Maria buried Isaac and William Robert next to one of those big oaks. She would not have had time to have caskets made, so I suppose she just wrapped them in something. A sheet perhaps."

"Yeah. I suppose that's what she would have done. Makes sense," Jew added.

"Well, that being the case, I know this doesn't sound, let's say pretty, but that being the case, their bodies would have decayed. They would return to dust as we know. But supposing in doing so the oak by which they were placed picked up some of the traces of their bodies."

Jew smiled and raised his hand. "I think I see where you are going. By golly, it makes sense. It really does."

"Sure. Both of them still live on in a different way, but they still live on. Their souls may and probably did go somewhere else but their bodies helped one of those trees flourish. So even after death, they did some good to one of God's creation. That's not such a bad thing to have to your credit, is it?"

"Not at all. In fact I think you have found the answer I have been looking for."

She stood up and poured another cup of coffee.

"How about you?" she asked as she held up the pot.

"No thanks. Something else has occurred to me. I mentioned it to Jeff today. Suppose, just suppose, the night Isaac died, he went outside to defend his home. He rushed and hurried so that he did not have his medicine bag with him. That charm was important to him. You could tell in the story Maria wrote that he credited it with saving his life at least three times. In her haste to bury the two of them, she probably forgot to put it in the grave. Or maybe she just wasn't superstitious like Isaac and didn't put any stock in a small leather bag filled with stones. At any rate, that bag was important to Isaac.

"When Jeff and I find his grave, I'm going to place that bag next to his remains." He hesitated. "If there are any. If there isn't, I'll place it in the spot where he was buried. I feel so sure that is what he has been looking for all these years."

Chapter 21

It was almost 10:00 in the morning when Jeff arrived. Jew was out back walking the fence row next to the field, looking for some sign of where Isaac and William Robert could have been buried.

"Surely Maria would have placed some rocks or something on the graves," Jew said to himself.

"Jew," Jeff called as he came across the field holding up the metal detector. When he reached Jew he was puffing. "Boy, am I out of shape. Think how bad it would be if I smoked."

"What do you mean? You do smoke."

"I do?" Jeff asked.

"Yeah."

"Darn. I must have run out of cigarettes then." He laughed. "Give me a smoke, will you?"

Jew laughed and handed the pack to Jeff.

"Does that thing work?" he asked.

"You bet. I put fresh batteries in it this morning. If there is anything left of that crucifix or any other metal, like a belt buckle, we'll find it. I promise."

They searched slowly around the oaks. After an hour or two, Jeff stopped. The alarm was making a faint sound. It had detected something metal. They dug down very slowly, being very careful. Jew started to rake the loose dirt with his hands, when he uncovered a piece of black metal, rusty and clad with dirt. He was very gentle as he swept the dirt away. Once he had cleared the object, he found that Jeff's metal detector had picked up part of an old horseshoe. He picked it up and Jeff went over the spot again. No sound was heard.

"Damn. I thought we had found it," Jew said.

"Yeah, me too. I've got to tell you, Jew. It gave me the willies. It really did. When that alarm sounded, I got chills."

"I know, Jeff, but I've got to find it. I've just got to find those graves. Those two men need to be found. They deserve better than what they got. The least you and I can do is find them and mark their graves. But what's more important, I've got to get that charm to old Isaac. I'm convinced he will never find his way to wherever he is supposed to go if I don't get it to him. Hell, he's been wandering around here now for a hundred years. Something has to be holding him, don't you think?"

"I suppose you're right. I read several books over the years and sometimes . . ." Jeff stopped abruptly. He sat hunkered down looking into the woods with his back toward the field. Jew sat a bit to the left of the hole they had just dug.

"What is it, man? You are as white as a sheet? Are you OK?" Jew asked.

"Jew, don't turn too fast, but if you can get yourself to where you can see where I'm looking. Right over there by that big oak about twenty feet into the woods." Jeff's voice was low, almost a whisper.

Jew turned his head slowly. He caught the figure of a man standing by the tree. It was hard to make out any features because of the undergrowth, but both men could see him.

"That's him," Jew said softly.

"That's Isaac? Is that what you are saying, Jew? That's the ghost?"

"Yeah. That's him all right. This is the closest I've ever seen him, too. Always before it's been a glimpse. Never like this."

"Well, he's not moving. What the hell are we going to do?" The excitement was building up in Jeff.

"Steady, Jeff. If he wanted to hurt us, he would have done so long before we ever saw him. Besides, that man and I have an understanding. He's not going to hurt anybody. I think he's trying to tell us something."

"Look! Look!" Jeff said. "He's squatting down. Can you see him?"

"I see him all right. Know what he's doing, Jeff? He's showing us where to look. We have been looking out here near the field."

"I know, but it would have been easier digging for Maria."

"Maybe so, but it would also put her in the open while she worked, too. Remember she was frightened. Hell, she had her husband's brother blown away right next to her, then she had to cut her husband down from one of these trees. Man, if I would have been her, I would have drug them back up in the woods, too. For cover. Just in case one of those nuts came back unexpectedly." Jew turned back. Both he and Jeff said at the same time, "He's gone."

Jew picked up the metal detector and pushing the brush aside walked to where they had moments before seen what they believed to be Isaac. Jeff followed with a shovel and was ready to strike out if he was forced to.

Jeff stopped just short of where he thought the image was. He looked around. No sign of man or beast could be seen. The ground was bare of grass under the oaks because of the shade and the light sandy soil would show footprints, yet there were none.

Jew looked at Jeff. He was scared, but then so was Jeff.

"Are you as scared as I am?" Jew asked.

"Hell, yes. I almost wet my pants a second ago. My heart must be racing 200 miles an hour," Jeff answered.

Jew turned back toward the spot. He rested the metal detector on the ground. Not talking to anyone, he said, "Hey, brother, remember our talk the other day in the barn? That still goes. My friend here and I are trying to find the grave of a man believed killed a long, long time ago. All we want to do is mark it, so back off and leave us be or show us where it is."

There was silence.

"Who the hell are you talking to?" Jeff asked.

"Whoever or whatever is out here. I told you we had an understanding. I just wanted to remind him, just in case he forgot."

"What kind of understanding?"

"I'll tell you later. Right now, let's see what we can find here."

Jew switched on the detector and moved it back and forth. As he swung it to the left, a branch about the size of a man's arm fell from the tree behind them. It was a dry limb dead for several seasons. As it hit the ground, both men jumped.

Jeff gasped and said, "Shit."

The branch was about ten feet to the right and behind where they were standing. Jew had a feeling. He moved over toward it. Just as the detector was within two feet of the branch, it went off. Both men flinched. Jew hit the spot again. He moved the detector left and right. He picked up another signal about a foot from the first.

"I think we've found it this time," he said.

"You know what, Jew? I think you're right and for some reason, I feel so different. My fear is gone. Now, man, I was about to pee all over myself a couple of minutes ago and now I'm as calm as if I was sitting in church. You know what I mean?"

"Me, too," Jew answered. "Hell, man, I've been in the jungle with the enemy looking for me and I thought I was scared then. That wasn't anything like I felt back there when that limb fell. I almost broke and ran. I expect if you weren't here, I would have, too."

Jeff slapped him on the back. "I know where you are coming from and believe me, if you would have broke and run, I would have run right up your back trying to get out front."

Both men laughed as they got down on their knees and began to rake away the dirt, being very careful.

"I think I got something," Jew said as he dusted away what looked like the remains of some metal object.

"That's it, Jew! That's what's left of the crucifix." He lifted the metal detector and moved it over the second object. The speaker sounded.

Jew moved and started to clear away the dirt. As he dusted away the dirt, he asked Jeff, "What do you suppose would set it off here?"

"Well, if she placed the cross on his chest like she wrote, that's got to be about here." He moved his hand down his body. "Sure, it would be his belt buckle. I'll bet he still wore that brass buckle the Army issued. The one with US on it. I've seen them in souvenir stores in town."

"Of course. That's what it would be. His belt buckle. Uh oh, here's a bone. I'm not digging any further. This is Isaac's grave."

Both men stood up.

"Think we ought to call the Sheriff?" Jeff asked.

"Do you know him?"

"Yeah, he's my cousin."

"You think he would believe what we've found? I mean, the book and all."

"I don't know, Jew, but if word of this gets out, there could be trouble. And you were going to order those headstones."

"Yeah, I did on the way home when I left your place yesterday."

"He'll hear about it. That's for sure."

"OK, let's go up to the house and call him. We'll tell him the whole story and hope he won't have to exhume the graves."

Both men walked back across the field. They washed up and Jeff called his cousin. They sat on the front porch waiting for the patrol car, while Clara served them a sandwich and some iced tea.

It took about thirty minutes before Sheriff Joe Ellis drove up.

"What's up, cuz?" he asked as he got out of the car.

"I want you to meet a friend of mine," Jeff said and introduced Jew.

Clara came out on the porch and Jeff introduced her also.

"Sit down, Joey. The story I'm going to tell you is going to take a little while and I don't want to leave anything out that's going to affect your decision."

It took almost an hour to tell the whole story. When Jeff finished, he asked Jew, "Did I leave anything out that he ought to know? I tried to tell it all the best I could."

"No," Jew said. "I think you covered all bases. What do we do now, Sheriff? All I want to do is get that medicine bag in the grave and mark those two men's final resting place."

"Let's go take a look at the graves and let me study this a bit before I make a decision."

The three men went back to the oaks and looked at the grave sites.

"I know you don't want to disturb them any more than necessary, but I've got to satisfy myself that these are old graves, not some poor bastard that got killed and hid here a few years ago. I hope you understand, Mr. Williams."

"Sure. What do we do now?"

"Don't do anything. I'm going to get Doc Anderson out here tomorrow early. He acts as our County Medical Examiner. A couple of kids I know in town are students specializing in archeaology. Both are graduate students and have worked on projects in Mexico and South America. Between them and the Doc, we'll know for sure. After that, we'll decide what to do. Now don't do any more digging. If this is a murder, we need to look for evidence. So, again, I have to warn you. Don't do anything else, OK?"

"OK. I'll rope the area off," Jew said.

"That won't be necessary. I'll have the area patrolled heavily tonight and we'll get started at first light tomorrow. You don't rush those kids when they go to digging. I've seen 'em work before."

The Sheriff left. Jeff told Jew he would be back early and he knew Sara would want to be there, too.

That night the Williams family sat around and discussed what had happened and how they would deal with it.

"Dad," Ronnie said, "why don't we build a fence around the site and keep it clean as long as we live here. You know, it would kind of be like we are taking care of the past. Sort of like they were left in our charge. You know what I mean, Dad?"

"That's a good idea, son, and yes, I know what you mean. It's a very honorable thought." He reached over and rubbed Ronnie's head. "You know, I'm always proud of you kids. You are both my joy in life, but at times, I'm especially proud.

Now, get to bed. We have a big day tomorrow."

Chapter 22

Jew had a hard time sleeping that night and so at a little after four, he got up and went out into the kitchen and put the coffee pot on. He had been up about three quarters of an hour when he saw car lights pulling into the driveway. He walked on the porch. It was a Sheriff's patrol car. A young deputy got out and walked over to the porch.

"Morning. I'm Deputy Eddie Davis," he said. "You're up early this morning."

"Yeah, I couldn't sleep, so I thought I'd just get up," Jew said. "Got some coffee working. Come on in and have some."

"Let me check in and I'll take you up on that. Thanks."

It did not take long and Jew and the deputy were sitting in the kitchen. The young deputy had been a green beret in Viet Nam. Middle ground was found soon. They talked until almost daylight. The deputy told Jew he had better get back on the job. As he left he told Jew that one of the young people the Sheriff was going to bring out was his sister and the other was her husband.

"I'll tell you one thing, Colonel. Don't get in any hurry. That sister of mine doesn't move a stone until she has noted how, when and, if she can, where it got to where it was when she found it. One thing for sure, you can rest assured she is probably the best around these parts. She'll be able to tell you more about what's out there than you can ever imagine."

"Sounds good to me," Jew said. "By the way, Eddie, please don't call me Colonel. My name is Jew. When I left the military, I left my rank. All I look for now is my check."

They both chuckled. "You got it, Jew," he said as he closed the car door and drove off.

Just at daylight the Sheriff's car, followed by a van and a sedan, pulled up to the house. Jew met them in the yard. The Sheriff introduced everyone. Jeff had ridden out with Dr. Anderson. Bob and Sue Edwards had driven their van. They showed it to Jew, and he was impressed. In the back was a small but very complete laboratory, besides having a small kitchen for their use while engaged in a field study such as this. Their studies often took several days, sometimes weeks, Bob told him.

"We use it when we are on a site and motels aren't nearby," Sue told him. "The lab helps us make preliminary studies."

Clara had made a new pot of coffee and they all sat around outside talking for about a half hour, while Jew and Jeff filled everybody in on what the Sheriff had left out when he talked to them the night before.

"Let's go," Bob said. "I want to get to it."

They all walked over to the site. It was a warm day and Jew was thankful they would be working in the shade. Bob and Sue were the ones doing the work, but the others were helping by staying out of the way.

Clara brought tea down about mid-morning. Sara had been

busy in town, but got out to the farm about ten. She was as excited as the rest for she had read the story first and felt a real closeness to the writer. Maria, she felt, was a very special lady. Somehow she felt that she knew her or at least understood her and what she was doing when she recorded Isaac's life story.

Everyone stayed close by the diggings until around six that evening. Jew could see that Bob and Sue were not going to rush the job and were taking every precaution not to disturb the remains any more than necessary.

"Looks like we'll be here for several days, Mr. Williams. Hope you don't mind if I pull the van up closer and put our tent up out here," Bob said to Jew.

"Not at all. You're welcome to stay in the house with us while you do your study," Clara remarked.

"Thanks, but it's really better if we stay out here by the site. Bob has a habit of waking up at odd hours and going to work. I've awakened to find him at two or three in the morning working by the lamps when we are working at a site," Sue said.

Dr. Anderson had left around noon, but told the Sheriff he would check back from time to time and get his information from Bob or Sue for his report. The Sheriff had to leave and get on about his duties, but told them he would be on call and that his deputy would be patrolling the area if they needed him for anything.

Jeff and Jew talked about the tombstones Jew had ordered.

"The stonecutter said we could pick them up next Wednesday, if we wanted to," Jew said.

"I'll get 'em in my pickup, Jew. How much were they?"

"Don't worry about it. I took care of it, Jeff."

"No, Jew. I want to pay half. Remember I told you I go back to the Willard family. That means William Robert and I are kin. In fact, I'm related to Isaac, too. Remember they were half brothers. Maybe it's fifteenth cousins or uncle. Whatever. We are still kin and I want to pay half."

"OK, Jeff. I've got the receipt up at the house. I'll have to look to see what the final price was, but I'll split it with you."

He slapped Jeff on the back. "Ol' Isaac did good coming back here to his homeplace and a friend like William Robert. I guess that Willard family probably was OK even back then."

Both men laughed. Jeff and Sara left to drive back to town.

The digging, brushing and scooping tiny particles of dirt went on every day for eight days. It was after six on that eighth day when Bob walked up to the house and asked Clara to call the Sheriff and Dr. Anderson.

Jew knew they had completed their findings and asked Bob, "Well, what has all your work told you, Bob? Is that William Robert and Isaac out there?"

"Mr. Williams, I would rather wait until I've talked to Dr. Anderson before I really go into it. I hope you understand."

"Sure. Sure thing," Jew answered. His mind began to wonder what if it was some poor devil that got murdered and buried out there and we just lucked out finding his grave. "No, can't be. The crucifix was there. That's Isaac. I know it is. I just know it."

"Tell you what. I'm going to call Jeff," Jew said.

The doctor and the Sheriff pulled up together about an hour later. Clara had made a big pot of coffee and the Williams' family along with Bob and Sue were sitting down by the van. The Sheriff pulled his car up behind the van and the doctor followed. Jeff and Sara were right behind them.

"Well, Bob, what did you and Sue find out?" the doctor asked after the customary greetings.

"Want to step in the van? Sue has it all spelled out in there, Doctor."

Bob, Sue and the Sheriff and Dr. Anderson went in the

van. Jew walked over and looked into the two graves. What was left of the skeletons was a grim sight. No spooky, not scary, but a grim sight. Clara walked up and stood next to him. He put his arm around her waist.

"It seems like a shame, doesn't it?" he said.

"What seems like a shame, John?"

"Well, folks do all they can to get you off and running, making every effort to get ahead. Once you've learned how, seems like you spend a lifetime learning. You're always learning something and doing something with what you've learned. Then by some quirk of fate, your life is over. Someone puts you in the ground, then a hundred years later someone comes along and digs you up. Seems like a shame."

"You did what you had to do, John. No one, especially those two," she pointed toward the graves, "would ever blame you for disturbing their graves."

The van's side door opened and the doctor stepped out, followed by the others. They walked over to where Jew and Clara stood. Jeff, Sara and the Williams' children followed.

"Well," Jew asked, "can you tell who these people were? It's Isaac and William Robert, isn't it? I know it's them."

"I feel without a doubt," the doctor said, "it looks like those two gentlemen right there are who you said they were, Isaac Turner and William Robert Willard. We could take samples to the University and run Carbon-14 tests, but we all think that would be a waste of time and money. Seems like one of them was a Negro and the other a white, both males between 25 and 30 years old. The white male had his left arm missing. The Negro had a Yankee belt buckle on when he died. Both men had coins in their pockets when they were buried. The dates put them back around the end of the Civil War. A couple of them were even older than that. The one we'll call Isaac had received a pretty stiff blow to the left side of the head several years before he died. But the real evidence was the other one, William Robert. He had a .36 caliber ball lodged in the area of his medulla spinalis. It looks like it might have entered up from the front of the throat area. That's what one could expect if the victim were standing, as the story said, in the doorway and the person shooting the gun was lying on the ground. The height of the floor and the man would put the line of flight for the bullet just about right for the angle the bullet was lodged.

"Isaac had a head wound. Looks like about the same caliber, .36, but it's hard to say for sure. The bullet exited out the front of the skull. He was shot from behind. Of that, I'm sure. There were traces of lead on the skull, so I would surmise a soft lead bullet or ball did the damage. Probably a ball because there is not sign of it changing shape after impact.

"From what Jeff told me, the lady who wrote about the account heard a shot, then later saw him hanging in one of these trees. If that's the case and that's the way she saw it, I would have to say the man was already dead when he was hung. After all, it doesn't make sense to hang a man, then shoot him. On the other hand, if you hang a dead man, it might scare anyone left."

"Well, Doc, what do we do now?" the Sheriff asked.

"Well, as far as I'm concerned, Bob and Sue agreed there was foul play. Not any lately, but there was, of course, a long time ago. Anyone involved would be long dead themselves by now. There is no way to serve justice by moving those two men. They have earned the right to rest in peace. So I say, if it's all right with Mr. Williams here, we don't disturb them any more, but cover them up with the respect they are due." The doctor turned to Jew.

"I've already ordered markers for them and my son has suggested we build a fence around the grave site to protect it from being desecrated."

"Sounds good to me, Sheriff. Lots of family plots in these

parts. Got one out on my farm myself," the doctor said.

"That's it then," the Sheriff said.

"Let's cover them up and leave them alone. I've got the markers in the back of my pickup," Jeff said.

"Good idea," agreed the Sheriff who picked up a shovel.

"Wait. Before we do that, I have something I've got to place in Isaac's grave. I feel he would want it." Jew knelt down and placed the small leather bag next to the belt buckle still lying there. "Here you go, old friend. I suppose when you carried this, you had it tied to your belt or in your shirt. So that's where it ought to be." He stood up and picked up a shovel and started to cover up Isaac's remains. The soil was soft and the job did not take long.

Once the graves were covered, Jeff drove his pickup around the van and they placed the stones he had picked up in town the day before over the head of each man.

"I'd like to say a prayer, if you don't mind," Clara said to the group.

"No, ma'am. You go right ahead. I think that would be the fitting and proper thing to do," Sheriff Ellis said as he removed his hat.

Clara stood there for a moment getting her thoughts together, then said, "Oh Lord, these two young men were given but a few short years on this earth before they were called home. We now enjoy the fruits of their labors. Bless them and keep them in your care until we can someday meet them and give to each the thanks they so richly deserve. In Christ's name, Amen."

Everybody hugged each other. Bob and Sue promised to come back when they had time. The doctor and sheriff both had to get back to town.

The girls and the two children went back up to the house. Jeff and Jew said they would be along in a minute. They wanted a little time to be alone with two old friends as they had come to call Isaac and William Robert.

After about a half hour, the two men started up to the house. Night was coming on fast now that the sun had set. A mist was starting to form.

As they reached the back porch, Jew had a funny feeling. The hair on the back of his neck stood and a chill ran across his body. He stopped and turned around. A mist was forming over the field and into the woods. His eyes froze on a figure standing at the edge of the clearing where they had just been. It was a man in full uniform. He held up an object. It looked like the small bag Jew had placed in Isaac's grave, but the light was failing and the oak thicket was about a hundred yards away. The figure lowered its hand with the object and in a military manner gave a hand salute. Jew's reflexes took over and he returned the salute.

Jeff turned around. "What is it, Jew? We forget something?"

"No, no. Nothing at all." He looked back. The figure was gone into the night mist that was settling over the woods.

Two weeks went by and no sign was seen of the visitor as the Williams' family had come to call him. Old Cigar had been fishing at least once every week and had given them a couple of nice catfish each time. He could not remember having such good luck in all the years he had been fishing the creek.

It was a Sunday afternoon when the telephone rang. It was Jew's parents. They were coming down from Ohio for a visit. They would be down next Thursday for a two week stay. Clara started to pick up in the living room after they had hung up.

"What are you doing?" Jew asked her.

"This house is a mess. What kind of a woman will your mother think you married if she finds it looking like this?"

"Honey, they won't be here until next Thursday. That's almost a week away," he laughed.

"I know, but there is so much to do."

"Well, it can wait until tomorrow. Now come on and sit here with me and watch the rest of this show."

She joined him in front of the TV, but was still nervous. She loved Jew's parents, but his mother was the original Mrs. Clean and Clara was not about to have her come into a house that was not ready for an IG inspection.

The week went slowly for Jew, but seemed to fly by for Clara. She was busy every day. Windows had to be washed, the carpet cleaned, cookies baked.

"Honey," Jew said to her after dinner Tuesday night. "Enough is enough. The house looks great. It's my Mom and Dad. They are coming to see us, not the house. So tomorrow I want you to take it easy. In fact, why don't you go to town and have your hair done or something?"

"What? My hair? Does it look that bad?"

"No, no, no. It doesn't look bad. I just know you enjoy having it done. I just thought it would relax you some. You've got to unwind, girl. You've worked the kids and me to death this week. Now let's just decide to enjoy the folks. OK?"

"I'm sorry, John. I didn't realize."

"That's OK," he said as he put his arm around her. "You have been so busy these last several days, you haven't even stopped to watch your soaps," he laughed.

"Oh, my goodness, John. You are right. I wonder what has happened. The trial was going on and I know Beth Ann is innocent."

He laughed and patted her. "Tune in tomorrow. I'm sure you haven't missed a thing you can't pick up on in tomorrow's episode."

The next two days went very well. Clara had settled down and Jew looked forward to his parents' arrival. He spent more and more time in his shop just puttering around.

It was a little after noon Thursday when Jew's father pulled into the driveway. The entire family rushed out to meet them. After the greetings were over, Jew took his father to the barn he had turned into his shop and showed him the new coffee table he was making.

"Son, you do real fine work. This is a work of art. Where did you learn to do this?" They both laughed.

"Well, Dad," Jew said, "all those years you thought I wasn't paying attention to you while you were trying to teach me the cabinet trade, I guess I learned more than you thought."

"You did that all right, son. Good work. Yes, sir, good work."

The two went back to the house. Jew's mother was impressed with their home and the way Clara had decorated it. Jew could see the pride and satisfaction in Clara's face.

"You should have seen this place last week. Wow! What a mess!" Jew said and laughed.

"John Eric Williams," Clara said with a start.

"Now, Johnny, I can't believe Clara's house was ever a mess," Jew's mother said.

"Well, son, what has been going on since you moved into this house?" Jew's father asked.

"Well, Dad, it's a long story and I guess the best way to tell it is to start at the beginning."

"That is usually the best way, son," Bob chuckled as he spoke.

Clara noticed the similarity between Jew and his father's mannerisms. A smile was ever present even when they spoke.

"Let's see," Jew continued, "I guess it all started the day we moved in." Jew told about seeing Isaac, the loft collapsing and how he was pulled clear. As Jew spoke, his father became more and more entranced with the story.

"Then," Jew added, "a friend of ours and a friend of hers put the story on tapes for us."

"Do you have the tapes here, son?" Bob asked.

"Yes, sir, in my office."

"Then get them, John. I've got to hear what that lady wrote."

Jew went to his office and returned with the tapes and his recorder.

After they had heard the tapes, Jew remarked, "I've heard that story three or four times and each time, I'm even more intrigued."

"I can understand why," Jew's mother, Grace, stated. "That is an intriguing story, to say the least. We have come a long way from those times."

"That we have, Mom," Jew said, "but we can't afford to forget that people like Isaac, William Robert and Maria paid one hell of a price so we could enjoy the station in life we now find ourselves in. They are our very foundation."

Chapter 23

Jew and Clara sat on the porch drinking their evening coffee not saying much, just enjoying the cool breeze and quiet of the countryside.

"I suppose the kids are enjoying their vacation with the folks back in Ohio," Jew remarked.

"You know they are, John. Those two will be so spoiled when they come home we won't be able to stand them."

Jew chuckled, "Yeah, my mom has a way of giving them both whatever they want."

"Some things they never even thought of," Clara added.

Silence again prevailed. Only the night sounds could be heard and the squeak of the porch swing.

"It must have been a night like this when Isaac heard William Robert coming to warn him about the townspeople."

Jew turned his head in that certain manner he had—half turned, half tilted.

"What did you say?" he asked.

"It must have been an evening like this when those people came out here and killed Isaac. They shattered a happy family in a single blow, and for what?"

"You did it again, my love."

"Did what, John?"

"I was just thinking about Isaac and Maria myself. It's been close to a year now since we discovered the graves of Isaac and William Robert, yet every time I look at the grave site I swear someone is watching me. It is almost like Isaac is trying to say something to me. Perhaps there is something else we have got to do." His voice trailed off to a whisper "But what?"

Silence again prevailed between them as they sat there watching the sunset. The clouds had a pink and orange cast. Several minutes went by without either saying a word.

Then Clara asked, not to Jew, just asked, "Wonder what happened to her?"

"I don't know, but I've wondered myself a million times. I want to believe she made it back to Mexico."

"Maybe she did."

The phone rang and Clara went inside to answer it. John stood up and strolled down the front steps to the yard gate where he looked out across the field toward the place where Isaac and William Robert were buried.

Several minutes passed and Clara came back out on the porch.

"Who is it?" Jew asked.

"It was Sara. She and Jeff are coming out. Said they wanted to talk to us about something."

"Wonder what they want."

"I don't know, but Sara seemed excited about something."

Jew went inside and poured another cup of coffee, then returned to his chair on the porch. Slowly he smoked a

208

cigarette between sips on his cup.

Jew heard the car coming several seconds before he saw the lights as Jeff and Sara turned onto the lane that ran down to the highway.

"Here they come," Clara said.

"Yep. Wonder what's up that would bring them out here this late and with a summer storm building up, too."

"I don't have any idea, but I'm sure we will find out."

Jeff pulled the car up to the side gate and got out. "Well, I see you two are hard at it tonight," Jeff said.

"Ah, you bet. Country folks like us have to work hard at relaxing," Jew answered laughing.

"Sara, it's good to see you," Clara greeted Sara. The men shook hands and Jeff sat down in the porch swing.

"No house should be without one of these. No sir."

"Brrr." Clara made the sound one makes when one feels a chill. "Let's go inside for coffee. The evening chill is starting to set in early tonight."

Small talk followed for almost half an hour. Finally Clara could stand the suspense no longer.

"OK, you two. What brings you out here and what was it you were so excited about a while ago, Sara Sanders?"

"You want to ask them, Jeff, or do you want me to?"

"Go ahead, honey, it was your idea."

"Let's go find Maria." Sara's statement was straightforward—not a question, but a direct statement requiring action.

Jew turned to Clara. They stared into each other's eyes for a split second. A strong feeling swept over Jew. He turned toward Sara.

"We were talking about Isaac and Maria when you called a while ago. Now you want to go search for Maria. God knows the thought has crossed my mind many times."

"I think it's a great idea," Clara added. "And there's no

time like right now. Our children are in Ohio with John's parents and your daughter is away at camp. When do you want to go?"

Jeff sat up. "How about day after tomorrow?"

Jew went into his study and returned with a map of the United States. He spread it out on the coffee table.

"Let's try to trace Isaac's path all the way out to Fort Davis, Texas. There we'll try to find out what town or area of Mexico Maria came from. If she made it back, that's where she would have gone, I'm sure.

A loud clap of thunder shook the windows in the house.

With everyone in agreement, plans were solidified and a route was planned. It was past eleven p.m. when Jeff and Sara left.

"See you at seven sharp Wednesday morning," Jeff said as he shut his car door.

"We'll be ready," Jew answered.

Jew was up early the next morning. He had coffee brewing when Clara came into the kitchen. Jew poured her a steaming cup of his strong coffee.

"Here, my love, this will get your eyes open," he said as he placed the cup on the table before her.

"Thanks, honey. You sleep good last night?" she asked.

"I was awake at least five or six times. How about you?"

"I tossed and turned all night. I kept waking up thinking about things I have to get done before we can leave."

"Yeah, I know. Me, too. I'll go over and see old Cigar in a little while and get him to feed the chickens and the dog while we are gone."

Jew went out to the chicken yard and turned his flock out to do their daily foraging.

It was a little after ten a.m. when Jew pulled up in front of the old cabin where Cigar lived. The old man was working in his small garden. As the car stopped, Cigar looked up.

When he saw Jew's head rise above the top of the car, his old black, wrinkled face lit up. The smile that formed showed what few teeth Cigar had left.

"What are you putting in this time of year?" Jew asked.

"I'm getting ready for my winter roots. I likes to be ready."

"Hell, man, it's only August and you are planning a fall garden," Jew said.

"Them that plans get. Don't you know that? I mean, you being in the Army and all," Cigar responded.

"You know it was the Corps and I guess I don't know a lot about gardens, if you want to know the truth."

"What brings you over here to ol' Cigar's place this morning, Mr. Jew?"

"Cigar, I've told you a hundred times. It's not Mr. Jew. Just plain Jew. John, if you prefer, but please no more mister. OK?"

"Whatever you say, boy."

"I need a favor, Cigar. I need you to look after my place for a few days. You know, feed and water my bird dog. Close the chickens up at night and let them out in the morning. That sort of thing."

"Going to be gone, are you?"

"Yep. The missus and me are going to take a little trip."

"Come on, boy. Let's go up to the house. Got some coffee left over from this morning."

The cabin was in bad shape. It had been patched with boards and scraps of old metal roofing over the years. Jew wondered if it could have been a slave shack once.

"How long has this house been around?" he asked.

"Don't know. Fifty, sixty years. Maybe longer. Why?"

"No reason. I just wondered."

"Weren't no slave shack, if that's what you think. No sir, them's all gone. Burned 'em, they did."

"Who burned them?"

"The slaves. I was told when they were set free on this here place, they burned all the buildings down." He set two old mugs filled with coffee down on the homemade table.

"Who told you that?" Jew asked.

"My pappy, that's who. He told me he was a little boy and a bunch of crazy niggers from the north part of the country came down here and set this place to blazes."

"He say why?"

"Nope. Don't suppose he knowed why. So you wants me to feed your critters, huh?"

"Yeah, sure do. You can have the eggs, too. What you can't use, you can sell. I've been getting sixty cents a dozen. Right now, you'll get about two dozen a day."

"That many?" Cigar asked.

"That many. Maybe more."

"How long you folks be gone?"

"Two, maybe three weeks."

Cigar sipped his coffee studying the question for a full minute. His eyes met Jew's. In a very calm, but firm, voice, he asked, "You ain't seen that haint around your place lately, has you? I mean since you found them bones."

"Cigar, you can forget about that ghost or haint, whatever it may have been. I've told you the whole story. It's the truth, my friend. I wouldn't con you. There was a haint, but he's gone. He was searching for his charm. I found it and I put it in his grave. He has gone to wherever the spirit is supposed to go. So don't worry about that any more."

Cigar reached out his hand. "Let me have your hand on it, Mr. Jew."

Jew shook his head as he took the old man's hand and shook it.

Chapter 24

Jew was driving with Jeff sharing the front seat with him. Clara and Sara were in the back seat as they headed west in search of Maria.

"This lady was such a learned woman, I just know she made it back home," Sara said to Clara.

"God, I hope so; but a woman all by herself in a time when things were so unsettled."

Jew interrupted Clara, "You have to remember, honey, she was not unaware of tough times. After all, she had gone through that Indian thing and managed to survive. Sara is right. If anyone could make it back, I really believe Maria would be that person."

The first day's end found the four in Monroe, Louisiana. A motel was found. The night passed quickly and at six a.m., they were once again on the road headed for Houston, Texas.

Dark found the travelers nearing Houston. "Let's find a

motel on the other side of town so we won't have the traffic when we leave in the morning," Jeff suggested.

"Sounds good to me," Jew agreed. "I remember several years ago driving in Houston and it was a madhouse."

The drive through Houston did not disappoint anyone. The traffic was heavy and southern hospitality did not prevail.

"It seems like everyone is for himself and to hell with the other guy," Jew remarked as he worked his way through the throng of cars and trucks.

"John," Clara said from the back seat, "let's get off this freeway and wait until the rush hour is over."

Jew smiled and glanced toward Jeff, then back to the traffic. "Honey," he said, "this is the slow time for traffic. The rush hour is over."

"You have got to be kidding," Sara said.

"Nope, this is just an everyday thing." Jew broke off his sentence. "Look. There is a motel up there. I'll exit and we can spend the night there. We can get an early start and perhaps avoid this mess."

"Sounds good to me," Jeff agreed.

The evening was a quiet one. After dining in a small but comfortable cafe, the four travelers retired to their rooms after agreeing to start around six a.m. the following morning.

"Why don't we eat breakfast somewhere around Rosenberg?" Jeff suggested.

"That sounds fine to me," Clara responded. "I have our coffee pot, so I'll have coffee ready. I know John will need at least two cups just to get his motor running."

Early the next morning as Jew started the car engine, he said, "Well, folks, today we see the Texas Coast. From the looks of this map, we'll go down to Ganado and drop off there and go to Port Lavaca. Looks like Indianola is just south of there." As Jew spoke he traced the route with his finger.

Jeff looked up. "Sounds good to me, Jew. If we like the

looks of Port Lavaca, we just might come back some day and try their fishing. I've heard there is supposed to be some really good fishing water around those parts."

"That's a hell of an idea," Jew agreed. "Now's the time to check it out."

Jew pulled into a gas station on the edge of Port Lavaca. As the attendant checked the car's oil level, Jew asked him if the road to Indianola was nearby.

"Yep. You go down this here street to yonder red light. That one there. About three blocks. Take a left and that street, well, it's going to dead end into the old Indianola road." He paused. "Number's 316. It'll take you right to it." Again he paused and then added, "Can't miss it."

As they pulled away, Jeff was looking straight ahead. His voice had the tone of a question as he said, "Can't miss it?"

Jew laughed. "Don't be too sure about that. That statement has always served as a curse on me."

"I'm sure from the map Indianola has to be close by now," Jew said. As he pulled the car into an old service station, Jew looked around. "I'll ask here and see how far we have to go."

"Can I help you?" a young lady asked as Jew walked into the office.

"Yes, you can. How far is it to Indianola?" he asked.

She smiled. "You are standing in the middle of it," she replied.

"This is it?"

The young lady smiled. "Yes. This is it." She picked up a brochure and handed it to Jew. "Used to be a real big city. Had a seaport here once, you know."

"No, I didn't know that," Jew answered.

"Oh sure. Lots of German immigrants came in right here. A lot of Central Texas was settled by folks that landed right here, then traveled by foot to places like New Braunfels,

Boerne, Fredericksburg, even up to Mason. Yes sir, this was a big city once."

"Was there a storm or something that happened here a long time ago?" Jew asked.

Jeff had come in and was standing next to Jew. "Yeah, we heard that there was a big storm that almost wiped the city out. Is that correct?" Jeff asked.

The young lady had a deep tan from many, many hours in the Texas sun. She smiled and her teeth were very straight and gleamed like pearls against her tan face. "Yes sir, there was a storm. Two, in fact. The first one destroyed the city, but those who survived wouldn't give up and rebuilt it. Two or three years later, another storm came through. It was really a bad one. It killed several hundred people and about two thirds of the town was washed right out to sea. The town just died after that.

"Never had a really bad storm hit here again. Oh, some bad ones, but not like those two. Too bad, too. If they would have rebuilt, this could be bigger than Galveston is today. Funny, isn't it? Two storms, back to back, then nothing."

"Are there any markers or anything around?" Jeff asked.

"Sure. At the park over there." She pointed toward the south.

"Thanks," Jew said as he and Jeff went back to the car.

After a couple of hours everyone was satisfied that they had seen all there was to see.

Jeff said to Jew, "I'm ready to head for San Antonio. How about you?"

"You bet. Being here somehow brings a sadness to me."

"I know what you mean, John," Sara said. "When one thinks that hundreds of people died here and it was a port of hope for so many, it does bring on a sort of eerie despair."

As they drove past a monument, Clara turned to Sara. "I felt a sadness, yet a joy back there. I know a great many people died and the hardships had to be more than we can possibly imagine, but suppose, just suppose, that you had been cooped up on a sailing ship for weeks, maybe even a month or more, that little port had to look awfully good to those immigrants."

The trip to San Antonio was interesting. The girls played gin and read while Jew and Jeff relived things that had happened to them in their high school and college days.

After spending a day in San Antonio and seeing Fort Sam Houston, they visited the Alamo, then headed for the far reaches of West Texas. At Sonora, Jew asked if they were ready to stop, but all agreed to drive on until they had reached Fort Stockton. From there they could make Fort Davis in a few hours.

They pulled into the motel at Fort Stockton. The road had taken its toll.

"I can't believe this state is so big," Jeff remarked.

"My god, we have been driving since day before yesterday and we still have a ways to go. Even then we won't be close to the border," Sara said.

"It's big alright," Jew agreed, "but tomorrow we'll be in Fort Davis. The closer we get, the more excited I become."

They left after breakfast and started for their final destination—Fort Davis. The highway was smooth and flat. The Davis Mountains could be seen rising on the horizon.

"Can you imagine living out here a hundred years ago?" Jeff asked.

Jew looked out the side window and taking in the vastness of the desert plains said, "No, I can't. Those who survived had to be some kind of tough."

"As hard a life as it must have been," Sara joined in, "the American Indian flourished out here. They knew how to use the land, not fight it. I think when we look at this harsh, barren land all we see is how difficult it would have been to survive. They looked at it as a giving thing."

"You are right, Sara. If one only knew and totally understood that way of life, it probably would look good. We do have a built-in way about us to compare, I suppose." As Clara spoke, she was looking out the window. "Take that mountain over there. Look at it. There is a certain beauty about it. It's barren. There are no trees, only some small shrubs, weeds perhaps, but there is a beauty just the same. It reminds me of a very old person, one who has grown wrinkled with age yet retaining a certain dignity; a dignity I really can't explain. You have to feel it."

"I never thought of rocks as having dignity," Jew remarked. "Yet I do understand what you are saying."

"Look! There's Fort Davis," Sara interrupted.

Jew pulled through the gates of the old fort and drove slowly through the front of the park to the parking area.

They went first to the office, then slowly went through the museum, reading everything they saw. From time to time, one would call the others over to see something special.

A noise came over a speaker from outside. Jew's head snapped up from a showcase.

"What was that?" he asked.

"I don't have any idea." As Jeff spoke he saw a Park Ranger and walked over to him. They spoke for only a few seconds and Jeff motioned for the others to follow him as he went outside.

Once outside, the speakers that were placed in the nearby hills began to fill the air with the sound of a bugle playing the call for assembly. The sound of soldiers running could be heard. Orders were barked and Jew could see a parade forming in his mind's eye, though no soldiers were to be seen. The recording was meant to excite one's imagination and with Jew, it did just that. The order to pass in review was given. The troops began to move around the parade field. Jew closed his eyes. He could almost feel the presence of the troops. Once he was sure he smelled the perspiration from the horses. As he opened his eyes, he could see officers' row across the parade field. The houses were made of native stone. Several had been restored, but there were still several in only a state of ruin.

As he stood there listening to the recording of the band and the troops moving, Jew closed his eyes again. He thought for a split second that he could see Isaac on his mount riding by full of pride, his uniform and his corporal stripes bright yellow, shining in the sunlight.

Jew said to himself, "He was probably as proud of those two stripes as I was of my oak leaf." Jew was brought out of his fantasy by a friendly voice.

"You folks from out of state?"

Jew turned to see the smiling face of a park ranger.

"Yes, sir. Georgia."

"Well, we're glad you dropped by to visit our little fort. Used to be a busy place. Lots of troops did duty out here. Lot of them stayed right here, too."

"I'm sure they did. We didn't just drop by, however. I don't think anybody just drops by out here. You've got to mean to come by."

"You're right about that. You all staying up at Indian Lodge?"

"No, we haven't got a room yet. We just came straight into the fort when we got here. Where is Indian Lodge?"

The Ranger advised them how to get to the lodge and explained how it was built by the hands of young men in the CCC back in the thirties.

"You're in luck," the lady at the desk said. "We have a couple of vacancies. Normally, we are filled up, but there have been a couple of cancellations today. I can let you have two rooms for tonight only. As of now, we'll be full the rest of the week, unless, of course, there are other cancellations."

"That will be fine," Jew answered as he signed the register.

Jeff and Sara would be on the lower level. Jew and Clara were on the upper level.

"John, this place is darling. It's built like an Indian adobe. Look at the furniture. It looks like it's handmade."

"It is, honey. Those boys in the CCC did it all. They would clear the land and build an entire park with their hands. Very often, they would cut timber from the site and work it into furniture."

"Well, they did a great job. I'd like to see something you buy nowadays last this long. Remember the furniture at the motel in Houston?"

"Yeah, my back may never be the same." Jew laughed as he spoke.

As they passed out the door to meet Jeff and Sara, Jew bumped his head on the top of the door jamb.

"Damn," he said as he rubbed his forehead. "Whoever designed these doors must have been a short fart."

"John, watch your language. People will hear you."

Jeff began to laugh. "First time in my life I was ever glad to be short. You big guys got to watch us shorties. We'll get even sooner or later."

Jew just rubbed his head and smiled.

Early the next morning, the four of them were at the small, local Catholic church. A young man was at work making minor repairs to the front door.

"Excuse me. Is the priest inside?" Clara asked.

"No, ma'am. He's gone right now. Should be back in a little while. Can I help you?"

"No, thanks. We need to talk to the Father."

"He went to the post office. Should be back in ten or fifteen minutes."

"Fine. Mind if we go in and look at your church?"

"No, ma'am. You all go on in." The young man held the door open as they entered.

"It's small, but beautiful," Sara whispered. "Makes one feel close to God by just being here."

"It truly does, honey," Jeff whispered back.

Their wait was not long. A young priest, perhaps thirty, entered through a door close to the altar.

"Juan said you were looking for me. How can I help you?"

Jew introduced himself and the others, then asked, "Father, could we speak to you in your office? We have a favor to ask and it really doesn't have anything to do with religion. We are searching for someone, someone who passed this way a long time ago."

The priest smiled. "Sure. Follow me."

Once in the priest's office, they all found chairs and were seated.

"Now, what can I do for you? What is this favor you need?" the priest asked.

"Well, I guess the best place to start is at the beginning," Jew said.

"By all means, let's start at the beginning. Before you start, let me get us some coffee."

The priest stepped outside and returned in less than ten minutes with a pot of coffee on a tray. Cups were stacked on the tray next to the coffee pot.

"If you want to smoke, feel free to do so." As he spoke, he lit a pipe.

"Now, let's start at the beginning," he said as he poured.

Jew told the entire story from his first sighting of Isaac to the finding of the graves of Isaac and William Robert. The priest sat never asking a question, never making any comment, but not missing a word that was said by any of the four as they told the story.

His patience was remarkable. When he was sure the story was finished, he stood and walked to a window.

"I find your story most interesting. Yes, indeed, most interesting. As I am sure you have guessed, I am a student of early western history and the American Indian in particular. I have always been fascinated by that era of time. However, I still don't understand how I can help you. You seem to have solved your problem yourselves and now are only looking at the scene where the events took place."

"No, Father, we haven't finished with our quest. We want to find out what happened to Maria and thought you could help. Surely there must be records that would show where she was from in Mexico. We thought since they were married here and Isaac converted to Catholicism, surely there must be something recorded in the church records.

The priest stood up and walked to the window once again. He seemed to be in some sort of trance. Several minutes passed as he stood staring out of the window toward the mountains. He turned and faced the group.

"There may be something. It's a very unusual request and normally we do not give out information such as you ask, but I believe in this case, I'll make an exception."

"Thank you, Father," Jew said as he rose and extended his hand.

The priest shook Jew's hand.

"Don't thank me too soon, my son. I may not find anything. Besides, it will take me a little while to go through the records. Let's see, I think I can probably find it in say two or three days."

Jew looked at the others. "Think we can keep our rooms at the lodge?" he asked as he looked at Jeff.

"Are you all up at Indian Lodge or one of the motels in town?"

"We were at the lodge, but they only had rooms for last night."

"Let me see what I can do." The priest picked up his telephone and dialed a number.

"This is Father Carlos. To whom am I speaking, please?" he said to whomever answered the telephone. "Oh, Jane, I need a favor. I have four friends in my office and we will be working on a project that may take two or three days They have rooms up at the lodge, but were told that none would be available as you only had vacancies for last night. Can you see your way to extend their stay up there? I know, I know. Sure. Good. I'll tell them. It's John Williams and Jeff Sanders and their wives. Right. I'll tell them. Thanks."

He hung up. "You have rooms. Now, I'll need some help to search the records. Can you meet me in the morning, say about eight?"

"We'll be here, Father," Clara said.

"Fine. I will expect you then. Now, I have work to do. Will you excuse me?"

As they walked back to the car, Jeff said, "You know, I'd like to go back to the fort and look around one more time. How about you folks?"

"Sure. Fine with me," Jew answered. "How about you girls?"

They all agreed and spent the better part of the day walking, looking and reading.

"Tell you what, Jeff, how about walking with me and we'll take that trail marked over there that goes back to the lodge? Can't be more than a couple of miles."

"Sure. Sounds like fun."

"Well, you boys can go without me. I'm for going back to the lodge and taking a good hot shower," Sara advised them.

When Jew and Jeff arrived at the lodge, they were both

223

very tired. The trail was a little more than three miles and a great part of it was uphill.

"Boy, I need me a good cold beer," Jeff told Jew.

"Yeah, me too. We'd better take the ice chest in. I don't think they sell beer here at the restaurant."

Once in Jeff's room, they opened a beer. Jew flopped in a chair. "Man, that was some walk."

"I know. Why do I let you talk me into these things," Jeff mumbled as he fell across the bed. "My legs may never work again."

Both men laughed.

The morning following found the four, along with Father Carlos, going through old records, searching for either Maria or Isaac's name to appear.

Father Carlos closed the ledger he had been going through. "Well, what do you folks say we break for a few minutes and go grab a sandwich?"

"I'm ready. My stomach is growling like a bear," Jew agreed.

After lunch the five of them were back at it and nowhere had they found any mention of either Isaac or Maria.

It was almost four o'clock when Sara picked up a new ledger and began to go through it page by page. She was halfway through the book when her finger came to rest on a name.

"Aha! Eureka!"

"What is it?" Clara asked as she moved closer.

"Look, Isaac Turner II." Sara hesitated. "What's this mean, Father? It looks like it's a baptism."

The priest took the ledger. He studied it for a few seconds. "It is. This is for an infant. The date is June 21, 1884."

"Do you know what that means?" Jew said. "If Isaac was killed, say in September," he paused. "Remember, he was planning on his crop, so he would be getting ready to harvest.

That's about September, right?"

"Yeah, that's about the right time. Sometimes October. Depends," Jeff said. "The date is 1884. If I remember correctly, Maria finished her manuscript in 1882. Isaac and William Robert were killed in 1882. That date says 1884."

"I see what you mean," Clara said.

"Just suppose," Father Carlos said as he studied the writing in the ledger. "Just suppose her baby was born somewhere else and she waited until she completed her journey to Fort Davis to have her child baptized by a father she felt close to."

"Well, that makes as much sense to me as any of this whole thing has. Why not?" Jeff agreed.

Jew thought about that for a couple of seconds, then added, "This is proof she made it back this far anyway and that's what we were looking for. She had her child, named him after his father and the church baptized him. Right here in this church."

"Well now, we'll find out where Maria was from in Mexico," Father Carlos said as he went to another shelf of records and began looking for a particular one. "Here it is," he remarked as he pulled a big, thick, black bound book off the shelf. He flipped through the pages. "OK," he said. "There is a Maria Elena Estrada Pena Turner listed here. Her home parish was in La Palma, Mexico. I know that town. It's maybe thirty miles south of the Rio Grande."

"That's great. We'll get us a visa and go down there," Clara said.

"I said it was about thirty miles south of the river, but it's a lot farther by road. I'm only guessing, but I'll say seventy or eighty miles. Remember, those roads are not freeways either."

"Where would we cross, Father?" Sara asked.

"Well, you could drive back to Del Rio and cross the

bridge at Ciudad Acuna or you could cross the river at Boquillas and get a driver. That could be a problem, too. No, I'd recommend you go back to Del Rio. To make things easier for you, I'll call a friend of mine at the church. His name is Father Ramos. He will help you with your visas and I will ask him to find you a guide when I call him this afternoon."

"Will we need a guide?" Jeff asked.

"I strongly recommend it, Mr. Sanders. You don't know the customs and it just doesn't hurt to have a local along with you when traveling in Mexico."

"We'll drive over first thing in the morning," Jew stated. He extended his hand toward the priest. "To say thank you seems so little after what you have done for us, Father."

"Thanks is all it takes. I hope you find her. I would ask one thing. When you have finished your search, let me know what you find. I would be most interested to know."

"We will, Father, and we'll get you a copy of Maria's writings."

"I would appreciate that. Thanks. Now go. I have work to catch up on." He smiled, then added, "Vaya con Dios."

Chapter 25

The drive to Del Rio took longer than anyone of the four had expected. It was early afternoon when they found the local church. With the help of a friendly nun, they were shown into Father Ramos' office.

"Come in, come in," Father Ramos said. "Father Carlos called yesterday and told me to expect you. When did you leave Fort Davis?"

"This morning around seven o'clock," Jew answered.

"You made good time. I am Father Ramos and you have to be John." As he spoke, he pointed to each and named them. "Yes. Father Carlos told me your whole story. He and I were roommates at the seminary. We both have always been history buffs. If I could get away from here, I would love to go with you on this search."

"You are more than welcome to come, Father," Clara said. "Why don't you join us?"

"Oh, no. I can't. I would if I could, I assure you. But with summer school in full swing, I, as monsignor of this parish, cannot leave. Thank you just the same. I must ask you, as I am sure Carlos has, please let me know what you find."

"We will, Father. You can bank on it," Jew said.

Jew looked around the office. The walls were decorated with all sorts of Indian artifacts. He stepped over to a picture frame. The background was white cotton and placed in a design were fifty or sixty stone arrowheads.

"Did you find all of these, Father?" Jew asked.

"Yes, I did. Every summer between classes, I find myself on a hunt also. I love to seek out old camping sites. I have been quite lucky, too."

As they talked about the various things the priest had on the wall, the door to his office opened and a young man, very neatly dressed even though he was wearing blue jeans, appeared. His shirt was starched and ironed and his black cowboy boots had a fresh shine on them.

"Ah, Tony. Come in." Father Ramos beckoned with his hand for him to enter. "This, my friends, is Anthony de la Garza. He is my nephew and the best guide in all of South Texas. I trust him with my life."

Tony blushed. "Uncle Enrique, you give me too much credit."

"No, no. He knows much of the country you will be traveling. He has hunted down there for years with my brother-in-law. He knows many of the people and will be a great help to you, I am sure. Now, when do you plan to leave?"

Jew looked at the others for an answer.

Jeff placed his hand on his chin as if to ponder the question. "How long will it take to get to La Palma?"

Father Ramos looked at Tony and made a motion with his

shoulders as if he did not know.

"The road, it is sometimes not too good," Tony said. "Maybe six or seven hours."

"That long?" Clara asked.

"Si, maybe more," he hesitated, "maybe less. It is dirt or gravel for a long way. If it rains it could take even longer."

"John, are we sure we want to do this?" Clara asked.

Jew looked at her with his head tilted down, much as someone would look over the upper rim of his glasses.

"Oh, of course we do," she answered her own question. "We didn't come this far to be turned back by a little old dirt road, did we?"

"Nope," Jew answered.

Jeff snickered, then said, "It won't be bad, Clara." He placed his arm on her shoulder. "If Maria could do it, I know you can do it."

Jew chuckled, then added, "You are so right, Jeff. If Maria did it, we can do it."

Father Ramos laughed. "I understand from Father Carlos that you two have been involved on this adventure from the start. That somewhere way back there you had an ancestor, Mr. Sanders, that was related to Isaac Turner."

"That I did," Jeff said. "I am not sure just what the term for our kinship would be; but his father, Lucas Willard, was in my family tree."

Jew smiled as he put his arm around Jeff's shoulder and looking at Father Ramos said, "It's a shame, too, isn't it, Father?"

"What is a shame, Mr. Williams?"

"Well, look at Jeff here. I love him like a brother, but to be kin to Isaac Turner, ain't he light?"

Father Ramos could not help himself. He broke out with a laugh that probably shook the rafters of the church. After he regained control of himself, he wiped the tears from his eyes and gasped for breath.

"You two deserve each other," Clara said. "Now, when are we going to leave? As for myself, I would like to spend the night here. How about you, Sara?"

"Oh yes. I would like to see some of this little town and maybe if these two would, they could buy us a big, juicy steak tonight."

"I think that's a great idea," Clara agreed.

"And Father, we would be honored if you and Tony would join us," Sara added.

"I would be delighted. How about you, my son?" the priest asked Tony.

"Not tonight, Father. I've got a date. That is, if we are not leaving until in the morning."

"Young people and love," the priest said.

"We'll leave at eight o'clock in the morning," Jew said. "Want us to pick you up somewhere?"

"Well, why don't you meet me here at the church and I'll leave my pickup here."

The young man stuck his hand out and Jew shook it. Then Jeff shook hands with Tony.

The priest took the young man in his arms and hugged him. "I will see you in the morning for breakfast. You know what time. I will give you a letter to Father Thomas. He is an old friend. I need to drop him a note."

Tony kissed the priest on his cheek. "I will be here," he said and went out the door.

The next morning Tony was ready when Jew pulled up.

"Well, let's get started. We have a long way to go," Tony said as he slipped into the seat next to Jeff.

230

Chapter 26

A cloud of dust engulfed the car as Jew pulled up in front of a small but beautiful church.

"You sure this is it, Tony?" Jew asked their guide.

"Yes, sir. This is La Palma. I know it doesn't look like much, but this little village has seen a lot of history move through its streets. Monsignor said we were to ask for Father Thomas. While you get the dust out of your eyes, I'll go in and find him."

Tony was out of the car and moving across the front steps before Jew or any of the others could respond.

"I don't believe that road we just came over," Clara spoke as she stood up outside the car and brushed the wrinkles from her skirt.

"We've been driving for almost four hours and how far did we come, John?" Sara asked Jew.

Jew looked at his odometer. "Hmm, looks like above

seventy-one miles from the border." Jew said as he walked around his station wagon.

Jeff stretched as he strolled over to the steps leading to the church's front door. "The bad part, Jew, is that we have to go back over that trail. You know that don't you?"

"Jeff, don't remind me. Not now." As he spoke, Tony reappeared with a priest.

"Mr. Williams, Mr. Sanders, this is Father Thomas. Monsignor called and told Father we were on the way. He was waiting for us."

"How do you do? You made better time than I thought you would. I expected you much later this afternoon."

After introductions and handshakes were exchanged, the priest invited them into his office. A short, heavyset nun came in with a coffee pot and several cups.

"Excuse me, Father, I thought your guests might like to have some refreshment," she said as she set the tray down.

"Thank you, sister." The priest placed a hand on her shoulder. "Folks, this is Sister Madeline. She is my right hand, my left hand, and most importantly, my memory." He chuckled. Clara could see the nun was embarrassed.

"Thank you, indeed," Clara said. "We could use a good cup of coffee."

The coffee was poured and small talk followed for several minutes.

"Now, how can I help you? The monsignor in Del Rio said you are looking for someone and perhaps they are in my parish."

"Well, Father, that's partly true, but it's more like she could have been in your parish a long time ago. It's a long story. First let me ask if there is a ranch anywhere around here owned by someone named Pena."

"There are many ranches and many people named Pena." The priest frowned. "What do you want with this Pena anyway?"

"Let me start at the beginning and tell you the whole story." Jew told Father Thomas the story beginning with the finding of Maria's writings. He never mentioned the ghost of Isaac. He felt that might just complicate things. It was hard enough for him to believe and he had seen what he believed to be Isaac several times; but that had been over a year ago, and at times, it seemed like a dream.

After Jew finished, the priest smiled. "You don't want the Pena Rancho. You want the Turner Rancho."

"The Turner Rancho!" Jess and Jew said at the same time.

"You mean there is a Turner Ranch around here? Is it close?" Jeff asked the priest.

"Not too close." He paused and raised his hand to his chin as if to cradle his thoughts. "But then, not too far either." Again he paused. "Maybe two, three hours at the most."

"How's the road, Father?" Jew asked.

"Well, you should know better than me. You just came over some of it on your way from Del Rio."

"What? We have to go back?" Clara said.

The priest chuckled. "Yes, you do, but not far. Then you will have to turn. Here. I'll draw a map for you to use. It won't be hard to find. You passed the gate to the rancho on the way here. Perhaps you remember seeing a large gate with wheels set on top of the stone columns."

"Yes. We all remarked about the gate," Jew stated.

"Sure, I remember that," Jeff said.

"OK. That's it. Just go back there and turn in. You'll have a long drive to the main house and you will pass several adobes along the way where vaqueros live. Should you have any problems, just ask one of the ranch hands for help. They will see that you get to the main house."

The road had not improved on the return trip and Jew was

glad to see the gate even when it was still over a mile away.

Jew pulled through the gate and stopped. "Well, this could really get interesting before we get back home. Sara, you ever think of writing a book?"

"John, I wouldn't even think of it. Who would believe it anyway?"

"You're right about that," Clara remarked. "But I think it's a great idea."

The drive to the main ranch house was slow, but the road was in fairly good condition. When they pulled up in front of the house, Jew saw why the road was in good shape. Sitting out back were several large pieces of road equipment.

Jew turned the key off and looked up to see the front door to the house open. A man in his fifties stepped out on the porch. Behind him was a younger man.

Jew and Jeff both got out of the car, along with Tony. They walked to the front steps. "Hello," Jew said. The older man said something in Spanish. He could tell he was not understood and turned his head to the younger man and again said something in Spanish.

The younger man stepped to the side of the older man. "Can we help you?" he said in broken English.

"Perhaps. My name is John Williams. This is Jeff Sanders. And this is our guide, Tony de la Garza."

The older man took Jew's hand. The younger man spoke in Spanish. A smile crossed the sun-dried, wrinkled face. He spoke in Spanish again.

The young man turned to Jew. "Ask the ladies to come in. My father says it is too hot to sit in the car."

"He's right about that," Jeff said. "Must be a hundred and ten degrees in the shade."

They all went into the house. It was furnished in the manner that one would expect—large oak chairs, hand-carved tables, all massive in size. It was plain to see this was not just a rancher, but a very important and successful rancher.

"Now, how can we be of service? By the way, I am Julio Turner and this is my father, Isaac Turner."

A chill raced up Jew's back. Clara shot a look at John and her mouth gaped.

"What is wrong? What did I say?" Julio asked with a surprised expression on his face.

"We are at the right place," Jew said as he looked at Jeff. "We have come from a small town in Georgia. Hazel, Georgia. And we are trying to find out what happened to a lady over a hundred years ago.

"To make a long story short, Jeff here is a distant relative of a man named Isaac Turner who died in Hazel."

Julio raised his hand and spoke to his father. His voice rose with what seemed excitement as he spoke. Isaac's voice showed the same excitement as he spoke to Julio.

"My father says how can this be?" His voice seemed to lose some of its volume.

"It's a very long story, but we will be glad to share it with you," Jew informed Julio. "It will take a while and we will have to leave and go back to town. We didn't get a room before we left. Would it be OK if we came back tomorrow? We could tell you the whole story then. But believe me, it is true. Jeff here is related to you and your father also, from a long time ago. The events that took place were in Georgia. It really began with a slave girl who belonged to the Willard family."

Julio turned to his father again. Isaac waved his hand a couple of times and his voice was very firm. After he had finished he set his jaw and gave his head a nod as if to say, "I have spoken."

"My father said it is getting late and there is no place to stay in La Palma. You will do us the honor of staying with us. My father wants to hear your story. First we will have drinks out back under the grapes."

Tony said something to Julio in Spanish and Julio answered him. Julio then went outside for a few minutes. When he returned he spoke to Tony.

Tony turned to Jew. "Mr. Williams, I have asked Senor Turner if I could catch a ride with one of his people back to Del Rio and he has agreed to have me driven back if you do not need me any longer."

"No, that will be OK, Tony. I think we can find our way back when we get ready to leave," Jew responded.

"Thank you, sir. I have a girlfriend. We plan to marry next week. I hope you understand."

"Sure I do," Jew answered. "I don't blame you. In fact, I probably wouldn't have come in the first place if I had been you. Thanks, Tony. You were a big help at the border." Jew reached into his pocket and brought out his money clip.

"No, no. You don't owe me anything," Tony said.

"No, Tony, this isn't payment. Consider this a wedding present." Jew gave him two twenties and a ten. "You kids enjoy yourselves."

Jeff had also reached into his pocket and matched Jew's money. "Here, son, have a dinner or two on us and enjoy your wedding."

"Thank you both. I know we will. My wife-to-be will be very interested in your story, too. I will tell her. I must go now. Senor Turner has a driver waiting."

As Tony left, Clara said, "That is really a nice young man."

"He is, indeed," Sara agreed.

After Tony had left, the group followed Isaac and Julio through the house. Two women were sitting out back on a terrace. One was in her fifties and the other in her early thirties.

"This is my mother and my wife," Julio said as he

introduced the four.

"Please sit down. Would you like some coffee, a mixed drink or perhaps a beer?" Julio asked.

As they sat around a table sipping their drinks, Jew asked Sara if she would go over the story in Spanish. "This time, Sara, tell them all about Isaac. Don't leave out anything."

Isaac did not move as Sara told the entire story. When she finished, she turned to Jew. "I hope I didn't leave anything out."

"This story is, how you say, almost unbelievable," Julio said. "But you have told us details no one else would know. My father was told about his great-grandfather and how he killed the Indian Victorio, how he married my great-great-grandmother and returned to his homeland only to be killed. We know what you tell us is true. Would you give us a copy of the story? I would like to have it for my son who is yet unborn, but I am sure will want to know about his ancestors."

"Of course. As soon as we get home, we'll have it copied and mail it to you," Jew said.

Isaac began to speak and Julio translated.

"Once we had a book. It was a daily account of my great-grandmother's life. This book told about the killing of her husband and how my great-grandmother traveled back after that terrible act."

"What happened to the book?" Jew asked.

"It was lost in a fire, but I had read it and remember some, if not most, of the events up until the disappearance of my great-grandmother, Maria," Isaac said.

"Wait a minute. She disappeared?" Jew questioned.

"Yes, but let me tell you my story from the start." As he smiled, his eyes lit up and one could tell he was enjoying the company of his long lost relative.

"You wait, Isaac," Julio's mother interrupted. "These people are tired. They have traveled a long way and they need to rest. Come. Follow me. I will show you to your rooms and you can freshen up. Isaac will have someone bring in your bags. We can talk after the evening meal. Until then, you rest." She was firm in her tone of voice. Julio translated and added, "She thinks you look tired."

It was plain to see who had control inside the house. Isaac controlled and ran a big, busy ranch, but it was his wife, Irma, who ran the house. Of this there was no question.

After dinner, Irma had coffee served in a large sitting room. "Now, Isaac, you may tell your story, but please no cigar in the house."

"She doesn't let me smoke in here," he said with a sheepish grin.

Jew grinned and winked at Jeff, who was smiling at Isaac's remark.

"Now, let me tell you about my great-grandmother, Maria. That was a lady—strong, smart, mean and beautiful, all at the same time. The most beautiful young lady in this whole end of Mexico, I was told. Her hair was long and black as night. The sun made it look blue like steel. Her skin was fair, except when the sun had turned it brown. I remember seeing a picture of her in a dress with the sleeves out. I could not believe how white her skin was. Most of her days, you know, were spent running the rancho."

"The story, Isaac, get to the story about Maria," Irma said.

"Oh, yes. Please excuse me. I get to remembering sometimes, the things my father told me." He became silent as he got his thoughts together.

"Maria, my great-grandmother, left the home of her husband on a bay mare and rode for four days, stopping only to rest and let the mare feed and water. She was sure the ones who killed her husband would be coming after her. After four days of travel, she felt safe, but still very alone. She knew she would need help. So somewhere near the Chattahoochee River, she met a family who was moving west. They had lost their farm and were looking for a new place to start over again. I suppose the war was the cause of them losing their land. I never knew for sure, but it would seem logical.

"Maria traveled with them for several weeks. Then she joined up with another family in Mobile. This family was moving to a farm in East Texas where they had relatives. There were three wagons. They, too, had lost their farms somewhere in Georgia.

"This is when Maria learned she was with child. They were moving too slowly. She knew she had to get back to Mexico before the child was born. This would protect him in her efforts to regain her rancho, should there be a legal battle.

"Outside Mobile she met a lady in a wagon train of colored people and rode with them to somewhere close to Baton Rouge, Louisiana. From there she traveled alone until she was in Texas, somewhere close to Houston she thought. It was here she met with a cattle buyer who was going to San Antonio. He let her ride along with him and his three sons to San Antonio. They pushed the trail hard, but she did not mind. She spoke of this gentleman and called him Colonel. He had known Isaac's commanding officer and for that reason, she always believed he befriended her.

"In San Antonio she knew her time was running out. She would not be able to travel much longer. She knew she would never make it home in time, so she followed an Army troop to Fort Clark where she hired a wagon to carry her to Del Rio.

"My grandfather was born in Ciudad Acuna, which made him a Mexican citizen. Maria had no problems. The birth was an easy one and she was, as I said, very strong. She came from good stock.

"After my grandfather was born, she wrote several letters to people in high places that she had known. They went to work on getting her rancho back, but it would take time. She traveled back to Fort Davis, where she had been happy in those early days. There, I suppose, from what you have said, she had my grandfather baptized. I never knew that before. I did know she spent several months at Fort Davis where she worked in the hospital.

"Word came from Mexico City that her land had been returned to her. That pig, Manuel Lopez, it was him that killed her mother and father, not the Indians like he had said. He spent his last days in Mexico City where he was hung. That was too good for him, but that's another story.

"Where was I?" He paused. "Would you like some brandy?"

"I would," Jew said.

"Sounds good to me," Jeff agreed.

"How about you ladies?"

"No thanks, but do you have any sherry?" Clara asked.

"But, of course," Isaac responded. He poured sherry for Clara and Sara. Julio poured some coffee for his mother and his wife, then poured a brandy for himself.

"Now, where was I?" Isaac asked again.

"She found out Lopez had killed her parents for the rancho and she was to be given back her land," Julio advised his father.

"Oh yes. Well, she did get the rancho back and started to build the brand again. She worked right along with the men. She was not what you would expect of a Mexican lady of means. I suppose those years with her husband had taught her that if you want something, you have to get right in the middle of it and make it come true. She kept a record book on her life. Each day she made another entry. The last one,

I remember well.

"One day two vaqueros came in and told her that they had seen a black man up in the mountains. He was on a spotted horse. She ordered her horse saddled and took a rifle with her as she rode out to see who it was they had seen in the mountains."

Jew interrupted. "She rode out alone?"

"Si, this lady was tough, as I have said before. One story was that she broke a Vaquero's jaw once when he backtalked her. She was a tough lady. A couple of vaqueros wanted to go with her, but she said no. Her last words in the book were, 'They have seen a black rider in the hills. I must see who it is.'

"My grandfather was a very young man then. He told me she did not return and when it started to get late, he had six or seven vaqueros ride with him. They searched the mountains. About midnight a storm broke and it rained so hard, they had to give up the search. It rained for two days. There was flooding in the low lands. Normally, it can go two, maybe three years in those mountains without any rain. Most of the years it will rain maybe three or four inches all year, but that year it must have rained seven or eight inches in two days.

"When the rain stopped, they went back and looked again. They found her horse and a spotted stallion grazing in a valley. Both horses were bare. No saddles, bridles, nothing. They appeared to have been turned out to graze. We still have horses in our herd from that spotted stallion's line.

"Well, after two weeks of looking without a trace of his mother, my grandfather came to accept the fact that maybe she was swept away by flood water."

"Didn't they ever look any more?" Jeff asked.

"Si, my grandfather would go back every chance he had for five or six years, but never was there a trace. I also remember in her writings she said several times she wished that there was some way she could be buried next to her beloved Isaac. My grandfather felt sure she would return to her home in the United States once she was married and could run the rancho. She loved that man she married. She loved him very much, indeed."

"We could tell that from her writing," Sara said. "She probably loved him more than life itself. I can just imagine how hard it had to be for her when she buried him at the edge of the field and then was forced to flee in fear for her own life."

"It had to be very hard, but death was no stranger to her. People were always faced with violence, pain and uncertainty in those times, I suppose." Isaac's observations were subtle, yet there was a note of caring in his voice.

"So, they never did find even a trace, except for the mare and the spotted stallion?" Jew asked.

"That's right, not so much as a trace. Some used to say, the vaqueros that is, they said that Senora Turner still rode the hills looking for her black man. Of course, we of the house knew that was just superstition." His voice trailed off. "But one can never be sure of such things."

"Could you, I mean, would you show us the valley where the horses were found?"

Isaac thought about it for a few seconds. "Well," he said, "I can't. Because of my back I can no longer ride a horse, but Julio knows where it is and I am sure he would not mind taking you to the Valley of Two Horses, as it has been called for many years."

"We will get started in the morning," Julio said. "We can go most of the way in a truck and pull the horses in a trailer. We have to travel by horseback for maybe two or three hours. We will plan on spending the night. Maybe two. I will have a couple of vaqueros follow us with the necessary camping equipment and food. I think you will like spending a couple of nights in the mountains."

Clara looked at Sara. Her expression was clear. "Well, suppose you boys count Sara and me out on this one. I think I for one will stay here at the rancho and enjoy sitting out under the grapes."

Sara laughed. "I couldn't have said it better myself."

"Fine. You two stay here. Jew and I will go see some of this beautiful back country," Jeff said as he stood and stretched. "If we are going to get started in the morning, I think I'll turn in. I need some rest. These old bones tell me I was never cut out to be a traveling man."

"I think that's a good idea," Julio said. "We will start at five o'clock."

Jew looked at Jeff. The both said, "Five a.m.?"

"Si, we will be there by early afternoon. I will go tell my vaqueros so they can have the horses ready for us after breakfast.

"So it's five a.m., for sure?" Jew asked.

"Si. Did you want to start earlier?"

"No, no, five o'clock will be fine," he answered.

As they went upstairs, Clara was holding Jew by the elbow. "It's the early bird that gets the worm, you know."

"I know, but I get to ride a horse. I hope I can walk after we get to wherever we are going," Jew replied.

"You'll walk and I feel sure you will find whatever it is you are meant to find. Somehow I have a strange feeling that you, my dear, are nearing the end of this quest and you will have true peace of mind when it is over."

"Honey, I hope so. I truly do hope you are right."

Chapter 27

"It's five o'clock, senor," a female voice called softly through Jew and Clara's door. It was followed by a soft, but firm, knock. "It's five o'clock. Are you awake?"

"Yes, yes, I'm coming," Jew answered in as soft a voice as he could without disturbing Clara.

Jew slipped into his jeans and pulled a slipover shirt over his head. It was still dark outside and Jew fumbled around until he found his sneakers that he had laid out the night before.

The light coming under the door guided him to the hallway. Once out of the room Jew put on his shoes and headed for the bathroom at the end of the hall. He met Jeff coming out of the bathroom.

"Morning," Jeff said.

"Yep. Maybe we should say night," Jew answered as he stretched.

"Makes one appreciate city life, doesn't it?" Jeff said.

"I guess so, but man, I slept like a log last night. I'll bet I didn't move a muscle all night. A good cup of coffee and I'll be ready to saddle up and ride for them there hills out there, pardner."

Jeff smiled. "I hope we both feel that way tonight after we have ridden a while. I'm afraid to think how my old butt is going to feel."

"Don't worry about it, Jeff. Anything has to be better than the road we traveled to get here."

After breakfast, Julio led them out to where his pickup truck was parked. The air was fresh and a bit crisp.

"Is it always this cool in the early morning out here?" Jew asked.

"Si, it gets very hot sometimes in the day, but the nights are always nice and cool. In the desert to the south, it is much cooler at night and, of course, much hotter in the day."

The ranch road was in fine shape, but there were areas Jew wondered if the pickup would get through with the horse trailer. Julio knew what he was doing and never had to stop. He just kept moving, sometimes slowly, but moving.

They had traveled almost two hours when Jeff asked, "How much farther?"

"Not far now," Julio answered. "Just over that next hill we will park and ride toward those twin peaks over there." He pointed to the southwest.

"Hell, how far are those peaks?" Jew asked.

"Ten, maybe twelve, miles," Julio smiled as he spoke. "Not far. We should be in Two Horse Valley by one or two this afternoon."

"I thought you said you were going to have a couple of your vaqueros follow us," Jeff said.

"I was, but they wanted to leave last night. They will have camp set up when we get there. See, over there is their pickup and trailer."

Jew saw an old four-wheel drive pickup. Hooked to its rear end was a rather large trailer.

"What did they bring with them in that trailer?" Jew asked.

"Oh, they had their horses and the pack animals."

"Oh, I see." Jew turned to Jeff in the rear seat of the crew cab, then back toward Julio. "The pack animals?"

"Si, it took three pack animals for the equipment. We may be here two or three days. This is a big valley. We can go back whenever you want, but if you want to see it all, it may take that long." He hesitated, then said, "Don't worry. My wife and my mother will keep your wives busy. They will enjoy themselves." He laughed. "How long since you have ridden a horse?" he asked as he pulled the truck up next to the old one already parked.

"A long time," Jew said.

"Me, too," Jeff added. "Hell, I bet it's been twenty years or close to it since I sat in a saddle."

"Well, senores, I think your wives will enjoy much more what they will do than your butts will what you are going to do." He chuckled.

"Don't worry. We will take it easy. I have picked our two best riding mares for you. It will be like sitting in a..." he paused searching for a word, "...a rocking chair."

"Yeah, a rocking chair. I'll bet," Jeff said as he got out of the truck.

Jew pulled himself up into the saddle and adjusted his weight. "Hey, Jeff, this ain't half bad," he said.

"Tell me that tonight," Jeff answered as he swung into the saddle.

"Look at the scenery," Jeff remarked as they topped the first ridge.

"God, it takes your breath away," Jew said. "Julio, is

this all part of your ranch?"

"Si." He flashed his ever-present smile. "The rancho goes over those mountains over there." He pointed to a range of mountains Jew knew had to be twenty-five miles away.

"How many acres do you and your father have?" Jeff asked.

Julio seemed to think about that question for a couple of minutes. "Senor Jeff, I don't know how to say this without making you feel bad. Understand I do not mean to embarrass you, but you know when you are talking to a rancher, it is best not to ask how many acres he has. It is like me asking you how much money you have in the bank." Julio smiled.

Jeff did feel embarrassed, but thought of Julio's answer and it made sense. "You are right of course. I'm sorry," Jeff said.

"No, no, do not be sorry. Not for something you did not know. Next time, be sorry." Julio laughed. "I will tell you this, the rancho is the third largest in all of Mexico. You can ride on a horse for four days and not cross from north to south. From east to west, it is not so big."

They moved on down the mountain they had just crossed.

Julio turned his head and told Jew, who was behind him, "It's always easier going up."

Jew thought he would fall over his mount's head, the grade was so steep. "You are right about that. I hope this old gal knows her business."

Julio laughed. "She does. She is, like I told you, one of our best."

As the land leveled off, Jeff rode up beside Jew. "Well, old friend, I'll tell you one thing. I wouldn't have missed this for anything. These mountains are beyond my imagination. I've never seen so much beauty and the air is so fresh. Smell that. Would you smell that clean air?"

"It is better than nice, I have to agree," Jew said.

"You know what was the best part, Jew?" Jeff asked.
"What's that?"
"Watching you trying to pull your mare out of a dive back there on the mountains. Man, I got to laughing so hard, I almost fell out of the saddle. You almost pulled that saddle horn off."

"There they are," Julio said, pointing toward two men in a grove of mesquite trees. Two tents were pitched and a small fire was already going as they rode up.

The vaqueros greeted Julio and pointed to a mountain lion hanging in a tree. Julio jumped from his saddle and went straight to the animal. He examined it closely. Jew and Jeff were right behind him.

"This is why they wanted to come out last night. This cat has been killing our cattle and Pedro knew he would be on the prowl. Look at him. He is old and can no longer catch deer. He has to live and cattle are easy prey. I don't really like it, but he had to be killed."

"How can you be sure this is the same animal that has been killing your livestock, Julio?" asked Jeff.

"This cat is old, like I said. He also has been hurt and hurt bad in the past. Maybe by a cow or maybe by another mountain lion. Look at this front paw." Julio picked up the left front paw so Jeff could see.

"There." He pointed to the side of the paw. "This one's been hurt, perhaps broken. See how he has dragged it when he walked. The hair is worn and a callus has grown. I suspect as he has grown older, this leg has stiffened up some and added to his inefficiency along with his age to catch and kill his prey. So he had to turn to something he could catch. Cattle. Calves mostly. One thing is certain. His hunting and killing days are over forever."

Julio dropped the paw and turned to his vaqueros. "Bueno," he said.

After lunch the three of them, Julio, Jew and Jeff, began to stroll down the valley. Jew had asked Julio if he knew where the two horses had been found many years ago when Maria disappeared.

"No, I do not know. Nor does my father. We only know in this valley somewhere. Perhaps right where we stand."

Jew squatted down and picked up a rock. He tossed it underhanded toward a large cactus.

"What did you expect to find, Jew? It's been so many years and Maria's son looked so long and with so many. What could we find that they couldn't after all these years?" Jeff asked as he squatted down close to Jew.

"I don't know. I really don't know. It was just a feeling I had. I thought maybe, just maybe, I was somehow being guided. Sounds stupid, I know, but I've felt it before back on the farm when we were looking for Isaac and William Robert."

"Look, Jew, I know how much this means to you, but we just got here. Let's take it one step at a time. If you...No, if we," he corrected himself, "are meant to find anything, we will. If we don't, that's the way it is. At least we now have the satisfaction of knowing what happened to Maria. She made it home safe and sound."

"Oh, yeah? What really happened to her?" Jew asked, not in an angry manner, just matter of factly.

"Senor," Julio said as he walked over to a spot across from Jew and sat down on the heel of one boot. As he sat he picked up a stone and tossed it at the same cactus at which Jew had earlier tossed a stone. "Senor John, you know she made it back to her home. Home to her rancho. She had a child—my great-great-grandfather. Because of her, my father and his family have enjoyed a very good life, and my son and his son will also. That, you know, is the most important thing. It is all because of her and the first Isaac Turner.

Somehow we have to accept the things we cannot change."

Jew looked away, then back at Julio. The smile was there that Jew had come to expect. Jew smiled and shook his head. He stood up and put his hands into his front pockets.

"By damn, you are right. Now let's get mounted up and ride some of this beautiful valley."

The three of them rode until the sun began to get close to the rim high overhead.

"We had better get back to the camp. Pedro will have supper on the fire when we get there and, as for me, I'm so hungry I could eat that cat hanging back there in the mesquites."

"I'm hungry, too, but not quite that starved," Jeff said.

Back in camp, one of the vaqueros took charge of the horses. Jew, Jeff and Julio sat around the fire after supper and drank coffee. Julio told them a story about roving bandits who had in the past roamed the mountains. This had been many years ago, however.

"Every now and then," he added, "there will still be two or three would-be bad men caught in the mountains by the Federales. That's why we bring the dogs." Julio pointed toward three old hounds lying next to the smaller tent. "They will let us know if anyone comes close to our camp."

Jeff looked at Jew, then back to Julio. "Do I understand you right? That there could be bandits out there somewhere?" He paused. "Right now? Watching us?"

"It is true," Julio answered. He saw a touch of fear creep into Jeff's face. "But I would not worry about it."

"That may be easy for you to say," Jeff remarked.

"Senor Jeff, you are a merchant, right? I mean, you own a store or something back in your town, don't you?"

"Yeah, a hardware store," Jeff said.

"Then how do you know some robber isn't looking you over when a stranger comes into your shop? Does that cause you any fear?''

Jeff poured himself another cup of coffee. He looked up with his eyes, but his head stayed bent down. "I guess you've got a point. What the hell. I'm out here with a rancher who knows every inch of the land, two vaqueros who could probably whip a half dozen banditos by themselves and a jarhead who could take care of anything they couldn't. So to quote an old saying by one of my heroes, 'What? Me worry?'"

They all laughed.

During the night the dogs barked a couple of times, but Julio told them that it was probably just a coyote or fox checking out the camp.

Morning came early. When Jew opened his eyes, he could see the flicker of a fire coming through the tent door. He sat up and stretched. He looked over at Julio's cot. It was empty, so he slipped into his jeans and sneakers. He stepped outside. Julio was sitting next to the fire talking to his vaqueros. He saw Jew and stood up.

"Good morning. Did you sleep well last night?" he asked.

"Not bad, not bad at all. In fact, once I fell off to sleep, I don't think I moved all night."

"How are your legs?"

"A bit stiff, but they will loosen up."

A moan came from the tent.

"Hey, Jeff, you awake?" Jew asked.

"Oh, my god, I can't move." Another groan.

"You OK?" Jew asked with concern.

"Yeah, I'm OK. But my poor legs and butt will never, I mean never, be the same."

Jeff staggered out of the tent. Jew looked over his coffee cup at Jeff as he struggled toward a camp stool. First, there was a smile, then uncontrolled laughter, first by Jew, then followed by Julio and the vaqueros. Jeff sat down very slowly and shook his head.

"If you know what pain I feel. Oh, if you only knew," he said. Then he began to laugh. "Oh, it hurts. Damn, it really hurts. If I don't laugh, I'll cry."

Julio and Jew went to get their horses. After the sun had peeked over the rim, Jeff said he would stay around camp today and maybe he would be ready to ride out tomorrow with them. Maybe he would wait until they headed back to the truck.

"It all depends on my joints and what they have to say."

Julio rode over toward where Jeff was seated. "Senor Jeff," he said, "maybe later this morning you should try to walk. It will help the stiffness. It will hurt at first, but you can walk a lot of it out. Pedro has some salve he will give you later. Rub it on your legs before you walk. It will help."

"Thanks, Julio. I'll do that."

It was after nine and Jeff had seen Jew and Julio on the side of a mountain earlier, but they had moved back down into the valley.

"Pedro," Jeff said to one of the vaqueros. "You have some salve for my legs?"

Pedro looked at him and smiled and hunched his shoulders as if to say, "I do not understand."

"Salve," Jeff said and rubbed his legs.

"Oh, si, Bean Gay." He went to the first aid kit and returned with a tube of Ben Gay.

"Oh, do your magic," Jeff said as he rubbed both legs with the cream. "I'll walk for a while and see if it helps. Sitting around here is just making me stiffer."

Jeff strolled over to an outcropping of stone. He picked up a small one and looked it over closely. "Hmm. This looks like part of that black line up there on the top of the rim." He stepped back and shading his eyes, he looked up, then down toward the pile of stones. "This pile must have broken off from that overhang and landed here at the base of the mountain."

Jeff moved on out into the valley looking at the ground. "Maybe I'll find an arrowhead," he said. "Probably were a lot of Indians in here once." As he walked, his legs began to feel better. He saw a stick and picked it up. As he walked he turned rocks over without bending down.

It was almost two thirty when Jew and Julio came back to camp. Jeff was sitting under one of the larger mesquite trees petting one of the dogs when he saw them coming down the trail.

"How's the legs?" Jew asked as he slowly raised his right leg and stepped down. He reached down and rubbed the inside of his thighs.

"Better, but it doesn't look like yours are doing too good," Jeff laughed.

"Hell, I would have been better off if I would have stayed in camp with you this morning. Man, they hurt," Jew said as he slowly walked around camp.

Julio patted his horse's neck. "You want to call it off and go back?"

"No, no," Jew said. "We've come too far to just give up now. If you can put up with us two greenhorns, I would like to look around some more."

Julio laughed and said something in Spanish to the vaqueros, who also laughed.

"What did you tell them?" Jew asked.

"Nothing. Nothing of importance anyway."

"Come on. What did you say?"

"I told them you may be a candy ass, but you had guts. I would have walked back to the rancho before I would have gotten back up in that saddle this morning if I hurt like you did."

Jeff and Jew both laughed.

"What is this we are eating, Julio?" Jeff asked. "I saw it when Pedro put it on the grill, but what cut of meat is it?"

"It is fajita. You may know it as skirt steak."

"I'll tell you what," Jew said. "It's good, whatever you call it. And these tortillas. Did your men make them, too?"

"Oh, sure. These two are my best range cooks. I always take them with me when I stay out on the range."

"What did you do today?" Jew asked Jeff. "I mean besides hurt." He chuckled.

"I covered this end of the valley pretty much. I walked over to that cut in the mountain." He pointed to the west where a ravine had cut its way down the mountainside.

"Find anything?" Jew asked.

"Yeah, as a matter of fact, I did." He reached into his pocket and handed a small silver disc to Jew.

"Found this. What do you think it is, Julio?" Jeff asked.

"Let me see."

Jew handed it to Julio. He studied it, then turned it over in his hand. Without looking up he asked, "Where did you find this?"

"Over there by the side of the mountain."

"Can you show me where?"

"What is it, Julio?" Jew asked.

"It is a concho."

"What in the world is a concho?"

Julio said something to Pedro, who rose and went to where the horses were tied. He pulled the bridle off Julio's horse and brought it back and gave it to Julio.

"See this silver thing on my bridle? That's a concho. This design is only on the rancho owner's bridle or his heirs'. There has never been one lost to my knowledge." He went silent. "Except for my great-great-grandmother. When she was lost, so was her saddle and bridle. Her horse when it was found was bare of all tack. Can you show me the place?" Julio asked as he looked at Jeff.

"The exact spot. I marked it with my handkerchief."

"Let's go." Jew was on his feet and headed for the area Jeff had pointed to.

Jeff led them to the spot where he had placed a rock in his handkerchief. "It was right there. I turned a rock over and there it lay."

Jew began to rake some of the dirt away from the area with his hand.

"It could have washed down from up there," Julio waved his arm toward the mountainside.

"I saw something else very interesting over there. Come on. Let me show you," Jeff said.

They followed Jeff to the pile of rocks that he had seen earlier.

"What did you see?" Jew asked.

"Look here." Jeff picked up another stone with a little of the black sedimentary stratum. "Look up there, almost at the top of the cliff. See that small black line?"

"Yeah," Jew answered.

"Well, I believe this is part of that stratum and this pile of rocks sometime or other broke off up there and fell down here. Suppose the night Maria was out here..." he hesitated. "Isaac told us the other night that there was a hell of a rain the night that she disappeared. It rained, for what, Julio? Two days and two nights?"

Julio nodded his head. "Si," he answered. "That is the story."

"Suppose, just suppose, she sought shelter in a cave and that cliff up there..."

Jew interrupted. "You mean she could have been sealed in a cave hidden by these rocks?"

"I don't know, but it's possible."

Julio said, "Wait here." He went back to camp and returned with his two vaqueros.

"Now we will see if there is a cave back of these stones."

The five of them started to move stone by stone. When one was too large, Pedro went back to camp and got two horses. They tied ropes around the large stone. Pedro, along with Armando, then pulled the stone clear two or three feet. Once the stone had moved, Jew saw only another behind it.

"We could move this whole mountain and there may or may not be a cave," Jeff said.

As Jeff spoke they all heard the sound of a cracking limb. Jew and Jeff's heads both turned in the direction of the sound.

High on the cliff about three hundred yards up the canyon were the remains of what had been a very large tree. It was dead now and as the large branch broke away, it fell crashing into small bits and pieces. Some of the larger parts slid and rolled until they came to a stop.

Jew looked at Jeff. "We've been here before," he said.

"Over there, Julio, we have got to look over there." Jeff's excitement was overwhelming. He and Jew both started in a quick walk to where the remains of the old limb lay.

With renewed vigor they started rolling stones. Jew wedged a part of the old limb behind a large stone and gave it a good shove. It was too heavy to move easily.

"Here," Jeff said as he fixed a rope to the stone. He pitched the free end to Armando who wrapped it around his saddle horn. Jeff climbed to the uphill side and placed his feet against the stone.

"Move off to the side," he said to Jew. "When this baby goes, it's going to roll all the way to the bottom."

Jew fixed his pry pole behind the stone. "Now," Jeff shouted and began to shove with his feet. The stone gave way and as Jeff had said, it rolled to the bottom. Armando had to kick his horse and jerk her aside to prevent being hit.

Jew recovered from the force of his efforts and looked into the cavity the stone had been nestled in. He looked up at Jeff.

"You were right."

"What do you see?" Jeff asked.

"There is an opening back there."

"Let me see," Julio said as he crawled up and looked. He shouted something to the vaqueros and Armando loosened his rope and rode toward camp. He returned and handed a flashlight to Julio. Julio turned the light on and shined it into the hole. He pulled back and handed it to Jew.

"Take a look," he said.

Jew pointed the light into the hole and without turning around, he said, "Oh, my God, sweet Jesus."

"What is it, Jew?" Jeff asked.

Jew turned and facing Jeff, he said, "You found her, my friend. You have found her. After all these years, she has been found."

Jeff took his turn and the five of them sat in silence for a few minutes.

"What now? We need help," Jew said.

"Yes, we need help. I will send Pedro back to tell my father and we will get more help to clear these big stones."

Julio spoke to Pedro in a rapid voice. When he had finished, he turned back to Jew. "My father will be here probably in the morning with help. Let's clear a few more stones and then wait for the others."

"How is your father going to get here with his bad back, if he can't ride a horse anymore?" Jew asked.

"He will call my older brother. He will be here. You can bet on that and be safe."

Chapter 28

When the sun came over the ridge, the four were sitting around the early morning fire drinking coffee.

"It won't be long now," Julio said.

"You mean before Isaac gets here?"

"Si, I'll bet he is on the way already."

"What do we do in the meantime?" Jeff asked.

"We wait. My father will be here. It won't be long."

Jew filled his cup again and stretched out, resting his back against a tree. His wait was short.

Jew heard it first. A sound out of his past. He sat up, then stood cocking his head from side to side. He said, "I hear a chopper."

"A helicopter?" Jeff asked.

"Yeah, hear it?"

Jeff listened, "Yeah, I do."

"That will be my brother. He will be bringing my father,"

Julio said.

The chopper rose over the mountain and came straight in toward the camp. The pilot was skillful and set the aircraft down in a clearing down wind from where Jew, Jeff and Julio stood.

"I'm glad he picked that spot," Jeff said.

"Yeah, me too. As dry as it is here, we would have been choked to death with the dust," Jew agreed.

Isaac opened the chopper door and stepped out holding on to his hat. The blades were slowing down, but the air was still being churned by the rotating blades.

From around the front of the aircraft came a young man. He was larger than Julio but one could see the family resemblance. As the two men advanced toward camp, Jew asked Julio, "Is that your brother, Julio?"

"Si, that is Isaac the fifth. We call him Pepe. He is older than I by three years." As Julio spoke, Jew could feel the pride Julio had for his older brother.

The greeting was something neither Jew nor Jeff had expected. First Isaac gave Julio a hug and kissed him on the cheek. Then the two brothers hugged each other and kisses were exchanged. The embrace was genuine and sincere. Jew could see the strength of family love among the three men.

Julio introduced his brother and when the formalities were over, Pepe looked at Jeff and said, "My father tells me we are related."

"I suppose we are," Jeff said. "It was a long time ago, but we all have the same Lucas Willard in the beginning."

Isaac stepped up and placed his hand on Pepe's shoulder and spoke to him in Spanish.

"Let's see what you have found. There are several vaqueros coming to help. They are just down the canyon and should be here in half an hour. They rode out last night when we got word of your find. My father wants to see for himself." He turned to Julio who started walking toward the pile of stones at the base of the mountain.

First Isaac looked, then Pepe. Julio looked in once again. It seemed like a dream. Was this really happening? Julio looked at Jeff who was himself feeling somewhat confused.

"What do we do now?" Jeff asked.

"Well," Pepe said, "we wait until help gets here and then we can clear these rocks out of here. After that we will see for sure who it is we see in there." His voice became very soft. "Do you believe it is our great-great-grandmother?"

"Yes, I do," Jew answered. "I believe the night she disappeared she sought shelter in this cave. The rains were so heavy that a part of that cliff up there," he pointed to the rim, "broke away and sealed her inside. That is why no one could ever find any trace of the senora."

Jew's voice was most sincere as he continued, "Pepe, I've seen things I would never have accepted if someone would have related them to me. I've felt feelings I have never before experienced. I not only believe that is Maria Elena Estrada Pena Turner we see lying in there, I also believe with all my heart that Isaac Turner somehow has guided us to this spot and showed us where his beloved wife has been entombed all these years. What I do not know nor can I understand is why.

"Why have we, after all this time, been shown these things? What are we to do?" His voice was very soft as he repeated, "What are we to do?"

"I had my doubts as I flew my father here," Pepe said. "But somehow I believe you. I, too, am sure that the mystery of our great-great-grandmother's disappearance has been solved."

"They come," Julio said as he pointed toward the end of the canyon they had entered two days before.

"Now we will know for sure," Pepe said.

The work took the better part of the morning. As the last of the stones were cleared away, making the entrance safer, Pedro called from the camp area that lunch was ready.

Jew looked at Jeff, then at the others. Several of the workers turned to walk toward camp.

"We've come too far and waited too long to find this tomb. I don't plan on leaving here until we have gone in there and checked this out," Jew said to Pepe.

"Nor would my father leave until we have seen for ourselves."

Isaac started in, followed by his two sons. Jew and Jeff followed close behind. Once in the cave, the light from outside grew dim. They walked over to where the body lay.

"Would you look at that? What has happened to her?" Jeff asked.

Isaac touched the face of the body. He looked up and spoke to Pepe who was standing by his side.

"The dryness of the cave and the lack of air in here with the sealed entrance has, as my father thinks, caused the body to mummify. It has just dehydrated. It did not decay as one would expect."

"Look at this saddle," Julio said. "This is from our rancho. There can be no doubt about it. This is our great-great-grandmother."

Isaac rose and walked to the entrance. He reached into his back pocket and pulled out a handkerchief. He blew his nose and wiped his eyes.

"Come," he said in broken English, "we will talk about this outside. We must give respect to this great lady."

Jew looked at Jeff, whose mouth was open. "He spoke in English," Jeff said.

"You do speak English?" Jew said to Isaac as they reached the outside.

"Si, but not too good. I prefer to speak my native

language. I know now I can trust you two gentlemen. You are, in fact, part of our family." He placed a hand on Jeff's shoulder. "And I feel you, too, are a part of my family." As he spoke he placed his free hand on Jew's shoulder. "I owe you the courtesy to speak to you, not at you. I hope you understand. I am old and set in my ways." He hesitated. "Even old people can learn new ways."

Jew smiled and placed his arm around Isaac's waist. "We do understand, Isaac. We have a lot to talk about, a lot of catching up to do."

They turned to walk away from the cave. Jew took three or four steps. He stopped and turned. "Let me see your flashlight," he said reaching for the light in Julio's hand.

Julio handed the light to Jew as he headed back into the cave. Standing just inside, he shined the light next to the wall where it was darkest. Something gleamed as the beam of light crossed it.

"Look here! Look!" Jew's voice was quivering. "Would you look at that!" He pointed to an object on the floor.

Jeff was next to him as was Pepe. Jew bent down and picked up the object and handed it to Isaac, who had re-entered with the others.

"That's a spur. It is a spur just like the Army used when Isaac was in the cavalry stationed at Fort Davis. We saw several when we were in the fort museum."

"Over there, Jew. Shine your light right there." Jeff was pointing to Jew's left. Jew moved the beam. There lying on the floor of the cave was a pipe. Jeff picked it up. He slowly stood up holding the pipe in both hands. His eyes met Jew's.

"Now we know why we had to come, Jew."

"This has to be some kind of dream. I know I'm going to wake up any time now," Jew said.

They moved outside again.

"This just adds to the mystery," Isaac said. "Who was

the black man on that spotted horse she came to find so many years ago."

"I think we all know who he was, my friend," Jew said as he placed his hand on Isaac's shoulder. "I truly do."

"I think you are right, John. We do know who he was and, now, why he came. I also know why he came to you; so we could find her. It was through you that he has shown us the way."

Back in camp, Jew found no one ate very much, although it was very tasty. Hunger had escaped everyone involved.

Pepe flew out to get an official and to arrange for a coffin in which to remove Maria's body back to town.

While they waited for Pepe to return, the coffee pot was drained and Pedro quickly had another one working. Isaac seemed to loosen up and began to relate stories of his childhood. He spoke in broken English and at times searched for a word. If he could not come up with it, he would turn to Julio for help. As Isaac spoke, Jew's mind kept drifting back to that night in Georgia so very many years ago when Isaac and Maria's happiness came to an abrupt end. Then he remembered something Isaac had said back at the ranch.

"Isaac," Jew said in a voice of concern. "You mentioned back at the rancho the other night about Maria keeping a diary."

"Si, she wrote something in it each day if only to say it rained today. Along side of each entry she also placed the date and which day of the week it was."

Jew was sitting on a small stool and with a stick he was making marks in the dirt between his feet. He looked up. His eyes met Isaac's.

"You also said that several times you remembered seeing where she had written that she wished to be buried next to her husband."

Isaac raised his hand as though he could see Jew's thought.

"No, senor," he said. "We could not do that. She is Mexican. She belongs in Mexico. She belongs to us and this land. This land, she belongs to this land." He stood up and walked toward the cave. He stopped a half dozen steps and plunged his hands deep into his pockets.

Silence followed for a couple of minutes. Jew sipped his coffee, but his mind was working. He was trying to see Isaac's point of view, but somehow he knew he had to convince Isaac that Maria had to be returned to Georgia and laid to rest next to her husband.

"Isaac," Jew said as he rose and walked toward the older man. "That lady in there saw hell through a keyhole when she was alive. First, she was captured by the Apache, Victorio. She was beaten, raped and treated worse than a dog. Then after she was saved by Isaac Turner, she found that her mother and father had been murdered. The son of a bitch she was to marry stole her ranch and even kept her from returning to Mexico, her home. These are facts we both know."

"She stays in Mexico." Isaac's voice was stern.

"Of course, Isaac, but let me finish."

Isaac made a sound as if to say "OK".

"At that point of time in her life, she must have thought the world was coming to an end. The world she had known had ended. What she didn't know was that a whole new world was opening up. She fell in love with a very brave, strong man that loved her for herself, not her land nor her money. The name Pena did not mean a thing to him. The soul, the mind, the warmth of Maria was all he saw. Their life together was short, too short. They deserved better times, but they were not to be. It is a shame, too. The way I see it is if Isaac had not been killed, you probably would be living in Georgia yourself right now. Not here on the rancho. Your boys would also be Americans living in the United States."

"What are you trying to say? We all know that." Isaac seemed to be less sure of himself. Jew could feel it in the tone of his voice.

"What I am trying to say, Isaac, is that we—you and I—we can see to it that Maria and Isaac are never, never separated again. They can sleep all the rest of time side by side."

Isaac walked past Jew back toward the fire and handed his cup to Pedro and motioned him to fill it with hot coffee. He sipped on his cup, not saying a word, for what Jew thought was an eternity.

Finally he said, I will talk of this matter with Pepe and Julio later. For now, I do not wish to talk about it anymore."

His voice was that of the patron. There was no doubt in Jew's mind that Isaac was in charge.

"Fair enough," Jew said. As he spoke, the chopper could be heard coming down the valley.

It settled down with a large cloud of dust. Jew was thankful the steady breeze dispersed the dust and carried it away from where they were waiting.

Pepe climbed out of the pilot's seat. As he did, an older man opened the passenger door and stepped out. He dusted himself off and coughed. Isaac met him and they shook hands. Then they walked over to where Jew and Jeff stood with Julio.

"This is my friend, Dr. Gonzales. He is, I believe, the equivalent of what you would call the. . . ." he was again at a loss for the word and motioned for Julio's help.

"Medical examiner," Julio said.

"Si, medical examiner," Isaac said. "We will need his report before we can move the body. You will excuse us. I wish to be alone with the doctor when he examines the body."

Once they had gone into the cave, Jew turned to Julio and

asked, "Julio, how is it you speak such good English and never seem to be at a loss for a word. Medical examiner? That's not a term one hears too often in Mexico, is it?"

Julio smiled. "No, it is not. My brother here," he placed an arm around Pepe's shoulder, "is an Aggie. I...well, I am a graduate of the University of Texas. Pepe's degree is in animal husbandry, while mine is in accounting."

"How about the chopper?" Jew asked. "Where did you learn to fly as well as you do?"

Pepe smiled and reached for a cup of coffee that Pedro had offered. "I was trained in the States. For three years I flew for the Mexican government."

Jeff had walked over to the helicopter. "Pepe," he called.

Pepe walked over to Jeff.

"You plan on carrying Maria under the chopper like this?" As he spoke, he pointed to a casket fixed firmly to the under side of the helicopter.

"Si, I have men back at the rancho waiting for my return. They have a station wagon to transport her to the church in town. Our priest, Father Thomas, will also be there. By the way, Mrs. Sanders asked me to remind you not to forget your blood pressure pills."

"She did, did she? That Sara. She's always worried I'll forget. I never do, but she worries just the same. Thanks. What have the girls been doing since we left?" Jeff asked as they walked back toward the others.

"I think my mother and Julio's wife have taken them shopping and sightseeing around town. Wherever they went, Mrs. Williams has used four or five rolls of film," he chuckled.

Isaac and the doctor came out of the cave. They were talking in a low tone. They stopped for a few moments. Then Isaac called Pepe and Julio over.

"Wonder what that's all about?" Jeff asked.

"I don't know. I suppose they are trying to figure out what to do now. Can you imagine the paperwork that has to be filled out once we get back to civilization?"

Isaac walked over to Jew and Jeff. The others followed.

"John, we have discussed what we were talking about earlier." He cleared his throat. "The spur and the pipe that were found and the fact that it was Jeff here who found the concho which, of course, led to the finding of this cave after all these years has given me reason to reconsider my earlier point of view. I do not want this talked about outside of the family after we leave here. There are some who would think we were all mad. Between your story and what has happened here in the Valley of Two Horses, I'm not too sure we are not mad. However, I have come to believe as you do, John. You have been led here for a reason. That reason, I am sure now, is to return with Maria Turner and place her next to her husband, the first Isaac Turner."

Jew felt a true calm come over him. The satisfaction he felt escaped any ability he had to describe it. He just smiled and extended his hand toward Isaac. As they shook hands, both men could see the other only through the mist that filled their eyes.

Chapter 29

"It's been three weeks now and we haven't heard a word from Mexico. You don't suppose Isaac changed his mind after we left. No, he wouldn't do that, not after he gave me his hand," Jew remarked.

Clara put her knitting down in her lap. She could feel the anxiety in Jew's voice.

"Honey, these things take time. You don't just walk into an office and say, 'Hey! I found my great-great-grandmother after a hundred years of looking. Now I want to send her to Georgia.' and expect some bureaucrat to jump to it, now do you?"

"No, I guess you don't. But Isaac has pull. God, their ranch is the third largest in Mexico. Julio told Jeff and me that when we were riding on the trail."

"I'm sure it is," Clara agreed, "and I'm sure the Turners have a great deal of political influence. However, I am just as sure these things take time."

"Of course, I know you are right. There probably isn't anyone closer than Mexico City who knows how to handle a situation like this either."

"That's probably the real problem," Clara agreed.

"Hell, I'm going to check the mail." As he spoke he went out the back door and headed for the highway where their mailbox was located.

Jew was halfway to the box when he saw Cigar cross the highway and start down the lane. He had his fishing pole thrown across his shoulder.

Jew greeted him. "Going after that big one today?"

"Yep, thought I might. Got me some good blood bait. Made it up yesterday afternoon. You wantin' to come?"

"Naw, too many things I have to do around the house," Jew answered.

"Better come," Cigar said as he started to walk off.

Jew shook his head and started for the mailbox. He had taken only three or four steps when he stopped and turned around. He saw the old man slowly walking away.

"Hey, Cigar, wait up a minute. Let me check the mail. I'll walk up to the house with you."

The old man turned around and nodded his head, but did not bother to answer.

Jew jogged to the box. "Aha," he said as he went through the mail. "Here's what I've been waiting for." The letter was postmarked Mexico City, Mexico, and had Isaac's return address on it. "I'll open this when I get back to the house. Right now, I've got a deal for that old man up there," he mumbled to himself.

Cigar and Jew strolled on toward the house. A few trivial things were discussed, but nothing of importance. They reached the front gate and Jew opened it.

"Come on in and have a cup of coffee with me," he asked

the old man.

"Best not. Need to get on down yonder, before it gets too late."

"Naw, you don't. Come on in. I have something I've been thinking about and I want to talk to you about it."

"Well, maybe for a quick cup, but I gots to get my hook wet 'fore it's too late."

Jew opened the door and asked Clara if she would bring them some coffee. When she came out Jew was opening the letter.

"What do you have there, John?" she asked.

"It's from Mexico," he replied.

"Hmm. OK. All right." Jew said as he read the letter.

"What's it say?" Clara inquired.

"They'll be here the sixth of next month. They will fly Maria to Macon and want Jeff and me to provide transportation from the airport to here."

"Who's coming here?" Cigar asked.

Jew told him most of the story and how they had decided to bring Maria's body back to be buried next to Isaac's. The old man listened but never asked any questions nor did he make any comments except, "That's nice," after Jew had completed his story.

"I gots to get, man. Them fish are waiting on me down yonder." The old man rose to leave.

"Wait a minute. I haven't talked to you yet."

"What you got to say, Mr. Jew? I ain't got all day like some folks. I got fish to catch."

"That's what I'm trying to tell you. You do have all day. I've been thinking I need some help around here from time to time. Clara and me, well, we want to travel some. Ronnie will be going to college this year and Rhonda will go next year. We are going to be here all alone and I was thinking about buying a nice trailer house and putting it out back by the shop."

"What's that got to do with me?" Cigar asked.

"Well, Clara and I were thinking maybe you could see your way clear to moving over here and working for us. Wouldn't be any hard or heavy work. Just helping with the chickens and..."

Cigar shook his head, "Man, you want me to move over here? Well, hell. Excuse me, ma'am." He tipped his hat toward Clara. "Don't mean no disrespect."

"None taken," Clara answered.

The old man set his jaw and looked Jew in the eyes. "You folks are nice. I likes you. I likes you a lot, but you done dug up two sets of bones over there," he pointed toward the graves of Isaac and William Robert. "Now that there letter says you're planning on putting another dead person in to boot. You wants me to stay here in a graveyard while you runs all over the place?" He shook his head. "Does I look crazy to you?"

"Crazy has nothing to do with it and you know it. Don't give me that old Uncle Tom act either. You are about as afraid of those dead people as you are of a catfish. What I need is a hand to help me out. Look at yourself, man. You are not as young as you used to be. Hell, I'll bet when you get home tonight you'll be so damn tired you won't even eat supper."

"I ain't going to get home if I don't get started," Cigar said as he turned and started for the gate.

"Well?" Jew asked.

The old man stopped and half turned as he spoke. "Well, what?"

"Are you going to take the job?"

"Have to think about it," he said as he turned and walked toward the creek.

"You would take Sunday dinner with us, but fix your own

meals the rest of the week," Clara called.

The old man shook his head as he kept on walking toward the creek.

"Think he'll make the change, John?" Clara asked.

"Probably. It'll take him a couple of days to think it over, but I believe he'll do it. That old man may be old, but he isn't stupid. He knows he is getting old and it won't be too many more years before he just can't get along by himself any more. He knows that. Nope, he's not stupid. Not at all. He'll come around."

Jew slapped his empty hand with the letter from Isaac in Mexico. "Got to call Jeff. I'm going to call my folks, too. I know Dad and Mom both would like to be here for this event," he said as he went inside.

Jeff made the necessary arrangements and had a hearse waiting when the plane landed at 11:05 a.m., the sixth of August.

Jew's parents had arrived the day before the plane was expected from Mexico. Jew's mother pitched in and helped Clara with the baking, as Clara went about getting her home ready for the group from Mexico. They enjoyed each other's company and spent hours talking. It was as though they were making up for all the years they were so far apart while John was in the service.

As the plane taxied to a stop, Jew said, "It's been a long trip, but she's home at last."

Isaac saw Jew and Jeff standing with the driver. He waved. They greeted each other like long lost relatives.

"Isaac, you and Irma will ride with me. Pepe, Julio and the ladies will ride with Jeff. We have about a hundred mile trip so plan on about three hours."

Isaac turned and related this information to his wife, Irma. She said something in return. Isaac chuckled.

"What did she say?" Jew asked.

273

"She said that's almost how long it took us to get here from San Antonio."

Jew chuckled. "She's probably right about that."

Clara, Sara and Jew's parents were waiting when the two cars pulled onto the lane. "Here they come," Sara said.

"Oh, I hope the house is clean enough," Clara remarked.

"Don't worry about it, girl. After all, you are not the owner of a huge ranch with servants running all over the place. They'll love your home. Stop worrying."

"I hope so," Clara responded.

"They will. Your home has a certain charm about it. No one, but no one, could not enjoy being here. Believe me and stop worrying."

Everyone enjoyed the meal that was waiting for them. After dinner, the men sat on the porch and sipped brandy. The women cleaned up the dishes. Irma was fascinated with Clara's dishwasher. Julio's wife, Rosa, told Clara that Irma was going to get her a dishwasher before they left the United States. She had heard of them but this was the first one she had seen.

It was about ten o'clock when everyone started to bed.

"We will have the service at nine thirty in the morning," Jew told Isaac. "Father Arnold from Hazel will be out and he has agreed to officiate."

"That is good. I am glad a priest will be here to pay the honor to a fine lady."

The service was small. Besides the family, there was Father Arnold, Sheriff Ellis, Dr. Anderson, and Bob and Sue Edwards. Jew saw Cigar as he came from behind the barn where he had taken a shortcut. The old man moved up to the group, his hat in his hand. Jew knew this old man would never admit it, but he felt a kinship to those who had died so many years ago.

After the service was over, the small group returned to

the house. Cigar just moved away without talking to anyone. The old man walked over to the shop. Jew stepped onto the porch and watched him for a couple of minutes as he seemed to be stepping off something.

"Bet that old man is looking over where he would like me to put his trailer," he said to himself as he went inside.

Jew, along with his father, Jeff and the Turners from Mexico, settled down in the living room where small talk followed. Jew's mother brought in a tray heaped with sandwiches and set it down on a table.

Clara handed a cup of coffee to Jew's father, as Sara served the others. Bob took the cup from Clara and smiled a thank you. As he stirred the sugar, his eyes met those of his son.

"John," he began, "when your mother and I visited you and Clara about a year ago, you told me that incredible story about Maria, Isaac and William Robert."

"Yeah, I sure did, Dad, and I guess today marks the end of that story."

"No, son, I'm not too sure the ceremony out there was the end of the story."

"What do you mean?" Jew asked as he sat up in his chair.

Isaac's head turned to hear what Bob was driving at.

"I do not understand, Bob," Isaac said. "John has found the graves, returned the charm, and between John, Jeff and Julio, Maria has been found and returned to her beloved husband's side. What more could there be?" The question could be seen on Isaac's face.

"I'll explain," Bob said. "John, if you will remember, I mentioned our Aunt Ola."

"Yes, sir, I remember. We were in Japan when she died," Jew answered.

"Right. I also mentioned she had no relatives except for us. None that I know of anyway."

He turned his head so Isaac was now the focal point of

his attention. "This old lady was an aunt of ours, Isaac, who lived in Illinois. She was married once to a fine man and they had two children. One died very young, less than a year old, I believe. The other child, a girl, was killed in a car wreck along with her husband. She never remarried. When she died, the lawyer handling her will sent me a letter and informed me that I was named a beneficiary in her will.

"Poor thing only had a few things to her name. Grace and I went over and signed the necessary papers and picked up a few mementos. I meant to bring a few objects to John on my last trip, but as usual forgot them."

"What's that got to do with Isaac and Maria, Dad?" Jew asked.

"That's what I'm getting to, son," Bob answered.

"John, you should know by now you do not rush your father when he has a story to tell," Grace informed Jew.

Jew nodded his head in agreement.

"As I was saying," Bob continued, "I forgot those things I had planned to bring on the last trip, but I did bring them with us this time. Let me run out to the car and get them.

"I'll get them, Grandpa," Ronnie said as he moved next to his grandfather.

"They are in a cardboard box in the trunk. The box is about this big," Bob held up his hands approximately a foot apart. As he spoke, he handed the car keys to Ronnie.

Ronnie went out to the car. Bob turned again to face Jew.

"Well, son, Father Arnold said something out there that set me to thinking and I think I have put two and two together and come up with four. Yes, several things came together that did not make sense; but then none of this story makes sense."

Ronnie came back in. "This one, Grandpa?" he asked as he handed the box to Bob.

"That's it, son." Bob set the box down and opened it.

All eyes followed his action as he took first one and then another item out, each one wrapped with tissue.

"Ah, here it is," Bob said as he pulled a folder out from the bottom of the box. He handed it to Jew.

Jew recognized it as a paper picture frame.

"Open it, John," Clara said.

Jew opened the frame and looked at the photograph. It was of a black soldier dressed in a cavalry uniform.

"I don't know who it is, son. The strange thing is that out of all the pictures she had, this is the only one I saved. I suppose perhaps because it probably was a relative a long time ago. Someone in our line, I guess. Must be a hundred years old, I'd guess, from the looks of the uniform. Wouldn't you say?"

"Yeah, I'd say, at least." Jew's hand was shaking. Isaac moved in closer and looked over Jew's shoulder.

Clara had moved over next to him. She placed her hand on his. "It couldn't be, John. It's a small world, I know, but it couldn't be," she said.

"What are you two talking about?" Jew's mother asked.

"Mom, if you will remember, Isaac Turner was a soldier. This picture is of a black cavalry corporal." Jew shook from the chill that ran through his body. "This is really a coincidence," he said as he laid the photo down.

"Is there any writing on it, Daddy?" Rhonda said.

"I don't see any, honey," he answered as he picked it up again and turned it over in its paper frame.

"Slip it out of that frame, Jew. See if someone put a name of the studio or something on the back of the frame under the photo. I think they used to do that," Jeff said.

"Yes, John," Isaac said as he placed a hand on Jew's shoulder. "Open the frame. Let us see if there is a name or maybe a date."

Jew felt the seam with his fingernail. The glue was still

very rigid. He reached into his pocket and pulled out his pocket knife.

"Be careful, John," his mother said.

"Oh, I will, Mom. I surely will." As he said this to his mother, the blade slid along the seam. The glue line popped loose.

Jew folded the frame back and lifted the photo out. He turned it over. There was writing in pencil on the back of the picture. Jew's hands began to shake. Before he read what it said, he recognized the writing. He had seen it before.

"I don't believe this," he said. "This has to be some kind of joke. This can't be happening. It can't be true."

"What does it say, John?" Jew's father and Clara said at the same time.

Clara reached out and took the picture from Jew's shaking hands. She read out loud, "Corp. Isaac Turner, Scout, 9th United States Cavalry, Fort Davis, Texas." She looked at Jew. "It is a small world," she said.

Clara looked at Jew. There was a look of real satisfaction, an expression of passion that she, in all the years of their marriage, had never seen in his eyes.

"You know," Jew said, "from the first time we set foot on this place back when we first came out here, I had this feeling that I had been here before. This man, Isaac Turner, had to be a distant relative of ours and somehow, I wonder, did we have help in finding this out-of-the-way farm? The one place out of all the others we looked at, there was never any question but we would settle here.

"Honey, you are right. It is a small world and I suppose it goes to show us once again that we are all just branches of a tree."

"Yes, we are," Isaac said. "We are. I mean, all of us in this room are branches from the same tree. We are—how you say?—bound by blood."

SUNDAY HELL

BY BUTCH HOLMES

Rocket Hunter is the most gifted black quarterback ever to play college football. He can make a pigskin talk pig latin! And his burning ambition is to be the first black superstar quarterback in pro football—the Sunday game—and make a few million dollars. Two obstacles stand in his way: Lena, a sweet sixteen sexpot who is determined to bed down with Rocket—even if the act breaks the rules and the law; and Leda, a voluptuous white chick who is convinced that love is more important than any ambition. Sunday Hell is a hard, gritty journey into the world of the black superjock and the success-crazy men and women who manipulate big time athletics.

HOLLOWAY HOUSE PUBLISHING CO.
8060 Melrose Ave., Los Angeles, CA 90046-7082

Gentlemen I enclose $ _____ ☐ check ☐ money order, payment in full for books ordered. I understand that if I am not completely satisfied, I may return my order within 10 days for a complete refund. (Add $1.00 per book to cover cost of shipping. California residents add 33¢ sales tax. Please allow six weeks for delivery.)

☐ BH391-2 SUNDAY HELL $3.95

Name _____

Address _____

City _____ State _____ Zip _____

THE ROOTWORKER

BY GLENDA DUMAS

Sissie was in love for the very first time, deeply and completely. Dano was everything she'd ever dreamed of and more. But he was an outsider...and outsiders were looked on with something worse than suspicion in the small North Carolina town where Sissie grew up. Her parents begged her not to bring him there, not to bring him home with her. But she felt it was important. Her parents were good people and had raised her to be. They couldn't hurt anyone she loved. But Sissie was wrong. They were waiting and watching and they destroyed for the pure pleasure of it! They were members of a Satanic cult, a cult devoted to evil, the cult of the Rootworkers.

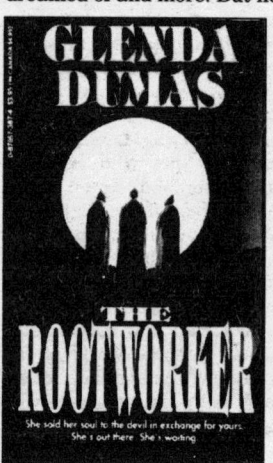

HOLLOWAY HOUSE PUBLISHING CO.
8060 Melrose Ave., Los Angeles, CA 90046-7082

Gentlemen I enclose $ _____ ☐ check ☐ money order, payment in full for books ordered. I understand that if I am not completely satisfied. I may return my order within 10 days for a complete refund. (Add $1.00 per book to cover cost of shipping. California residents add 33¢ sales tax. Please allow six weeks for delivery.)

☐ BH387-4 THE ROOTWORKER $3.95

Name _____

Address _____

City _____ State _____ Zip _____

WHITE MAN'S JUSTICE, BLACK MAN'S GRIEF

BY DONALD GOINES

Goines' classic novel of prison life, it has been called "one of the most revealing books ever written about prison life and bigotry built into our system." This is the story of Chester Himes, who thought he was the baddest man to come down the street. Behind prison walls he was nothing more than fresh meat.

DONALD GOINES, savagely gunned down at the age of 39, was the undisputed master of the Black Experience novel. He lived by the code of the streets and exposed in each of his 16 books the rage, frustration and torment spinning through the inner city maze. Each of his stories, classics in the Black Experience genre, were drawn from reality.

HOLLOWAY HOUSE PUBLISHING CO.
8060 Melrose Ave., Los Angeles, CA 90046-7082

Gentlemen I enclose $ _____ ☐ check ☐ money order, payment in full for books ordered. I understand that if I am not completely satisfied. I may return my order within 10 days for a complete refund. (Add $1.00 per book to cover cost of shipping. California residents add 29¢ sales tax. Please allow six weeks for delivery.)

☐ BH184-7 WHITE MAN'S JUSTICE, BLACK MAN'S GRIEF $3.50

Name _____

Address _____

City _____ State _____ Zip _____

CRIME PARTNERS

BY DONALD GOINES

In this powerful novel Donald Goines lays bare the bloody, brutal world of crime in the black ghetto. *Crime Partners* is a gutsy, sometimes shocking story of Billy and Jackie, ex-prison buddies hot on the trigger to pull any job that pays the bread; of Benson, a black detective and his white partner Ryan, companions in the right against black organized crime; and of Kenyatta, a ghetto chieftain torn between two ambitions: cleaning the ghetto of all the drug traffic and gunning down all the white cops! This is a book that will grip you from first page to last!

HOLLOWAY HOUSE PUBLISHING CO.
8060 Melrose Ave., Los Angeles, CA 90046-7082

Gentlemen I enclose $ _____ ☐ check ☐ money order, payment in full for books ordered. I understand that if I am not completely satisfied. I may return my order within 10 days for a complete refund. (Add $1.00 per book to cover cost of shipping. California residents add 29¢ sales tax. Please allow six weeks for delivery.)

☐ BH183-9 CRIME PARTNERS $3.50

Name _____

Address _____

City _____ State _____ Zip _____

KENYATTA'S LAST HIT

BY DONALD GOINES

Ghetto chieftain Kenyatta, the living black legend, concentrates his army's ruthless forces to rid the black community of rampant drug traffic. With the help of Elliot Stone, a black football star and latest recruit to the army, Kenyatta discovers the identity of the number one man... the fat cat king of the drug pushers!

The crack black and white detective team, Benson and Ryan, follow Kenyatta's trail of blood across the country. They're not sure now whether their target is the hated butcher they've believed him to be, or the savior of the black community.

But Kenyatta doesn't give a damn. He has only one goal; the fight to the death with the smack king.

This book is the last in the great Kenyatta adventure series written by the late Donald Goines under the Al C. Clark pseudonym.

HOLLOWAY HOUSE PUBLISHING CO.
8060 Melrose Ave., Los Angeles, CA 90046-7082

Gentlemen I enclose $ _____ ☐ check ☐ money order, payment in full for books ordered. I understand that if I am not completely satisfied, I may return my order within 10 days for a complete refund. (Add $1.00 per book to cover cost of shipping. California residents add 29¢ sales tax. Please allow six weeks for delivery.)

☐ BH198-7 KENYATTA'S LAST HIT $3.50

Name _____

Address _____

City _____ State _____ Zip _____

DOPEFIEND
THE STORY OF A BLACK JUNKIE

BY DONALD GOINES

Donald Goines is a talented writer who learned his craft and sharpened his skills in the ghetto slums and federal penitentiaries of America. **DOPEFIEND** is the shocking first novel by the young man who would go on to write sixteen books; books that made him a household name among readers of black literature.

DOPEFIEND exposes the dark, despair-ridden, secret world few outsiders know about—the private hell of the black heroin addict. Trapped in the festering sore of a major American ghetto, a young man and a girl—both handsome, talented, full of promise—are inexorably pulled into the living death of the hardcore junkie.

DOPEFIEND is an appalling story because it rings so true. It is also a work of rare power and great compassion. **DOPEFIEND** will draw you into a nightmare world you will not soon forget.

HOLLOWAY HOUSE PUBLISHING CO.
8060 Melrose Ave., Los Angeles, CA 90046-7082

Gentlemen I enclose $ _____ ☐ check ☐ money order, payment in full for books ordered. I understand that if I am not completely satisfied. I may return my order within 10 days for a complete refund. (Add $1.00 per book to cover cost of shipping. California residents add 29¢ sales tax. Please allow six weeks for delivery.)

☐ BH190-1 DOPEFIEND $3.50

Name _____

Address _____

City _____ State _____ Zip _____

SWAMP MAN

BY DONALD GOINES

Rape and murder sets off a savage manhunt through southern backwater country! George, a young black living in the samps of Mississippi, never had an easy life. As a child he, along with his sister Henrietta and his grandfather, stood by helplessly as the honkie hillbillies castrated and murdered his father. After his sister escaped the swamps with a scholarship to college, George learned to live with the evils of the southern swamps, whether it slithered like the water moccasins or walked on two legs like the vicious Ku Klux Klan.

But then Henrietta returns for a visit—a visit that becomes a bloody nightmare of rape and murder!

HOLLOWAY HOUSE PUBLISHING CO.
8060 Melrose Ave., Los Angeles, CA 90046-7082

Gentlemen I enclose $ _____ ☐ check ☐ money order, payment in full for books ordered. I understand that if I am not completely satisfied. I may return my order within 10 days for a complete refund. (Add $1.00 per book to cover cost of shipping. California residents add 29¢ sales tax. Please allow six weeks for delivery.)

☐ BH191-X SWAMP MAN $3.50

Name _____

Address _____

City _____ State _____ Zip _____

CRY REVENGE

BY DONALD GOINES

Crap games and smack pits the blacks and the Chicanos against each other in bloodbath of vengeance!

Young Curtis Carson doesn't mean to rip off the Chicanos in his back yard crap games. He just rolls the dice better. But the Chicanos don't see it that way, and when one of their brothers is brutally slaughtered in a shootout, because of Curtis's dealings with heroin pusher Fat George, the Mexicans cry revenge on Curtis, leaving his brother with a wrecked body that will forever prevent him from being the basketball star he'd always dreamed of being. Curtis swears vengeance of his own, as the ghetto streets run red with the blood of Black-Chicano warfare!

Author Donald Goines, whose established Black Experience best-sellers such as **Street Players, Dopefiend, White Man's Justice: Black Man's Grief** and **Black Gangster**, have ripped apart the curtain camouflaging Black life myth and fact, now reveals the bloody, gut-level truth of Black-Chicano hatred!

HOLLOWAY HOUSE PUBLISHING CO.
8060 Melrose Ave., Los Angeles, CA 90046-7082

Gentlemen I enclose $ _____ ☐ check ☐ money order, payment in full for books ordered. I understand that if I am not completely satisfied. I may return my order within 10 days for a complete refund. (Add $1.00 per book to cover cost of shipping. California residents add 29¢ sales tax. Please allow six weeks for delivery.)

☐ BH196-0 CRY REVENGE $3.50

Name _____

Address _____

City _____ State _____ Zip _____

DEATH LIST

BY DONALD GOINES

Donal Goines continues the gripping, gritty story of crime in the black ghetto begun in CRIME PARTNERS. They're all back for blood: Kenyatta, the ganglord with an army of brothers to deal deadly with crooked cops and dope dealers; Benson and Ryan, a black and white detective team, desperate in their fight to stop the black crime wave. It's doomsday when Kenyatta joins them in a war against a secret list of junk pushers.

DONALD GOINES, savagely gunned down at the age of 39, was the undisputed master of the Black Experience novel. He lived by the code of the streets and exposed in each of his 16 books the rage, frustration and torment spinning through the inner city maze. Each of his stories, classics in the Black Experience genre, were drawn from reality.

HOLLOWAY HOUSE PUBLISHING CO.
8060 Melrose Ave., Los Angeles, CA 90046-7082

Gentlemen I enclose $ _____ ☐ check ☐ money order, payment in full for books ordered. I understand that if I am not completely satisfied. I may return my order within 10 days for a complete refund. (Add $1.00 per book to cover cost of shipping. California residents add 29¢ sales tax. Please allow six weeks for delivery.)

☐ **BH195-2 DEATH LIST $3.50**

Name _____

Address _____

City _____ State _____ Zip _____

THE NAKED SOUL OF ICEBERG SLIM

BY ROBERT BECK

NON-FICTION Don't cry for his soul because he's Black. Though Black is pain. Black is death. Black is despair. Black is the ghetto where he was born. And lived. As a pimp, dope addict, brutalizer of women—and other Blacks, but he cured himself of the ghetto rot. To write—as no other man ever has—about his people and his life. His name is Robert Beck. Better known by his ghetto name, Iceberg Slim. His first three books brought him fame. **PIMP: THE STORY OF MY LIFE, TRICK BABY,** and **MAMA BLACK WIDOW,** a tragic bitter family portrait. They were honest books—sensitive portraits of ghetto life and people. But this book, is his most disturbing. Because it has hope. Because it is now. Because he searches the artist's soul in a collection of personal essays that are full of passion and razor-sharp perception. And when his soul is naked, you see the hurt of a man who feels too much and cares too much.

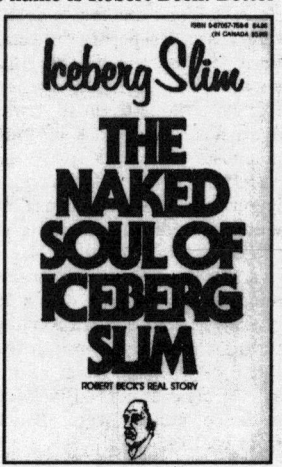

HOLLOWAY HOUSE PUBLISHING CO.
8060 Melrose Ave., Los Angeles, CA 90046-7082

Gentlemen I enclose $ _____ ☐ check ☐ money order, payment in full for books ordered. I understand that if I am not completely satisfied. I may return my order within 10 days for a complete refund. (Add $1.00 per book to cover cost of shipping. California residents add 41¢ sales tax. Please allow six weeks for delivery.)

☐ **BH758-6 THE NAKED SOUL OF ICEBERG SLIM $4.95**

Name _____

Address _____

City _____ State _____ Zip _____